William in Trouble

Richmal Crompton was born in Lancashire in 1890. The first story about William Brown appeared in *Home* magazine in 1919, and the first collection of William stories was published in book form three years later. In all, thirty-eight William books were published, the last one in 1970, after Richmal Crompton's death.

'Probably the funniest, toughest children's books ever written'
Sunday Times on the Just William series

'Richmal Crompton's creation [has] been famed for his cavalier attitude to life and those who would seek to circumscribe his enjoyment of it ever since he first appeared'
Guardian

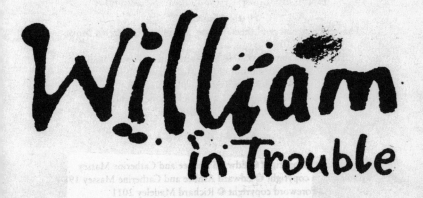

William in Trouble

RICHMAL CROMPTON

Foreword by Richard Madeley

Illustrated by Thomas Henry

MACMILLAN CHILDREN'S BOOKS

First published 1927
This selection first published 1984 by Macmillan Children's Books

This edition published 2016 by Macmillan Children's Books
an imprint of Pan Macmillan
20 New Wharf Road, London N1 9RR
Associated companies throughout the world
www.panmacmillan.com

ISBN 978-1-4472-8556-4

A CIP catalogue   ry.

Typ
Printed and bound by CPI Group (UK) Ltd, Croydon CR0 4YY

CONTENTS

FOREWORD

If William Brown had been able to break free from fiction's unbreakable time lock and allowed to age along with the rest of us, not only would he have long ago qualified for his state pension, he would certainly have been the star turn on television's *Grumpy Old Men*.

Rereading Richmal Crompton's wonderfully crafted short stories, one realizes just how grumpy her William was. His world-weary cynicism; his profound distrust of almost all aspects of the social order; his impatience and impotent fury with authority in all its forms . . . yes, William was the prototype Grumpy Old Man all right, long before he even became a teenager. He stalks through his rural, middle-class world with a near-permanent cloud of irritability and exasperation floating just above his head.

And yet, and yet . . . William is ever the optimist. William Brown may often be down: he is never out.

If he now seems to us a putative grumpy old man, he is also surely a model for *Blackadder*'s Baldrick; William always has a cunning plan.

Fate and grown-ups may conspire against him: William unfailingly meets the challenge. He refuses to kowtow to authority, and his is a very British kind of resistance: polite, almost regretful, insouciant, but deadly. Pity the figurehead who William decides must be challenged, whether it be headmaster, priest or parent.

Perhaps the real mark of Crompton's achievement is that so many of us enjoy her William stories as much as adults as we did as children, and we often find ourselves nodding in recognition at some scenes that could have been drawn from our own childhood. That is an extraordinary thing for any writer to pull off. There is nothing twee, or patronizing, or knowing, or dated (apart from fascinating and factual period detail) in these pages. Crompton has an instinctive grasp of humour too. Her timing, as she moves from paragraph to paragraph, is beautifully judged. In another life I'd bet Richmal Crompton would have made a terrific stand-up comedian.

Well, enjoy what follows. Remember that what you are reading was written in another age: forgive some of the inevitable hostages to history. But relish the timelessness of William's baffling, frustrating and hilarious wrestling-bouts with what each day throws at him. Enjoy the deceptive simplicity of Crompton's storytelling.

But most of all, forgive William his trespasses. Whatever the stern, exasperated Mr Brown may think, it is Mrs Brown who is in the right of it. She knows her son is, fundamentally, a 'good sort'.

And so do we.

Richard Madeley

CHAPTER 1

WILLIAM AND THE EARLY ROMANS

WILLIAM and Douglas and Henry and Ginger, commonly known as the Outlaws, were coming home from school together. There was violent excitement in the village. A real, true Archaeological Society was excavating down in the valley and had discovered real true traces of a real true Roman villa. The Outlaws had decided to watch operations. Douglas and Henry were thrilled by the stories they had heard. William and Ginger were incredulous and rather contemptuous.

'An' they're findin' bits of broken pots an' things,' said Henry.

'Not much use if they're broken,' said William.

'Yes, but they stick 'em together with glue, I bet.'

'Pots don' hold water stuck together with glue,' said William scathingly. 'I've tried 'em. I don' see what use findin' bits of broken pots is anyway. I could *give* 'em lots of broken pots out of our dustbin if that's all they want. Our housemaid, she's always breakin' pots. She'd've made a fine ancient Roman, she would. Seems to me these ancient Romans wasn't much use spite o' bein' cracked up so – spendin' all their time breakin' pots.'

'They *didn't*,' said Henry, exasperated. 'The pots only got broken with bein' buried.'

'Well,' said William triumphantly, 'think of that – buryin' pots! 'S almost as silly as breakin' 'em. Think of a race of men like what the ancient Romans is supposed to have been, spendin' all their time *buryin'* pots. . . . I always *knew* there was something fishy about those Romans. Their langwidge is enough to put you off to start with – hic haec hoc an' stuff like that – fancy *talkin'* it – an' then we're s'posed to think 'em great an' all they did was to bury broken bits of pot . . . I've *never* liked 'em. I'd rather have pirates or Red Injuns any day.'

Henry felt that William's eloquence was taking him, as usual, rather far from the matter in hand.

'Well, they're findin' money, too,' he said, stoutly defending the reputation of the departed race.

'*Real* money?' said William with interest. 'Money you can spend?'

'No,' said Henry irritably. '*Roman* money, of course – they're findin' it all over the place.'

'Breakin' pots an' throwin' money about what other people can't spend,' said William with disgust.

But he went with the others to watch the

excavations. They were not allowed near, but from their position behind the rope that partitioned off the site of the excavations they had a good view of operations. Some workmen were digging in a trench where they kept stooping down and throwing pieces of pottery or coins on to a little heap by the side. A little old man with a beard and spectacles wandered up and down, occasionally inspecting the piles of coins and broken pottery and giving instructions to the workmen.

The Outlaws watched for a time in silence, then boredom settled upon them. The Outlaws did not suffer boredom gladly.

'I bet,' said William, slowly taking his catapult from his pocket, 'I bet I could make every one of those coins in that heap jump into the air with just one knock.'

He took a small stone from the ground and aimed. He missed the coins, but got the little old man in the small of the back. The little old man threw up his arms with a yell and fell head first into the trench. The Outlaws fled precipitately from the scene of the crime, not stopping to draw breath till they were in the old barn.

'I s'pect you killed him,' said Douglas the pessimist. 'Now we shall all get hung an' all your fault.'

'No – I saw him movin' afterwards,' said Ginger the optimist.

'Well, he'll write to our fathers an' there'll be no end of a fuss,' grumbled Douglas.

'It's all those beastly ancient Romans,' said William gloomily. 'I never did like 'em. Well, who else in the world'd have a langwidge like "hic haec hoc"?'

The nest day was a half-holiday, and most of the school was evidently going to watch the excavations.

Benson minor had great hopes of seeing the Roman soldier who figured in the illustration that formed the frontispiece to Cæsar IV. dug up whole and entire, and Smith minor thought that with luck they might come upon a Roman eagle. Smith minimus accompanied them under a vague impression that the ghost of Julius Cæsar was going to arise from the earth at a given signal. The Outlaws would have liked to watch the excavations too. It was a hot day and there is a great fascination in standing in the shade and watching strong men digging in the heat.

But the Outlaws dared not again approach the scene of the excavations. Douglas was gloomily certain that the little, white-haired old man was dead, in spite of Ginger's assertion that he had 'seen him movin''. He had decided that all the Outlaws must sportingly share the murderer's fate and was already composing touching last messages to his family. But whether the old gentleman were dead or not, it was certain that his underlings must have seen and marked the perpetrators of the crime, and that a second visit would be unwise.

Yet so full was the air of Roman villas and excavations that pirates and Red Indians seemed tame and old-fashioned in comparison.

Then William had one of his great ideas.

'Let's find a Roman villa 'f our own,' he said. 'I bet we can find one as good as that ole place, anyway.'

Their gloom lifted. The Outlaws had a pathetic trust in William's leadership which no amount of misfortunes seemed able to destroy.

They assembled as many gardening tools as could be filched from their various families' gardening sheds without attracting the attention of their rightful owners. William had a real gardening spade. He had had an unfair advantage, because he knew that the gardener had gone home and that his family was out, so he had boldly fetched the largest tool he could find. The cook certainly had seen and objected. She had come to the door and hurled vituperations at William. But William wasn't afraid of the cook. He had marched off, his spade over his shoulder, returning the vituperation with energy and interest as he went.

Ginger had a small trowel. He had secreted it in his overcoat pocket under the gardener's very eyes.

Douglas had a large and useful-looking fork and Henry had his little sister's wooden spade.

Henry had found the gardener working in the potting shed among all his tools, and Henry's family's gardener was a large and muscular man with whom one dealt carefully. Henry had hung round for a long time hoping that the gardener would be called away on urgent business. He had mentioned to the gardener casually that he had seen his wife that morning and that she looked very ill indeed. The gardener did not, as Henry had hoped, hasten home at once. On the contrary, he seemed quite unmoved by the news, and after a humble request for the loan of the big spade 'jus' for a few minutes', which was brusquely refused, Henry wandered indoors.

He had chosen and already taken the most murderous-looking of the morning-room fire-irons, when his mother met him going out with it and ordered him to put it back. He did so murmuring pacifically that he was 'only jus' lookin' at it'. He then went up to his small sister's nursery and finding her unattended, seized her wooden spade and ran downstairs with it before her yells of fury could summon assistance. He was proud of having achieved his object but aware that, compared with the others, it savoured of the unmanly. He anticipated any mockery of it, however, by stating at once that he'd fight anyone who laughed at it, and so the excavators, who did not wish to waste their time fighting Henry (a thing they could do any time), abstained from looking at it more often than necessary.

They set off, proudly carrying their tools over their shoulders – except Henry, who carried his very unostentatiously down by his side.

It was William who chose the site for the Roman villa, down in the valley not far from the white-haired gentleman's preserves. There was a ploughed field by the roadside and here the Outlaws began operations.

Ginger and Henry and Douglas set to work with energy upon the soft soil. William walked to and fro beside them in the manner of the white-haired gentle-man, examining with a stern frown and an air of knowledge, the stone and chips they threw up as 'finds.' William had brought with him six halfpennies which, having been previously buried, were discovered by the diggers at intervals. He had also brought some broken pots, to obtain which he had deliberately broken two flower-pots. These, previously deposited in the soil, made excellent 'finds'.

This performance could be seen distinctly from the real site of excavation. Things were rather dull, there. Spectators were roped off to an inconvenient distance from the scene of action, and no coins had been found since yesterday and very few pieces of crockery.

The audience – consisting chiefly of school children – was growing bored. They began to turn interested eyes to where William in the distance strode to and fro issuing orders to his perspiring trio of workers. A group of three detached itself and went slowly over to William's preserves. William saw them coming and hastily buried all the halfpennies and bits of broken pottery again. William's spirits rose. He loved an audience.

'That's right, my men!' he called lustily and cheerily. 'Dig away there. Ahoy there! Tally ho! Dig away there.'

Ginger threw up a piece of pot. William seized on it and examined it closely.

'This, ladies and gen'l'men,' he said in his best showroom manner, 'is part of an ole Roman teapot, prob'ly the very one what King Julius Cæsar drank out of when he was in England.'

'He wasn't a king,' objected one of his audience.

William looked at him crushingly.

''Scuse *me*,' he said with withering politeness, 'Julius Cæsar was one of the seven hills – I mean seven kings – of Rome, an' if you think he wasn't – you can jus' come an' fight me for it.'

The objector looked at William. He'd fought William before.

'All right,' he said pacifically. 'He was, if you like.'

Ginger had thrown up a halfpenny now. William took it up and rubbed the earth away with his handkerchief (it did not make any appreciable difference to the colour of his handkerchief) and made a pretence of examining it with great interest.

'Ladies an' gen'l'men,' he said. 'This – why – I really believe it *is*!'

There was a gasp of interest and suspense.

'Yes, I b'lieve it *is*,' he repeated. William knew how to hold his audience's interest.

'Yes, it *certainly* is.'

'What?' said a boy.

'Kin'ly don' interrupt,' said William sternly. 'Ladies an' gen'l'men, this coin is actually the one what Balbus used to buy stuff to build his wall with.'

'How d'you know?'

'*You* wun't know,' said William condescendingly, '*you* wun't know if you looked at it all day, but I know because I know about that sort of thing. Why d'you think I'm doin' diggin' here if I don' know about that sort of thing? That man over there he *thinks* he's got where the ole Romans were – but he's not. It's here where the old Romans were, where I am.'

Gradually the other spectators had left the scene of the Roman villa and wandered over to where William was holding forth. The fifth halfpenny had just been discovered, and William was holding it up still covered with mud for the admiration of his audience.

'This coin, ladies an' gen'l'men,' he said, 'is a very valu'ble one. It's far more valu'ble than any *he's* found,' he jerked his head in the direction of the other now deserted excavator. '*He's* only findin' very ord'nery things. This coin is the mos' valu'ble old Roman coin what it's possible to find. It's part of what the Roman parliament useter give to the Roman king for pocket money, like what the parliament gives the king pocket money today, like what Mr Bunker said they did in the history lesson.

'This, ladies an' gen'l'men,' he went on impressively, 'is off the top of the wall what Balbus built.'

This information was lustily cheered by members of the class that was engaged in turning the account of Balbus' solitary exploit into Balbus' native tongue.

But William felt that the imminent approach of tea-time and the paucity of his material made a temporary suspension of proceedings necessary.

'Ladies an' gen'l'men,' he said, 'this show will now close down for tea. These,' he paused while he mentally chased the errant word 'excavations.' 'These execrations,' he finally brought out, 'will begin again at 6 p.m. prompt.'

The crowd melted away. The little old man, Professor Porson, who was in charge of the excavations, was watching curiously. When William and his friends had finally departed, he came over to William's hole and looked about it but, finding nothing of interest, he returned to his own.

William did not spend the time before the opening of his 'show' in idleness. He and the other Outlaws might have been seen in the interval carrying down baskets full of various objects, which they concealed in the soil of their hole. There was little time, and the presence of a suspicious family at home gave little opportunity for the collection of very numerous or very interesting 'finds,' but they did what they could. William found time in the interval for a hasty glance at his Latin book.

At six o'clock a large audience had assembled round William's hole and William began operations.

Ginger first of all unearthed an old sardine tin which he handed up to William. William wiped away the mud with his long-suffering handkerchief, then made a pretence of careful examination. This pretence had gained greatly in dramatic force since before tea. He placed upon his nose a pair of blue glasses which the doctor had once ordered Ginger's mother to wear, and which Ginger had long ago appropriated to his own use, and approached the tin closely to them, making exclamations of interest and surprise as he examined it. The audience watched breathlessly.

'Why,' he said at last, 'this is the very tin what the Roman wolf drank out of.'

'What wolf?' demanded a small boy at the back.

William looked at him in horror through his blue spectacles.

'You meanter to say,' he said, 'that you've never heard of the Roman wolf – the one what sucked Romus an' Remus?'

It may here be remarked that all William's knowledge of the animal in question had been gleaned hastily from his illustrated Latin book before tea.

'Who was *they*?' piped the stubbornly illiterate small boy.

'Well!' said William in a tone that expressed horror and surprise at the revelation of such depths of ignorance. 'Fancy not knowing 'bout Romus an' Remus. Romus an' Remus was – they was – they was two Romans an' they went out walkin' in a wood an' they met a wolf an' – an' it sucked 'em.'

'Why'd it stick 'em?' said the small boy.

'Wolfs don't suck folk,' said a boy in front, 'you're thinkin' of bears huggin' folks.'

'I'm *not*,' said the excavator pugnaciously. 'You ever met an ole Roman wolf?'

The objector had to admit that he had not had this experience.

'Well then,' said William triumphantly, 'how do

12

you know how they useter go on? I tell you that all ole Roman wolfs useter *suck* folks. It *says* so in the book. It's just like dogs *lickin'* folks to show that they're pleased. Well, this tin is the tin what the wolf what sucked Romus an' Remus useter drink out of—'

Henry with his little wooden spade had unearthed a small dish. William carefully wiped it and examined it, adjusting his blue spectacles with a flourish and uttering the while his dramatic exclamations of surprised interest. Any member of William's household would have recognised the soap-dish from William's bedroom, but, fortunately for William, no members of his household were there.

'Why, this is the basin where Julia washed the sailors' hands,' he said at last.

There was a murmur of pleased recognition. That came in Exercise II. Most of them had got so far.

'There's a bit o' soap still left in,' said William, holding up a fragment of coal tar soap for inspection, 'so that *proves* it.'

Then he hastily passed on before anyone could challenge his deduction.

Douglas was holding up a piece of wood.

'Part of an ole Roman mensa,' said William with an air of conscious scholarship which was both deprecating and proud.

Next came the gem of the collection, a battered,

once white cloth goose with a broken yellow beak, which Henry had taken, together with the spade, from his furiously protesting small sister.

William rubbed this drooping creature with his earth-sodden handkerchief, and gave a well-simulated start of amazement.

'Why, this,' he said, 'is one of the geese what woke the Capitol.' He held it up. Its head drooped limply on to one side, 'dead now, o' course,' he added.

The boys in front demanded to handle the body, and were sternly refused.

''Course not,' said William. 'You don' know how to hold the things. It'd drop into dust 'f you caught hold of it. Don' you remember in that Tootman's tomb the things dropped into dust? You've gotter be very careful. I know how to hold it so's it won't drop into dust an' you don't.'

'Why'd it wake the Capitol?' piped the small boy at the back.

William had merely read the title of the story in his book, but as the story itself was in the Latin language, he had not been able to make himself further acquainted with it. But William was never at a loss.

''Cause it was time for him to get up, of course,' he said crushingly.

The next 'discoveries' followed thick and fast – a Roman hatpin, a Roman pipe, a Roman toasting fork and a Roman tennis ball. Upon all of these the excavator held forth eloquently with great *empressement* if little accuracy. The audience was warming to the game. Each 'discovery' was cheered loudly and the account of the excavator challenged at every detail. The excavator liked that. His eloquence thrived on contradiction. He proved conclusively that the little figure of the Lincoln Imp upon the hatpin was the figure of one of the Roman gods, 'Joppiter or Minevus or one of 'em – or I don' say it isn't Romus or Remus or the wolf.'

'Or the goose,' put in the small boy at the back.

'Yes,' said William kindly, 'I don' say it isn't the goose.'

He proved too, from the presence of a pipe among his other 'discoveries', that smoking, far from having been discovered by Sir Walter Scott, as the small boy insisted, had been one of the favourite pastimes of Julius Cæsar during his residence in England. An empty match box, lying not far from the other discoveries, said by the excavator upon examination, to be 'mos' cert'nly ole Roman,' was admitted by most of those present to be conclusive proof of this.

The 'discoveries' might have gone on indefinitely had not Farmer Jenks appeared upon the scene. The sight of the Outlaws had that effect upon Farmer Jenks that the proverbial 'red rag' is supposed to have upon the proverbial bull. When the Outlaws weren't climbing his fences, they were treading down his meadowland, or walking through his corn or climbing his trees or birds' nesting in his woods. They didn't seem to be able to live without trespassing on his land.

Farmer Jenks spent a good deal of time and energy chasing the Outlaws. On this occasion he first saw a crowd of boys (he hated boys) on the public path that bordered his ploughed field. He then noticed that the crowd was distinctly encroaching upon his ploughed land. Finally he saw 'that boy' (thus always in his mind he designated William) and the rest of them actually digging up his field. He rushed at them with a yell of fury.

The chief excavator, with great presence of mind, caught up the basket in which his 'finds' had been placed, jumped across the ditch, and scrambled through a hole in the hedge. The others followed.

Farmer Jenks had outgrown the youthful slimness of his earlier days. Even the occasional physical exercise which the pursuit of the Outlaws gave him had done little to keep down his weight. He was just in time to seize the smallest boy (who was the last to attempt the hole in the hedge) by the scruff of his neck.

The smallest boy, though of inconsiderable stature, possessed well-developed teeth which, with a quick twist of his neck, he planted firmly in Farmer Jenks' detaining hand. Farmer Jenks released him with a yell, and the small boy, smiling sweetly to himself, scraped through the hole and trotted as quickly as he could after the others, who were already disappearing in the distance.

Farmer Jenks turned wrathfully and began to kick back the earth into the hole.

William reached home breathless, but, on the whole, satisfied with his afternoon. He'd given them a better show than that ole man with the white beard, anyway. He didn't seem to know how to make things *interesting*. Fancy digging up nothing but bits of ole pot and dirty ole halfpennies. Anyone'd get tired of watching that all day.

William carried the basket containing his 'finds' up to his bedroom, and there amused himself by taking them out one by one and holding forth to an imaginary audience. He thought of a lot more things to say. He wished he could do it all over again. He could do it heaps better. He heard his father come in with a visitor and stopped a dramatic account of the meeting of Romus and Remus and the wolf in the wood to go and lean over the banisters to see who it was. Crumbs! it was the little old man with the white beard.

He returned very slowly to his bedroom. He did not continue the account of the meeting of Romus and

Remus with the wolf. Instead, he tried to express to an imaginary accuser the fact that p'raps he *might* have shot the catapult by mistake. Yes, he remembered distinctly holding it in his hand, and he admitted that it *might* have gone off by mistake when he wasn't looking. They did sometimes. He was very sorry if he hit anyone, very sorry indeed. He remembered when it went off by mistake hoping that it hadn't hit anyone, because he always tried to be very careful with it and hold it so that if it went off by mistake it wouldn't hit anyone.

William practised in his looking-glass for a few minutes the sort of face that went with the foregoing sentiments, and having achieved a look of blank imbecility which he fondly imagined to express concern and contrition, he went downstairs, his features still carefully composed.

Determining to get the worst over at once, he entered the drawing-room where his father sat conversing with the visitor. William sat down by the door and stared at the visitor. On his entrance into the room his features had, unknown to himself, taken on an expression of pugnacious fury, and the ferocious glare which he turned on the innocent old man would have reduced any of William's own followers to instant subjection. The old man, however, met it blandly enough.

'Is that the little boy?' he asked. 'Come nearer, my little fellow,' he said. 'I'm afraid I can hardly see you over there. I'm so near-sighted that I can hardly see across a room.'

William's expression softened. He liked old men who were so near-sighted that they could hardly see across a room. It meant that they were so near-sighted that they could hardly see across a field at the end of which a small boy might stand with a catapult which had a habit of going off by mistake.

William shook hands with the benign old man, who then immediately went on with his conversation with William's father.

'Yes, we've got some most interesting exhibits – most interesting. Your valley has proved indeed a most fruitful field.'

'When do you finish?' asked Mr Brown.

'On Saturday. The discoveries cannot, of course, be moved till next week. I shall send off the bulk of them on Friday, but the half-dozen or so more valuable ones I shall take up myself on Saturday. The vicar has asked me to be present at the Village Social on Saturday evening and give the people a little talk with an exhibition of the chief discoveries before I take them away. It will, of course, be highly educative for them. A few came to watch the excavations, but on the whole I was disappointed – disappointed. A good many boys came on Wednesday afternoon. It would have been an experience – a cultural experience – that they would have remembered all their lives – but they soon tired of it and went over to another part of the valley to join in some childish game, I suppose. The modern child lacks perseverance. I fear that it was one of those children who projected some missile across the field the evening before, which precipitated me into the trench and obliged me to swallow a large amount of moist earth.'

William's father threw a quick glance of suspicion at William, who had hastily composed his features into their expression of blank imbecility in readiness to receive that glance.

It was arranged, before William left the room, that the Professor was to dine at the Browns' on Saturday evening before he went on to the Village Social.

William's pride as an excavator was piqued. If that old man was going to give a show of his finds so would William. He lost no time in making preparations. The old barn was jolly well as good as the Village Hall any day, and while the adults of the village were listening to the old man lecturing on his discoveries in the Village Hall, William decided that the youth of the village should be listening to him lecturing on his discoveries in the old barn.

Moreover, he'd be able to prepare a few more

'discoveries'. It was duly announced that William was going to hold a 'show' of his discoveries and lecture on them, and it seemed as though the youth of the village meant to be there in force. Anything might happen at one of William's 'shows.' They were things not be missed. They rarely turned out as they were meant to turn out, and there was always a chance of their ending in a free fight.

Saturday evening arrived and Professor Porson arrived at the Browns' house for dinner. He left his bag of 'exhibits' in the hall and went into the drawing-room. William never scorned to learn from an expert. He wanted to do the thing properly. As soon as the drawing-room door shut, he hastened to examine his rival's preparations. William's own exhibits were still in the basket in which he had brought them from the field. He examined the bag first of all. Why, his father had a brown leather bag just exactly like that. He'd 'borrow' his father's bag for his things. He opened the bag. They looked a mouldy lot of things, anyway. His were a jolly sight more exciting.

But he noticed that to each of them was attached a number. All right. He'd stick numbers on all his things, too. He went upstairs, 'borrowed' his father's leather bag from his dressing-room, and some labels from his desk, and then set to work fixing the labels on to his exhibits.

Soon he had them all labelled and arranged in the brown bag. He took it downstairs (fortunately meeting no one on the way), put it in the hall near the old Professor's, looked at it with deep and burning pride, and then went to join his family.

William always insisted that he was not to blame for what happened.

He didn't take the wrong bag. The old man did that. The old man went out of the house first and he took up the only brown bag he could see, which happened to be William's father's bag 'borrowed' by William.

His own bag happened to be in the shadow of the hall table – exactly where he himself had put it, as William later repeatedly told his accusers. He insisted that he hadn't touched the old man's bag, he'd only put his down near it, and he couldn't help it if the old man took the wrong one. It wasn't his fault. Well, and if his bag spoilt the old man's show, he could jolly well tell them the old man's bag had jolly well spoilt his.

But all this comes afterwards. The Professor was rather late for his lecture, as the result of having talked too long to Mrs Brown on the subject of hypocausts in Roman villas. The conversation had been very one-sided, because Mrs Brown was somewhat vague as to the exact meaning of the term. At the beginning of the conversation she thought that they were prehistoric animals, and at the end had a vague idea that they had something to do with kitchen flues. But the professor had four cups of her excellent coffee, and drank them with leisurely enjoyment while he wandered from hypocausts to tessellated pavements (Mrs Brown confused these with macadam pavement, and murmured that she understood that they were less dangerous for skidding), then, realising with a start that he ought to have departed at least ten minutes ago, he uttered hasty thanks and apologies and farewells, seized a bag from the hall, and fled out into the night.

About five minutes later, William might have been observed to creep downstairs, stealthily, seize the remaining bag, and also flee out into the night.

The Professor hurried up on the stage and faced his audience. The Village Hall was crowded. A Whist Drive was to follow the Professor's discourse, and upon the faces of most members of his audience was an expression of suffering patience. After all, the expressions seemed to say, it would only last half-an-hour. They might as well go through with it.

The Professor scuttled across the stage to the table in the centre, where waited a lanky youth who was to help him to display the exhibits. The Professor placed his bag on to the table.

'I must go and stand over there by the light,' he said in a hasty whisper. 'I'll read my notes from there. The exhibits are numbered. All you have to do is to find the number I call out and hold it up in sight of the audience while I read the appropriate remarks upon it. We are, I think, ready – I'll go over to the light.'

There was a feeble burst of applause as the Professor cleared his throat, took up his position beneath the light at the side of the stage and unfolded his little sheaf of notes. He then adjusted his spectacles. When wearing them he could barely discern an object two yards away. He held his notes close to his eyes and began to read.

'Exhibit No. 1?' he announced.

The lanky youth searched in the bag and finally, with an expression of interest and surprise, brought out the battered, grimy cloth goose which belonged to Henry's sister. It certainly bore a label on its neck with Number 1 inscribed upon it. He held it up to the audience. Its neck, which had lost most of its stuffing, hung limply on to one side. Its broken beak wobbled pathetically.

'This delightful little object,' read the Professor, 'must have been the pride of the Roman villa which enshrined it. We are lucky, indeed, to have secured it. It argues its possessors to be people of taste and culture. Its exquisite grace and beauty prove it, I think, beyond doubt to be of Greek workmanship, and make it, I may tell you at once, the gem of the collection.'

The hideous face of the goose upon its wobbling neck leered comically at the audience.

'Observe,' went on the lecturer, still reading from his notes, 'observe the grace of posture, the clarity of outline, the whole dignity and beauty of this little *objet d'art.*'

Someone applauded half-heartedly, and the audience seemed to begin to wake up. Some there were – earnest souls and seekers after knowledge – who at the Professor's words immediately gazed at Henry's sister's goose and conscientiously saw in it such an object of beauty as the Professor had described. Some there were who had a dim suspicion that something must be wrong and looked bewildered. Some there were who had a sudden glorious conviction that something was wrong, and from their faces the expressions of boredom were disappearing as if by magic. Some there were who had come to sleep and had already attained their object.

'No. 2,' called out the Professor.

The lanky youth examined the contents of the bag and at last brought out the toasting fork. There are some dainty toasting-forks that might grace a drawing-room, but this was not of that fashion. It was unmistakably a kitchen toasting-fork made to fulfil its

'THIS DELIGHTFUL OBJECT,' READ THE PROFESSOR, 'MUST
HAVE BEEN THE PRIDE OF THE ROMAN VILLA WHICH
ENSHRINED IT. ITS EXQUISITE GRACE AND BEAUTY MAKE
IT THE GEM OF THE COLLECTION.'

primary function of toasting rather than conform to
any known standard of beauty. It was large and stout
and rusty. It bore a label marked 2. The lanky youth
held it up.

'Exhibit No. 2,' said the Professor, his notes held
closely up to his spectacled eyes. 'This little article of
feminine adornment is a fibula or Roman brooch. It is,

SOMEONE APPLAUDED HALF-HEARTEDLY, AND THE
AUDIENCE SEEMED TO BEGIN TO WAKE UP.

you will remark, somewhat larger than the brooch of
the modern daughter of Eve, and the reason for that is
that it was used to pin the lady's garment together
upon the shoulder, and so a certain strength and
firmness was required. You will agree that its greater
beauty of design is sufficient recompense for its larger
size in comparison with its modern descendant. I want
you to admire in this the beauty of design and the
exquisite workmanship.'

These statements were received with ironical cheers

by some of the audience, but the Professor was on the staff of one of our great Universities, and was quite accustomed to his statements being received with ironical cheers.

The sleepers were awaking. Those who had realised that something was wrong were beginning thoroughly to enjoy the evening. Only the few honest seekers after culture were following the Professor's speech with earnest attention, looking with reverent eyes at Henry's sister's goose and Ginger's kitchen's toasting-fork, and seeing in them that strange beauty that they tried so conscientiously to see in things they ought to see it in. They knew that to be really cultured you had to make yourself see beauty in things that you knew in your heart to be ugly. Their only consolation for the effort this entailed was their feeling of superiority over the common herd that it left behind. . . .

'Exhibit No. 3,' said the Professor.

The lanky youth again dived into the bag. This time he brought out the old sardine tin. It was very earthy, but the paper bearing the name of a well-known manufacturer of sardines still adhered to it. The audience gave a howl of joy. The devotees of culture in the front row turned round reproachfully.

'Exhibit No. 3,' repeated the Professor, quite unmoved by the commotion (he found it, as a matter of fact, rather soothing. He was not accustomed to lecturing to silent audiences). 'This dainty piece of Castor pottery is the only piece, alas! that we have been able to obtain intact, but it is a very beautiful representation of its class. It—'

The Vicar was not present, but the curate was sitting in the front row. Up till now he had not been quite sure. He was young enough to wish to conceal his ignorance. He had, so to speak, swallowed the goose and the toasting-fork. But he could not swallow the sardine tin. He got up and ascended the three steps that led to the platform.

'Excuse me, sir,' he began.

The Professor did not like to be interrupted. He did not mind lecturing to an accompaniment of conversation or even of mirth. He was used to it. But he couldn't have people coming up to the platform to interrupt him.

'Any questions,' he said sharply, 'can be asked at the end of the lecture.'

'Yes, but, sir—'

The Professor grew still more annoyed.

'If you want to see the exhibits more closely,' he said, 'you will have an opportunity at the end of the lecture. Now, kindly refrain from interrupting me any more. This exhibit, ladies and gentlemen—'

'B-but—' gasped the curate.

The Professor turned on him in exasperation.

'Sit down, sir,' he said, 'and if you've anything to say to me say it at the *end* of the lecture, not the middle. Have the civility not to interrupt me any longer.'

The Professor always prided himself on knowing how to deal with undergraduates when they went too far. . . .

The curate retired in purple-faced confusion to his seat in the front row, where he sat mopping his brow and breathing hard.

The lecture proceeded with ever increasing hilarity on the part of the audience.

He described William's soap-dish as Samian pottery, and the hatpin with the Lincoln Imp at the end as a fragment of mosaic. The remarks he made on the piece of Balbus' wall and the mensa were unheard by most of his audience. Finally he bowed, and said: 'That is all, ladies and gentlemen.'

The audience applauded whole-heartedly, and then surged excitedly into the room where the Whist Drive was to be held.

Meanwhile in the other room the Professor carefully folded up both spectacles and notes and went to the table where lay the 'exhibits'. He took up the drooping goose, held it up close to his eyes. He gave a start and held it closer still. Frantically he seized the toasting-fork and the sardine tin and did the same with those. He put them down. A wild look came into his eyes. He turned to the lanky youth.

'W-what are these?' he said.

'The things out of your bag, sir,' said the lanky youth.

'No, they're *not*,' almost screamed the Professor. 'I tell you they're not. You – you didn't hold up *these*, did you?'

'Yes, sir,' said the youth blankly. 'They was numbered same as you said – they was all there was.'

The Professor searched wildly in the bag. Then he gave a scream.

'It's not my bag,' gasped the Professor. 'It's not my bag. It's—'

He bundled the things back into the bag and tore out of the building, and ran down the road to the Browns' house. At the gate he met two boys. They carried a bag almost exactly like his. One was talking indignantly.

'Well, I can't help it. I tell you someone's stole my things an' put these rotten ole things in instead. Well, I could've talked about the real things. I can't talk about these rotten ole things. There was jus' nothin' to say about 'em. I'd thought out things to say about the real things. Well, no one could say anythin' about *these* old things, I tell you. An' then they got mad – well, *I* din' want everyone to start fightin', I—'

The old Professor dropped his bag and seized upon the one William held and opened it. William seized upon the one the Professor had dropped and opened it. He looked at the contents and fixed a stern eye upon the Professor.

'So it was *you* stole my things, was it?' he said indignantly.

'The statuette!' screamed the Professor, searching through his bag. 'It's not here!'

'Oh, that doll thing!' said William contemptuously. 'A kid cried for it an' I gave it her. I din' think anyone'd want it.'

'Get it back! Get it *back*!' screamed the Professor.

'All right,' said William in a bored tone of voice. 'She's only jus' down the road. I'll get it for you 'f you want it.' He turned to Ginger. 'You stay an' see if all my things are all right,' he said sternly.

He departed. The Professor put on his spectacles and eagerly and suspiciously examined the contents of his bag. Ginger, with equal eagerness and suspicion, examined the contents of the other bag. At the end of ten minutes William returned. He held an ancient green bronze statuette and had a black eye.

'Had to fight her brother for it,' he explained briefly, 'he said she'd given it him. Here it is.'

The Professor snatched it eagerly and put it into the bag. Then he took out his watch.

'THE STATUETTE!' SCREAMED THE PROFESSOR,
SEARCHING THROUGH HIS BAG. 'IT'S NOT HERE!'

'Goodness gracious!' he said. 'I shall miss my train,'
and set off at a run down the road without another
word.

William and Ginger bent over the bag.

'Are they all there?' said William.

'Yes,' said Ginger.

'No *wonder* he pinched 'em for his show,' said William bitterly. 'They're a jolly sight better than his mouldy ole things. No *wonder* I coun't make anyone take any int'rest in 'em.'

'Well,' said Ginger optimistically, 'let's give another show with the real things.'

'No,' said William firmly, 'I'm *sick* of ole Roman things. Let's think of something else.'

The Professor was in a railway carriage speeding on his way to London. His precious bag was on the seat by his side. The Professor was thinking. He was remembering the nature of the objects which he had seen on the table in the village hall, and which had caused him such consternation. He remembered the numbered labels which were attached to them. He took out his notes and read them in the light of these memories. Then there came the sound as of the drawing of rusty bolts or the creaking of rusty hinges.

It was the Professor laughing.

CHAPTER 2

WILLIAM AND THE FAIRY DAFFODIL

THE Outlaws swung happily along the road. It was Saturday. It was a holiday. All the world was before them. . . .

'I went to the dentist, Wednesday,' said Ginger with a touch of legitimate pride.

'What'd you have done?' said Douglas.

'I bet you made 'nough fuss,' said William, who considered it his duty to deflate his fellow-creatures when he thought they were unduly puffed up.

'I had a tooth *out*,' said Ginger triumphantly, 'an' I *din't* make no fuss.'

'I bet you had gas,' said William contemptuously.

''*Course* I had gas,' said Ginger indignantly; 'd'you want me to die of pain? That's what people do what don't have gas – die of pain – it's not the *pain* I mind,' he added hastily, 'but it seems silly to go and *die* of it.'

'I bet you wun't die of it,' said William pugnaciously.

'Well, you go an' have a try,' said Ginger; 'you go

35

an' have a tooth out without gas tomorrow an' *see* if you die of pain.'

'I can't,' said William with an air of virtue, ''cause they'd make me pay, an' I haven't any money.'

'Don't see how they *could* make you pay if you died of it,' said Henry.

'Well, I'm not *goin'* to,' said William, irritated by the callousness of his friends; 'you'd only get hung for murder 'f I did.'

'No, it'd be the dentist what'd get hung,' pronounced Henry judicially.

'I'll lend you the money to go,' said Ginger.

'You can't,' said William with an air of finality, ''cause I know you haven't got any.'

This was irrefutable, and the subject died a natural death.

'My aunt sent me a box of tools yest'day,' said Douglas.

The Outlaws received this news with interest.

'What sort of tools?' said William.

'Fretwork tools,' said Douglas, with a swagger, 'a jolly fine box of 'em.'

'Well, where are they?' said Ginger; 'why din't you bring them along?'

Douglas' swagger dropped.

'Haven't gottem any longer. They've took them off me.'

The Outlaws' faces registered righteous indignation at this fresh example of adult tyranny.

'Whaffor?' they said simultaneously.

'I jus' did a nice s'prise for my mother,' said Douglas, with a mixture of resignation and indignation in his tones. 'She's gotter ole bookcase – all plain wood, you know – ugly ole thing – an' I got up early an' fret-worked it for her – made it ever so much prettier – for a nice s'prise for her – an'—' he sighed.

There was no need to complete the story. They had all experienced similar examples of almost incredible ingratitude from the grown-up world around them.

'Anyway,' ended Douglas simply, 'they took 'em off me.'

'Once when I had a tooth filled,' said Ginger, returning to the former subject, 'I din' have gas jus' havin' it *filled*, though, coo! . . . it *did* hurt. I did *nearly* die of pain – anyway, my father gave me a book after it called *The Jungle Explorers*, an' crumbs! it was exciting. They went on and on through woods which no white man had ever set foot in before an' they found an unexplored tribe livin' there what no one had ever found before – savages livin' in the middle of an unexplored wood. Crumbs! I wish there was places like that in England!'

There was a short silence. Then William said:

'Well, how'd you know there isn't?'

''Course there isn't. You'd read about it in the newspapers if there was.'

'P'raps the newspapers don't know about it. Jus' think,' went on William, warming to his subject, 'what a big place England is, an' jus' think of all the woods in it, an' d'you think that anyone's ever walked *right* over every inch of every one of those woods? Huh!' he gave a scornful laugh, 'I *bet* they haven't. Who'd do it, anyway? Everyone's too busy to go searchin' about every inch of every wood. I bet we'd find some unexplored tribes 'f we looked prop'ly for 'em. I bet no one's ever *looked* before. They jus' took for granted there wasn't any, but I just bet there is. I bet—'

The road was now leading them through woods stretching into the distance on either side. 'Look at those!' said William dramatically. 'Look at 'em! You can't see to the end of them. D'you think that anyone's ever took the trouble to walk *right* over every inch of 'em? I bet there's – there's – vast tracks of unexplored land there what no one's even set their feet in, an' I bet there's unexplored tribes, too, if only one was to look for them.'

The others gazed at him open-mouthed. Then Ginger gave vent to their feelings by a simple, but heartfelt 'Crumbs!'

Henry already had his foot on the lowest rung of the fence that separated the road from the wood.

'Come on!' he said.

'Of course,' said William, slightly disconcerted by the immediate effect of his eloquence, 'we don' *know* there is any.'

'No, but we can see,' said Ginger, assuming the grim expression he considered suitable to an intrepid explorer.

'They might be dangerous, you know,' cautioned Douglas, hanging back.

'All right, you stay behind 'f you're afraid,' said Ginger.

'I'm not afraid for myself,' said Douglas hastily, 'I was only thinkin' of you others.'

'Come on, then,' said William, assuming leadership and making an unsuccessful attempt to vault the fence. 'We'll have a jolly good look for 'em,' he added as he picked himself up from the ground and removed the bits of bracken from his mouth, 'we'll have a *jolly* good look!'

The undergrowth grew thicker, and they walked now in single file. 'Well, I bet no white man's ever set his feet *here* before,' said William as he forced his way through a bramble.

'I say,' said Ginger, 'wun't it be fun if we found a tribe of savage tree dwellers. You know, the sort that lives up in trees.'

'You're thinkin' of monkeys,' said Douglas gloomily.

'I'm not either,' said Ginger indignantly. 'I know what I'm thinkin' of, an' I'm *not* thinkin' of monkeys. I'm thinkin' of *people* what built sort of nests in trees.'

'It's birds what you're thinkin' of, then,' said Douglas.

'Well, whatever they are, let's join 'em,' said William, 'an' live a savage life with 'em, and not go back to school.'

'Let's hope they're not cannibals,' said Douglas, still gloomy.

'P'raps,' said Henry, 'they'll think we're gods an' make us kings. I once read a tale where they did that.'

The Outlaws did not seem to think this probable.

William put the matter succinctly. 'The people in your book must've sort of *looked* different from us if anyone'd think they was gods. . . . Anyway, I think we'll *join* 'em an' live a savage life with 'em.'

'I hope you're all keeping a lookout for wild animals,' said Henry. 'I think I saw a leopard vanishin' in the distance jus' then.'

''F I'd *known* what we were goin' to do,' said William, 'I'd've brought my air-gun.'

'Yes 'n if they hadn't took my fret-work tools off me they might've saved my life,' said Ginger, bitterly. 'They cut holes right through things.'

'*Coo!*' said Douglas, who had just fought his way through a thorn bush only to fall into a bog. 'Coo! it's *jus*' what they call an im-impenetratable jungle.'

'A what jungle?' said William.

'An impenetratable one,' said Douglas, firmly.

William had a vague idea that there was something wrong with the word, but not being sure, he let it pass.

They had walked for nearly an hour. Their clothes were torn, their collars awry, and they carried attached to their persons, at various points, a goodly load of mother earth – but though they were convinced that they had explored land where no white man had ever set foot before them, they had found no traces of savage tribes, and were beginning to lose hope.

'They may've all died of starvation 'cause there doesn't seem much to *eat* round here,' said William, who was feeling hungry.

'Well, wun't we have found their bones if they'd done that?' said Douglas the practical.

'Pity we didn't meet any wild animals. We might've killed and eaten 'em,' said Henry.

'We ought t've brought supplies,' said Douglas, 'we're miles off civilisation an' we've got nothin' to eat.' He looked round. 'I s'pose,' he went on, hovering between hope and despair, 'no one *has* got anythin' to eat?'

All searched their pockets. The only edible object was a stunted walnut that William found in his trouser pocket. They looked at it without interest.

'It'll be difficult to divide,' said William thoughtfully.

'Let's keep it till we're abs'lutely starvin',' said Ginger.

'We may be eatin' each other before we've finished,' said Douglas gloomily.

This suggestion seemed to enliven them.

'Drawin' lots so as to be quite fair,' stipulated Henry.

'You'd have a job to catch *me*,' prophesied William jauntily.

'Let's sit down an' have a rest,' said Henry.

They sat down and after a stone-throwing competition in which Ginger accidentally dealt himself a black eye, and William won, they began to consider the possibilities of the place.

'I don' feel like penetratin' any further, do you?' said Douglas.

'We ought to've brought a Union Jack to plant it here,' said Ginger, holding grass to his eye in the vague hope that it possessed medicinal properties. 'They do, you know. Jus' to show that they've discovered it.'

'We'll bring one tomorrow,' said Henry, 'my sister's got a little one.'

'I say,' said William, 'it's a fine place for Hide-an'-Seek. Let's have a game. Who'll be It?'

'Ginger,' suggested Henry unfeelingly, ''cause his eye's almost closed up to start with.'

'Anyone'd *think*,' said Ginger bitterly, 'that you weren't sorry for me.'

'I'm not,' said Henry simply. 'Why, people what explored Mount Everest got frozen toes an' things. You ought to think yourself jolly *lucky* to have only a black eye.'

'Well, what about *you*? You've got nothin'.'

'Yes, I'm luckier still,' agreed Henry, still unfeelingly. 'But *you* ought've brought along a bit of gas to stop you dyin' of pain.'

As a combat seemed imminent, William intervened.

'Come on,' he said. 'Ginger, count a hundred.'

Ginger closed his remaining eye and the others then scattered to hide.

After running a few minutes, William was disconcerted to find that he had reached a main road. It was the end of the wood. Doubts as to the unexplored nature of the land they had just claimed assailed him, but he dismissed them as irrelevant. The immediate business was to find a good hiding place. They could discuss the other question afterwards. There was a motor-car standing in the road, empty, unattended. It was a four-seater, but the back two seats were covered by a taut waterproof apron stretched from the back of the front seats to the back of the rear seats.

William's eyes gleamed. Crumbs! What a good hiding place.

He opened the door and slipped underneath the apron. He chuckled to himself. He was sure that no one would find him there. He waited gleefully—

Suddenly he heard voices. People were approaching the car. People were getting into the car. People were starting the car. He grew stiff with horror. He made an inarticulate sound of protest, but it was drowned by the noise of the engine. He realised suddenly that the car was now moving rapidly down the road. Very cautiously he peeped out. Two ladies, both elderly, both prim, both severe-looking, were in the front seats. They held large bunches of leaves and tiny bushes, evidently taken from the wood. One almost turned round, and at sight of her profile, William hastily decided not to reveal his presence, and dived beneath the macintosh apron again. The car sped along. There was a sinking sensation at the pit of William's stomach. How would his gallant braves fare without him in the virgin forest, and where – where – oh, where was he going—?

The car turned into a gate – it slid into a garage. The two ladies got down. 'I think the leaves are just what we wanted,' said one.

'Beautiful,' said the other, 'they will fulfil the purpose most admirably.'

They went out of the garage, still talking. William waited till the voices had died away in the distance, then very, very cautiously he climbed out of his hiding place. He was in a large garage. He realised with a sinking of the heart that he was not, to put it at its mildest, a reassuring object. The virgin forest had left its marks upon him, it had clutched at his collar and coat and hair with its thorn bushes. It had besmeared his face and clothes and knees and boots impartially with its bogs—

He crept out of the garage. It was a large garden and a large house. No, it didn't look quite like an ordinary house. Its windows were uncurtained. Within sat many girls of all sizes, with bobbed hair or plaits. Surprised and interested, he crept nearer.

A small woman wearing glasses stepped out of a French window and called him. 'Here, boy!' she said imperiously.

William was uncertain whether to obey or whether to turn and flee. But a small girl with a dimpled face and dark curly hair looked out of the window and smiled at him, and William obeyed.

He entered a class-room with a dais at one end. A large number of girls sat about the room at easels. The lady with spectacles took William by his ear and led him up the room.

'The little model I had arranged for is unable to come, girls,' she said, 'so I am going to ask you to draw the gardener's boy.'

'It must be a new gardener's boy,' said a tall thin girl, with interest. 'I've not seen him before.'

'Don't talk, Gladys,' said the mistress reprovingly; 'the point is not whether he is a new or old gardener's boy. The point is that you are to draw him. Sit down, boy.'

William, who had already picked out the dimpled dark little girl by the window, sat down quite meekly.

A girl in the front row gave a shudder.

'Isn't he *dirty*?' she said.

'Never mind,' said the mistress, 'I want you to draw him as he is – just an ugly, dirty little boy.'

She had apparently looked upon William as something as inanimate as a plaster cast, but the ferocious glare which he now turned on her informed her that he was not. She looked slightly disconcerted.

'Er – try to look a little more pleasant, boy,' she said faintly.

'I do hate having to draw *ugly* things,' said the girl in the front row with another shudder.

A look of apoplectic fury overspread William's face. He opened his mouth for an indignant rejoinder. But before it emerged the little girl at the window with the dimples and dark curls said, '*I* don't think he's ugly.'

William's expression of fury turned into a sheepish smirk.

'Don't talk about him, children,' said the lady. '*Draw* him.'

They worked in silence. William looked about him. The frowning critical appraising glare of sixteen girls did not embarrass him at all. Only when he caught the eye of the little girl with the dimples did a dark blush over-spread his earth-bedecked countenance.

'I think I've got his *ugliness* all right,' said a short, snub-nosed girl earnestly, 'but I can't quite get his *cross* look.'

'Let me look, dear,' said the mistress.

She took the sketch and examined it, standing accidentally in William's line of vision. William craned his neck and looked with interest at his portrait. Then his interest changed again to that intensity of fury that William's countenance could so ably convey. Certainly the sketch suggested a gorilla rather than a human being.

'Y-yes,' said the mistress doubtfully, 'you've caught a certain likeness—'

William opened his mouth again indignantly, when the girl by the window said suddenly, '*I* don't think he looks cross.'

William closed his mouth and his ferocity softened once more into a sheepish grin.

'He keeps looking *diff'rent*,' complained a girl in the back row.

'Stay the same, boy,' ordered the mistress imperiously.

At that minute a bell rang and there was a stampede of girls out of the doorway.

'Gently, girls,' said the mistress, preparing to follow them. 'Boy, stay and straighten up the room and put the easels away.'

William stayed behind, and to his joy discovered that the little girl with the dimples and dark curls was staying behind too. She remained at her easel gazing out of the window. William began to move easels about without any definite plan of campaign.

'I'm not the gardener's boy,' he said to the little girl.

She did not answer.

'I'm an explorer.'

She made no comment.

'I've explored places where no white man ever set his feet before.'

Still no answer.

'Runnin' terrible risks from starvation an' wild animals.'

Still no answer.

William picked up a sketch of himself from the

'I'VE EXPLORED PLACES WHERE NO WHITE MAN EVER SET
HIS FEET BEFORE,' SAID WILLIAM

floor, looked at it, blinked and swallowed, then
screwed it into a vicious ball and flung it into the
waste-paper basket.

'I once had all my teeth out without gas,' he went
on, with deliberate untruthfulness, but with a vague
desire to restore his self-respect.

Still no answer.

'I'm here disguised on a secret mission,' he went on darkly.

Suddenly the little girl put down her head on her arms and began to cry.

'Oh, don't,' said William greatly distressed. 'What's the matter? Have you got toothache?'

'No – o!'

'Has anyone been unkind to you?'

'No – o – o – o!'

'Tell me if they have,' he went on threateningly. 'I'll kill 'em for you. I don' mind how many people I kill. I've been where no white man ever—'

'I'm homesick,' wailed the little girl. 'I want to go ho-o-o-o-ome.'

'Well – well, you *go* home then,' counselled William encouragingly, almost tenderly, 'you *go* home. I'll – I'll *take* you home.'

'I c-c-can't.'

'Why not?'

She dried her eyes.

'Well, I'm in a play we're doing this afternoon, and if I don't turn up for it they'll know something's happened, and they'll c-c-catch me before I get to the station, and bring me b-b-b-back!'

'No, they *won't*,' said William. 'I-I'll help you. I tell you, no one'll ever dare stop me. I've been where no

50

white man ever set his feet 'n I've had my leg cut off without gas an—'

'Yes,' said the little girl quite unimpressed, 'but don't you see I can't go at once 'cause I've not had dinner yet, an' I'm hungry, an' if I ran away after dinner they'll find out at once and c-c-c-catch me.'

She burst into sobs again.

'No, don't,' said William desperately. 'Don't cry. It's all right. I'll take care of you. I – I say,' the light of inspiration shone suddenly in his face, 'I'll take your part in the play an' then they'll never know you've gone an' you'll get home all right.'

She stopped crying and gazed at him, then the hope died from her face and she burst into a wail.

'B-b-but you don't look like a fa-a-a-airy,' she sobbed.

'I could *make* myself look like one,' said William grimly. 'I bet I could— Look – look at me now.'

He gazed into the distance, his features composed into a simper that suggested to an impartial observer a mixture of coyness and imbecility.

'Oh, no-o-o-o!' she wailed. 'It doesn't— Oh, *don't*!'

Disappointed, William dismissed the expression which had been meant to represent the faëry for which in his heart he had such a profound contempt.

'Well,' he said, 'if it looks wrong, can't I cover my face or somethin'?'

Her tears ceased. Her eyes shone. She clasped her hands.

'Oh, I *forgot!*' she said, 'there's a veil. They won't see your face. Oh, you are a *nice* boy. Will you *really* do it? Listen, I'll tell you *just* what to do. I'm Fairy Daffodil – I'll get you the clothes in a second. There's a cap of daffodil petals, and a veil that comes down from them over your face, so *that's* all right. And you have to hide behind the green bank at the side of the stage behind a lot of green stuff and leaves. Miss Pink and Miss Grace went into the woods in the car this morning, to get the green stuff and leaves. You go there early, about two, and then when the others come they'll be so busy getting ready that they won't bother you. I'll leave you a book, and you can pretend to be reading, and when it begins you wait there till someone calls, "Fairy Daffodil," and then you come out and bow and say, "Here am I – speak, Queen." And when that bit's over you just sit down on the stool by the side of the queen's throne and you don't speak again. It's quite easy. Oh, it is *kind* of you, dear boy.'

William's freckled countenance flamed again.

'Oh, it's nothin',' he said modestly. 'It's nothin' to what I'd do for you, an' it's nothin' to what I've done. Why, I've been where no white man's ever set his feet before. This is *nothin'* to that. An' if they catch you and bring you back,' he gave a short sinister laugh, 'well, they'd better look out, that's all.'

She gazed at him with bright eyes. 'Oh, it *is* kind of you. I – I'd go now, at once, but I'm so hungry and – it's treacle-tart today.'

The guests swarmed into the school hall. In the middle of the second row sat William's father and mother, Mr and Mrs Brown. The room was tastefully decorated with leaves and bracken.

'I like to come to all these affairs, don't you?' said the lady next to Mrs Brown. 'I really didn't *want* to have a big girls' school so near the village, but now it's come it's best to be sociable, and I must say they're always very good about sending out invitations to all their little affairs.'

'Oh, yes,' said Mrs Brown vaguely, 'and it all looks very nice.'

The curtain rose and the two ladies continued their conversation in a whisper.

'Very pretty,' said Mrs Brown.

'Isn't it?' said the other. 'Oh, it's quite a nice change to come to a thing of this sort once in a way—'

'Well, I must say,' admitted Mrs Brown, 'I like to get right away from home sometimes, because, really, at home I'm on pins the whole time, not knowing whatever William's going to do next. At a place like this I feel *safe*. It's nice to be anywhere where I *know* that William can't suddenly rise up before my eyes doing something awful.'

'Fairy Daffodil!' called the fairy herald on the stage.

A figure arose from behind a leafy barrier, took an ungraceful step forward, tripped over the leafy barrier and crashed to earth – leafy barrier and all. The yellow headgear rolled off on to the floor revealing a tousled head over a stern earth-streaked freckled face.

'What's your boy like?' said Mrs Brown's neighbour, who was not looking at the stage. 'I don't think I've ever seen him.'

But Mrs Brown's smile had faded. Her face had become a mask of horror. Her mouth had dropped open. Her neighbour followed her eyes to the stage. The strange apparition was in no wise disconcerted by the contretemps with the leafy barrier. It did not even trouble to recover its headgear. It stood in the middle of the stage and said loudly and ferociously: 'Here I am—'

There was a dead silence. Fairy Bluebell, who stood near, inspired by a gallant British determination to carry on in spite of all disasters, prompted, 'Speak—'

William looked at her haughtily. 'I've just spoke,' he said.

'Speak, Queen,' hissed Bluebell desperately.

'It's not my turn,' hissed the Queen back.

Bluebell stamped.

'Say, "Speak, Queen,"' she said to William.

'Oh,' said William, 'I'm sorry. I forgot that bit. I forgot there was something else. Speak, Queen. That's all, anyway, isn't it? Where's the stool?'

He looked round, then calmly sat down on the stool, sublimely unaware of actors and audience completely paralysed around him.

Slowly, very slowly, the power of speech returned to Mrs Brown. Her horror-stricken eyes left the stage. She clasped her husband's arm. 'John,' she said hysterically, 'it – it – it's William.' Mr Brown, too, had gazed open-mouthed at this wholly unexpected apparition of his son. Then he recovered himself.

'Er – nonsense, my dear,' he said firmly. 'Never seen the boy before. Do you hear? We've never seen the boy before.'

'B-b-b-but we have, John,' she said. 'It's William!'

'Who's William?' said Mr Brown wildly. 'There isn't any William. Temporarily, I've disowned him. I've disowned him till we meet again under the shelter of our own roof. I don't know how he got here or what he's going to do, and I don't care. He's nothing to do with me. I've disowned him. I tell you – I've disowned him.'

'Oh, John,' wailed Mrs Brown. 'Isn't it *awful*!'

*

'WHAT'S YOUR BOY LIKE?' SAID MRS BROWN'S
NEIGHBOUR. 'I DON'T THINK I'VE EVER SEEN HIM.'

Everyone agreed afterwards that somebody ought to
have done something at once. But the headmistress
was out of the room supervising the tea arrangements,
and the mistress who was attending to the curtain was
shortsighted and deaf, and was thinking of something

WILLIAM LOOKED AT FAIRY BLUEBELL HAUGHTILY. 'IT'S
NOT MY TURN,' HE HISSED. 'I'VE JUST SPOKE.'

else at the time and didn't realise that anything was the
matter, and the mistress who was prompting said that
for all she knew it was some fresh arrangement made
behind her back, and if it had been, it wouldn't have
been the *first* time it had happened, so how was she to
know? Anyway, the play dragged on. But no one took

any further interest in the play. The whole interest of the audience was concentrated on the curious apparition inadequately clothed in yellow butter muslin, who had taken its seat at the foot of the throne.

The apparition itself seemed unaware that it was attracting any attention. It sat down and gazed around it, stern, bored, contemptuous – then a light as at some happy memory came into its face. It pulled up the butter muslin to its waist, revealing muddy boots, muddy legs and muddy trousers, plunged its hand into its pocket and brought out a nut, which it proceeded to crack with much facial contortion and bared teeth.

At this point the headmistress entered by the door at the back of the hall. Her face wore a proud smile. Her eyes wandered slowly to the stage. The proud smile dropped from her face. A look of startled horror succeeded it. The Fairy Daffodil had cracked the nut and was proceeding with every appearance of concentration and satisfaction to extract the edible part of it.

With the air of one dashing to a heroic rescue, the headmistress plunged up the hall and drew the curtain.

'Er – who is that boy?' said Mr Brown brazenly to a mistress who stood near.

It was the art mistress.

'He's our gardener's boy,' said the art mistress helplessly, 'but I don't know *what* he's doing on the stage.'

'You see, dear,' said Mr Brown to his wife, with a twinkle in his eye, 'he's the gardener's boy.'

'But he *isn't*!' wailed Mrs Brown, 'he's William. You *know* he's William.'

The headmistress, purple with rage, plunged behind the curtain and made a grab at the Fairy Daffodil.

'What is the meaning of this, you wicked boy!' she said.

The Fairy Daffodil abandoned his half-eaten nut, dodged what he rightly suspected to be an avenging hand and fled.

'Catch him!' panted the headmistress, 'catch that boy.'

The entire cast followed by the entire staff dashed after William and pursued him in a body. Gathering up his impeding yellow robe, William fled like an arrow from a bow – out of a door at the back of the hall, across the garden towards the front gate. He would probably have outrun his pursuers had he not collided with a little girl and a tall man who were just entering the gate. The three of them rolled on the ground together. Then they sat up and looked at each other. The tall man, who had received the full impact of William's bullet head in his middle regions, caressed those regions with his hands and moaned softly. But the little girl gave a cry of joy and said:

'Oh, it's the nice boy, Daddy.' Then to William: 'I met Daddy on the way to the station, boy. I didn't know he was coming and I feel *quite* happy now. He's given me a lovely tip, and I've remembered that I'm playing in the netball match next week and I'd *hate* to miss that.'

At this point the gym mistress, the vanguard of the pursuit, arrived and seized William by one ear, the art mistress arrived next and seized him by the other ear. The head girl arrived next, and, not wanting to be out of it, seized him by the scruff of his neck. The rank and file of the pursuers now arrived and seized him by any portion of his anatomy that happened to be unoccupied. Thus seized at all available points, he was marched off to the headmistress. A crowd of visitors was pouring out of the side door. Among the first came Mr and Mrs Brown. Mr Brown gave one glance at his son in this ignominious plight and plunged back to lose himself among the crowd. Mrs Brown, distraught and torn between husband and son, finally followed him.

'Oh, John,' she said wringing her hands, 'aren't you going to *do* anything?'

'Not I,' said Mr Brown. 'I told you I'd disowned him.'

It was an hour later. The visitors had been collected again. A concert and many recitations had been given. The prizes had been distributed. The head-mistress, at the earnest request of the tall man, had pardoned William's escapade. The visitors were having tea in the garden. William sat at a little table with the tall man and the little girl. He was blissfully happy. He was consuming unlimited quantities of cakes, and every now and then the little girl smiled at him very sweetly.

'I won't be so silly any more, Daddy,' she said. 'We'd had a midnight feast last night and I'd eaten thousands and thousands of mince tarts and that *always* makes me feel a little sad the next day and—'

'One minute,' said her father. 'I can see a business friend of mine there. Hello, Brown,' he called.

Mr Brown approached the table. William's jaunty air dropped from him. He blinked. His jaw dropped. Crumbs! His father! He bent down as if to pick something off the ground and remained in that position, hoping thus to remain undiscovered.

'This is my daughter, Brown,' said the tall man after greeting him. Then he seized William by the scruff of his neck and raised his head. William tried to avoid his father's gaze. 'I'm not sure who this young-ster is, so I can't introduce him properly. All I know about him is that he's been where no white man ever set foot before and he's had all his teeth taken out without gas – but perhaps you know him?'

'I didn't know either of those facts about him,' admitted Mr Brown drily, 'but,' his sardonic eye forced his son's to meet it, 'I *have* met him before.'

CHAPTER 3

WILLIAM AND THE CHINESE GOD

Mr Markson, the headmaster of William's school, was very large and very red-faced and very loud-voiced and very irascible. Behind this mask of terror Mr Markson was in reality a rather shy and very well-meaning man. He liked big boys and got on well with them. He disliked small boys and glared at them and roared at them on principle.

William and his friends came in contact with this ogre seldom, and on occasions of decided unpleasantness.

In their eyes he was all the fabulous masters of antiquity and all the ogres of fairyland rolled into one. They trembled beneath his rolling eye and booming voice. Which was just as well, because these were about the only things beneath which they did tremble.

They were discussing this grim potentate on their way home from school.

'He's the nasty temperedest man in the world,' said Ginger solemnly. 'I know he is. I know there's not another man as nasty tempered as what he is in all the world.'

'He swished Rawlings for jus' walkin' through the stream in the playground,' contributed Henry, 'an' Rawlings is short-sighted, you know. An' he said he din't *see* the stream till he'd got right over it, but ole Markie swished him jus' the same.'

'When he jus' *looks* at me,' admitted Ginger, 'it makes me feel kinder queer.'

'Yes, an' when he *yells* like what he does,' said Douglas, 'it makes me jump like – like—'

'Like a frog,' suggested Ginger helpfully.

'Frog yourself!'

'I din' mean you *was* a frog,' explained Ginger. 'I only meant you jumped like a frog.'

'Well, I don't jump like a frog more'n other people do,' said Douglas pugnaciously.

'Oh, shut up arguing,' said Henry, who had been enjoying the collective indictment of 'Old Markie', and did not wish it to tail off into a combat between Douglas and Ginger. 'I guess,' he went on darkly, 'that if some people knew what he was like really an' – an' the way he shouts an' swishes people an' – an' carries on, I guess he'd be put in prison or hung or something. There's laws,' he added vaguely, 'to stop people goin' on at other people the way he does.'

William had listened to this conversation in silence.

William disliked belonging to the majority of the terrorised. He preferred always to belong to the minority of the terror-inspiring, or at least of the intrepid. He gave a short, scornful laugh.

'I'm not frightened of him,' he said with a swagger.

They gazed at him, aghast at this patent untruth.

'Oh, *aren't* you?' said Ginger meaningly.

'No, *an'* I'm not,' retorted William. 'I wun't mind sayin' anythin' to him, I wun't. I wun't mind – I wun't mind jus' tellin' him what I thought of him any time, I wun't.'

'Oh, *wun't* you?' said Ginger disagreeably, piqued by this unexpected attitude of William's. 'Oh, no,' sarcastically, 'you're not frightened of him, *you* aren't. *You* wasn't frightened of him las' Tuesday, was you?'

William was momentarily disconcerted by this reference to an occasion when he had incurred the public wrath of the monster for scuffling in prayers, and had been summoned to his study afterwards. But only momentarily.

'P'raps you *thought* I was,' he conceded in a tone of kindly indulgence. 'I daresay you *thought* I was. I daresay you judge eve'body by yourself an' *thought* I was.'

'Well, you *looked* frightened,' said Henry.

'An' you *sounded* frightened,' said Ginger, and mimicked '"Yes, sir . . . No, sir . . . please I didn't mean to, sir."'

William looked at them with an air of superior pity.

'Yes, I daresay you *thought* I was frightened,' he said, and added darkly, 'you see you din't hear what I said to him in his study afterwards. I guess,' he added with a short meaning laugh, 'he'll leave *me* alone after that.'

The others were dumbfounded by this attitude. For a minute the sheer impudence of it deprived them of the power of speech. Ginger recovered first.

'All right,' he said, 'we're jus' at his house now. All right, if you're not frightened of him, go in. Jus' go an' ring at the door an' tell him you're not frightened of him.'

'He knows,' said William simply.

But they were closing him in around the gate, preventing his further progress down the road.

'Well go in an' tell him again,' said Douglas, ''case he's forgot.'

William, at bay, looked up at Mr Markson's house, inappropriately termed The Nest. He wished that he had not made his gesture of defiance in its immediate vicinity. Then a cheering thought occurred to him.

'An' I would, too,' he said, striking a heroic attitude. 'An' I would 'f he was at home. But he's at school. He's at school till six o'clock today.'

'All right, go an' walk into his house an' take

somethin' jus' to *show* you aren't frightened of him,' said Ginger.

'That'd be stealin',' said William piously.

'You could take it back afterwards,' said Douglas. 'You aren't fright'ned of him, so it'd be all right.'

'No, I'm not goin' to,' said William.

Henry crowed triumphantly.

'You're fright'ned of him,' they jeered.

Suddenly William's blood was up. When William's blood was up things happened.

'All right,' he said. 'I'll – I'll *show* you.'

Without waiting to consider his decision in the calm light of reason he went boldly up to the front door. There his courage began to fail. He knew that no power on earth would nerve his arm to knock on the ogre's dreaded front door. But there was a drawing-room to the right of the door. One of the French windows leading from this drawing-room on to the drive was open.

The drawing-room seemed to be empty. Steeling his heart and spurring his flickering courage by the thought of his jeering friends without, William plunged into the room, seized the first thing he saw, plunged out, and with a beating heart and unsteady knees ran down the drive to join the little crowd of boys gaping through the gate of The Nest.

His panic left him as he neared safety and his

swagger returned. He held out his booty on one hand. It was a small and (though William did not know it) very valuable Chinese figure of a god.

'There!' he said. 'I've been in his drawing-room and fetched that.'

They gazed at him speechless. William had once again consolidated his position as leader.

'Sorter pot thing out of his drawin'-room,' he explained carelessly. 'D'you think I'm afraid of him *now*?' he ended with a short derisive laugh.

Henry found his voice. 'Well, you've gotter put it back now,' he said, 'an' – an' p'raps that won't be 's easy 's takin' it.'

''F you think it was *easy* takin' it—' began William indignantly.

But at that moment a tall figure – ferocious-looking even in the distance – appeared at the end of the lane.

William had been wrong. Mr Markson was not staying at school till six.

By the time Mr Markson reached the gate of The Nest, William and his friends were mere specks on the horizon.

In the safe refuge of his bedroom William took the Chinese figure out of his pocket and looked at it distastefully. He didn't know how to get the beastly thing back, and he was sure there'd be a fuss if he didn't get the beastly thing back, and he wished he'd never taken the beastly thing, and he blamed Douglas and Ginger and Henry for the whole affair.

If only they'd taken his word that he wasn't frightened of old Markie, instead of making him go in and get the beastly thing – and ten to one old Markie would catch him as he was putting it back and – and – and there'd be a *norful* fuss.

He considered the advisability of giving it a temporary hiding place in one of his drawers among his handkerchiefs or shirts or collars, then dismissed the idea. His mother might find it and demand explanations. On the whole, his pocket was the safest place for the present.

He went downstairs feeling gloomy and disillusioned. All the people one read about in books – Odysseus and Tarzan and the rest of them – could do anything they liked and nothing ever happened to them, while he couldn't even say he wasn't fright'ned of old Markie without getting a beastly little pot thing shoved on to him, that there'd be an awful fuss about if anyone found out he'd got it.

He wandered downstairs, his mind still occupied with the problem of returning the china image before Mr Markson had discovered its absence. Suppose someone had seen him go in and fetch it and told old Markie, and old Markie summoned him into his study tomorrow morning after prayers. William turned hot and cold at the thought. That gesture of defiance and courage had been very effective and enjoyable at the time, but its consequences might be unpleasant.

'What's the matter, darling?' inquired Mrs Brown solicitously as William entered the drawing-room.

'Why?' said William guiltily, afraid that in some way his appearance betrayed his late escapade.

'You look so sad,' said his mother fondly.

William emitted his famous laugh – short and bitter.

'Huh!' he ejaculated. 'I bet *you'd* be sad if—'

He decided on second thoughts not to make any detailed explanation and stopped short.

'If what, dear?' said Mrs Brown sympathetically.

'If you'd got all the troubles what I've got,' said William darkly.

'Yes, but what sort of troubles, dear?' said Mrs Brown.

'Oh, people botherin' you an' not b'lievin' what you say an' – an' gettin' things you don't want shoved on to you,' said William gloomily.

At this point he caught sight of his reflection in a full-length mirror on the wall and was greatly disconcerted to discover that the Chinese figure made a bulge in his pocket that seemed to call aloud for comment. At any minute his mother might demand to know what it was. He took advantage of her turning to the window to transfer the figure from his pocket to a small table by the wall just where he stood. He put it well at the back of a lot of other ornaments. Surely no one would notice it there. It could surely stay there quite safely till the coast was clear for taking it back, anyway.

He heaved a deep sigh and passed a hand over his brow. Life was very wearing – and there'd certainly be a most awful fuss if anyone found out – an' all Henry's and Ginger's and Douglas's fault – it ought to be a lesson to them to believe what people said in the future. Anyway – he found great comfort in the thought – he'd *shown* 'em.

He joined his mother at the window, scowling gloomily. Suddenly his gloomy scowl changed to a look of rigid horror. Mr Markson was coming along the road with Ethel . . . now they were turning in at the gate of William's house. And there on a table in the drawing-room, which presumably they would soon enter, reposed Mr Markson's Chinese image. William had had many nightmares in his time but none as bad as this.

Ethel, although William's sister, was admittedly the prettiest girl for miles around, and Mr Markson, although William's headmaster, was beneath his mask of ferocity quite a simple-hearted man, who liked pretty girls and had been much attracted by Ethel when introduced to her the week before.

They entered the room almost immediately, followed by two old ladies who were friends of Mrs Brown. Mr Markson took no notice of William. He knew, of course, that there was a small boy in the room who might or might not be a pupil at his school, but out of school hours Mr Markson ignored all small boys on principle.

To William suddenly the Chinese image on the little table seemed to dominate the room. It seemed to tower above every other object, not excluding the grandfather clock. It seemed to yell aloud to its owner: 'Hi, you! I'm here! I'm here! I'm here! I'm here!'

Instinctively William stepped in front of the table, placing his small but solid person between the now hateful image and its rightful owner. Standing thus, red-faced with apprehension and determination, he glared fiercely around the room as though daring anyone to attempt to dislodge him. There was a How-Horatius-kept-the-Bridge air about him.

Ethel and Mr Markson and Mrs Brown and one of the old ladies sat at the other end of the room and began to discuss animatedly a forthcoming village pageant. The other old lady drifted across to William and sat down on a chair near him. She pointed kindly to another chair near her.

'Sit down, little boy,' she said, 'pray don't stand, though it's nice to see a little boy so polite nowadays.'

William's scowl deepened.

'I'd rather stand, thanks,' he said.

But the old lady persisted.

'No, do sit down,' she said with a pleasant smile. 'I want to have a nice long talk with you; I'm so fond of little boys. But you must sit down or I shan't feel comfortable.'

William was disconcerted for a minute, then he recovered his aplomb.

'I – I can't sit down,' he said mysteriously.

The lady gaped at him, amazed.

'Why, dear?' she said sympathetically.

'I've hurt my legs,' said William with a flash of inspiration. 'I can't bend my knees. Not for sitting down. I *gotta* stand.'

He scowled at her more ferociously than ever as he spoke.

'My poor little boy,' said the old lady sympathetically. 'I'm *so* sorry. Do you have to stand up all the time? What do the doctors say?'

'They say – they say jus' that,' said William lamely, 'that I've gotta stand up all the time.'

'But there's – hope of your being cured, I suppose, dear?' said the old lady anxiously.

'Oh, yes,' William reassured her.

'*When* do they say you'll be all right?' went on the lady earnestly.

'Oh, any time after today,' said William unthinkingly.

'You can *lie* down, I suppose?' said the old lady, evidently much distressed by William's mysterious complaint.

'Oh yes,' said William, who by this time had almost convinced himself of the reality of his disease. 'I can go to bed at night and that sort of thing.'

'Well, dear, won't you come and lie down now?' said the old lady. 'We'll go over to the window and you can lie down on the sofa and I'll sit on the chair near, and we'll have a nice little talk. It's so nice over there in the sunshine.'

William moistened his lips.

'I – I think I won't move, thank you,' said William.

'But you can walk, dear, can't you?'

'Oh, yes, I can walk, but—' he stopped and gazed around, seeking inspiration from the wallpaper and ceiling.

'It's so nice and light over there,' coaxed the old lady.

Inspiration came again with a flash. William's face cleared.

'I'm not s'posed to be in the light,' he said brightly, 'because I've got bad eyes.'

'I'VE HURT MY LEGS,' SAID WILLIAM, WITH A FLASH OF
INSPIRATION. 'I CAN'T BEND MY KNEES.'

The old lady gazed at him weakly.

'Bad – bad eyes, did you say?'

'Yes,' said William pleasantly, relieved to have
found another plausible excuse for not relinquishing

his post. 'I can't stand the light,' he explained earnestly. 'I've gotta stay in dark places 'cause of my eyes.'

'B-but how terrible,' said the old lady, horrified to the depth of her kindly old soul. 'Bad legs and bad— It's almost incredible.' She gazed in silence at his stolid and almost crudely healthy countenance, while a dim suspicion crept into her mind that it was, indeed, incredible. 'Can't sit down or bend your knees?' she repeated in amazement.

'No,' said William unblushingly.

'And can't bear the light on your eyes?'

'No,' said William, staring at her unblinkingly. 'Bad eyes.'

Well, of course, thought the nice old lady, it might be true. One did hear of sad cases of terrible illnesses among quite young children.

She crossed over to the other group.

'I'm so sorry to hear of your poor little boy's ill-health, Mrs Brown,' she said.

There was a moment's tense silence, during which the members of the other group stared open-mouthed from the nice old lady to the robustly healthy William, from the robustly healthy William back to the nice old lady. The silence was broken by William who, realising the moment was one that called for discretion rather than valour, fled from the room with the speed of an arrow from a bow.

Mrs Brown's bewildered demand for an explanation was lost in a sudden exclamation of astonishment from Mr Markson, who was staring in amazement at the little table of ornaments that William's flight had revealed.

'Er – excuse me,' he said, and going across the room picked up the little Chinese ornament. 'Most extraordinary,' he said, 'I have an exact replica of this at home and I was assured that it was absolutely unique. May I ask without impertinence, Mrs Brown, did you get it in England?'

Mrs Brown joined him and looked at the little ornament with a puzzled frown.

'My husband must have got it,' she said. 'I was away last week and hadn't noticed it before. But I'm always coming back and finding curios and antiques all over the place. My husband's mad on them. He's always bringing them home. . . .'

'Most interesting,' said Mr Markson, still examining the figure. '*Most* interesting . . . I must have a talk with your husband about it. I quite understood that mine was unique—'

There came the sound of the tea-gong, and Mrs Brown ushered them into the dining-room.

William's extraordinary behaviour was quite forgotten except by the kind old lady, who was so worried by it that she scarcely ate anything at all.

As soon as the guests were safely shut into the dining-room, William slid down the banisters and into the drawing-room. His face wore a look of strained anxiety. He must take the thing away at once before old Markie spotted it. He only hoped that he hadn't spotted it before tea, but he didn't think so because the tea bell had gone almost at once. But he wondered whether that old lady had told his mother about his eyes and legs. Crumbs, he simply didn't get a bit of peace – just one thing after another.

He slipped the little image into his pocket and, peering carefully around the hall to make sure that the coast was clear, crept stealthily out of the front door and set off at a run down the drive and into the road. He felt a great relief. The danger was over. Old Markie was safely at tea. He could easily slip the thing into its place again before old Markie returned.

'It's William Brown, isn't it? William dear!'

He turned with an inward groan. It was Mrs Franks, a friend of his mother's.

Unchilled by his expression, she greeted him effusively.

'Just the little boy I wanted to meet,' she said with an all-embracing smile. 'I want you to take a note to your mother, dear. Just come back to me and I'll write it out for you.'

William muttered something about being 'busy'

and 'in a hurry,' and 'come along later,' but it was useless. She put an arm affectionately upon his shoulder and gently drew him along with her.

'I know you want to be mother's helpful little man,' she coaxed, ignoring his ferocious scowl, 'and I won't keep you one minute longer than I must from your toys and little friends.'

William gulped eloquently and, his face flaming with fury, allowed himself to be led down the road. The only satisfaction he allowed himself was a vigorous ducking out of the circle of her arm. He accompanied her in silence, refusing even to satisfy her curiosity as to how he did and his mother did and how his father did and how Ethel did and wasn't it a sudden change in the weather.

The hateful image seemed to be shouting its existence aloud to all the world from its inadequate hiding-place in William's pocket. And every minute made the return of it more dangerous. Every minute old Markie might be going back to his lair. He sat, fuming inwardly in Mrs Franks' drawing-room while she wrote the note at her bureau, his hands on his bare knees, his muddy boots planted firmly on the carpet, his tousled head turned in the direction of the window, his freckled face set in a stern frown.

Then, suddenly, his eyes filled with horror and his jaw dropped open. Old Markie was coming down the road again; old Markie was coming in at the drive of Mrs Franks' house; old Markie was ringing the bell. A sudden panic came over William. Not only did the Chinese image protrude conspicuously from his pocket, but its head was distinctly visible. Anything rather than be caught by old Markie with the thing in his pocket. He took it out of his pocket and slipped it with feverish haste upon the top of the piano behind a small Dresden china shepherdess. Then he sat staring in front of him, his face vying with the Chinese image's in blankness and immobility.

Mrs Franks had not noticed his movement, she went on writing.

Mr Markson entered. He threw a quick glance at William and then proceeded to ignore him. Another small boy, perhaps a pupil at his own school – he didn't know and didn't care. The less notice taken of small boys the better. His business with Mrs Franks concerned the coming village pageant which he was organising. But in the middle of their conversation his eyes wandered to the piano and his voice died away. His eyes dilated. His jaw dropped open. William still stared fixedly in front of him. William's expression of blankness verged on imbecility.

'Er – excuse me,' said Mr Markson, advancing to the piano, 'but – er – most extraordinary. *Most* extraordinary.'

He picked up the little image and examined it. His perplexity increased. '*Most* extraordinary – three in the same village and I was *assured* that mine was unique.'

'To what do you refer, Mr, Markson?' said Mrs Franks pleasantly.

'This little Chinese image on the piano,' said Mr Markson. He sounded like a man in a dream.

'Oh, the shepherdess!' said Mrs Franks brightly, fixing her short-sighted eyes vaguely in the direction of the piano.

'It's not a shepherdess, pardon me,' said Mr Markson courteously, 'it's a Chinese god.'

'Fancy that now,' said Mrs Franks in genuine surprise, 'and I always thought that it was a shepherdess.'

'Not at all, not at all,' said Mr Markson, still examining the figure. 'Forgive the impertinence, Mrs Franks, but did you get the figure at a curio dealer's?'

'No, Mr Markson, my aunt left it to me, but' – Mrs Franks was certainly surprised – 'fancy it being a Chinese god, and all these years I've thought it was a shepherdess and so did my aunt.'

The striking of the clock of the village church reminded Mr Markson that time was getting on and that he wanted to take a short walk before dinner, so after receiving from Mrs Franks a repeated assurance that she would be *proud* indeed to impersonate an

WILLIAM STILL STARED FIXEDLY IN FRONT OF HIM AS MR
MARKSON PICKED UP THE LITTLE IMAGE AND EXAMINED
IT.

early Saxon matron, provided, of course, that the
costume was – er – suitable, Mr Markson departed
with one last long perplexed look at the Chinese image
on the piano. William, who had been holding his
breath for the last few minutes, emitted a long,
resonant sigh of relief which fluttered all the papers

MR MARKSON'S PERPLEXITY
INCREASED. 'MOST
EXTRAORDINARY!' HE SAID.

on Mrs Franks' bureau.

'William darling, don't *blow* like that,' said Mrs Franks reprovingly. 'I'll just address the envelope, dear, and then you can take it.'

She sat down again at her bureau, with her back to him, and William, seizing his opportunity, slipped the Chinese image again into his pocket.

'Here it is, dear,' said Mrs Franks, handing it to him.

Then she went over to the piano, took up the Dresden china shepherdess and examined it from every angle.

'A Chinese god,' she said at last. 'What an extraordinary idea! No, I don't agree with him at all. Not at all, dear, do you? A Chinese god' – her amazement increased – 'why, nothing about it even remotely suggests the Orient to me. Does it to you, dear? The man must suffer from some defect in his sight.'

William murmured something inaudible, took a hasty farewell of her, seized the note, and hurried out into the road.

Old Markie had said that he was going for a walk before dinner. That would give him plenty of time to put the thing back. Crumbs! He'd had an awful few minutes in Mrs Franks' drawing-room, but it was all over now. He'd just put the thing back where he'd got it, and – and – well, he'd never go into old Markie's house again for anything. He was pretty sure of *that*. Crumbs! he wouldn't, indeed.

He stopped at the gate of The Nest and looked up and down the road. The road was empty. With a quickly beating heart he went up the drive. The French windows were shut, but the front door was open. He slipped into the hall. He took the Chinese image out of his pocket, and stood for one moment irresolute holding it in his hand. Then, the door of the room at the back of the hall opened and Mr Markson came out into the hall.

Mr Markson had thought that the clouds were gathering and had decided not to go for a walk before dinner after all.

'Who's that?' he bellowed. 'What do you want, boy? Come in! Come in!'

William slowly advanced to the back room still holding the Chinese figure in his hand.

Mr Markson looked him up and down. William silently implored the earth to open and swallow him up, but the earth callously refused.

A light of recognition dawned in Mr Markson's eyes.

'Why, you're Mrs Brown's boy,' he said.

'Yes, sir,' said William tonelessly.

Then Mr Markson's eye fell upon the Chinese figure which William was vainly trying to conceal with his hands.

'What!' he began, 'you've brought her Chinese figure?'

William moistened his lips.

'Yes, sir. She – she's – she's sent it, sir.'

'*Sent* it?' said Mr Markson. His eyes gleamed with the greed of the collector. 'You mean – *sent* it?'

'Yes, sir,' said William with sudden inspiration. 'She's sent it to you – to keep, sir.'

'But how *extraordinarily* kind,' burst out Mr Markson. 'I must write to her at once. How very kind! I must – wait a minute. There's still the third. I'll write to Mrs Franks, too. I'll ask Mrs Franks if she can possibly trace the origin of her piece.' He was speaking to himself rather than to William. 'I'll just hint that I'd be willing to buy it should she ever wish to sell. Sit down there and wait, boy.'

William sat down and waited in silence while Mr Markson wrote at his desk. William stared desperately in front of him. Crumbs! Things were getting in more of a mess every minute. He didn't see how he could possibly get out of it now. He was in it – right up to the neck. But – Mr Markson fastened up the envelope, addressed it, and turned to William.

Just then a maid entered with the evening post on a tray. Mr Markson took it. She retired and Mr Markson read his letters.

'Bother!' he said, 'here's a letter that *must* be answered by tonight's post. Do something for me, boy. Take this figure and put it on the table in the front room with its fellow and then take this note to Mrs Franks, will you?'

'Yes, sir,' said William meekly.

Mr Markson sat down at his bureau. William went quickly and gratefully from the room. In the hall he stopped to consider the situation. Mr Markson would expect an answer from Mrs Franks. He might even ring her up about it. There would be awkward complications, awkward for William that is – And suddenly yet another inspiration came to him. He pocketed the image again and set off down the road.

He walked for a few yards, turned back, walked up again to the front door of The Nest and into the back room. Mr Markson was still writing his letter. William took the Chinese figure out of his pocket.

'Mrs Franks sent you this, sir,' he said in his most expressionless voice, staring in front of him fixedly.

Mr Markson's face beamed with joy.

'*Sent* it?' he gasped.

'Yes, sir,' said William, speaking monotonously, as though he were repeating a lesson. 'An' she said please will you not write to her about it or thank her or ever mention it to her please, sir.'

At the conclusion of this breathless speech William paled and blinked, still staring fixedly before him. But old Markie beamed with joy.

'What delicacy of feeling that displays,' he said. 'A lesson indeed to the cruder manners of this age. How – how *exceptionally* kind!' He held the china piece on his hand. 'The third! What almost incredible good fortune! The third! Now to put it with its two fellows.'

He walked across to the front room and entered it. He looked from the image in his hand to the empty table where that image had stood only a few hours ago. He looked from table to image, from image to table, and again from table to image. Then he turned for an explanation from William.

But William was no longer there.

CHAPTER 4

ALL THE NEWS

CONTINUOUS rain had put a stop to the usual activities of the Outlaws. The game of Red Indians, if played in a perpetual downpour, palls after an hour or two, and even the absorbing pastime of Pirates loses its savour when it has reached a certain pitch of dampness.

So the Outlaws assembled in the leaky old barn and from its inadequate shelter watched the rain despondently.

'Seems 's if it's goin' on for ever,' said Ginger with gloomy interest.

'P'raps it is,' said Henry. 'P'raps it's the end of the world comin'.'

'I bet I'm the last person left alive if it is,' said William boastfully, ''cause I can float on my back for hours an' hours, an' *hours*!'

'*Floatin'* won't be no good,' objected Douglas, 'you'd get et up by fishes and things.'

'Oh, *would I*!' said William with scornful

emphasis. 'I'd take a big knife in one pocket an' a pistol in the other an'—'

'It wun't shoot, all wet,' said Ginger firmly.

'It would. I'd have special bullets,' said William pugnaciously. 'I *bet* it would.'

'Oh, shut up about bullets an' fishes an' things,' said Henry, 'let's try 'n think of something to *do*.'

'Well, what *is* there to do?' said William irritably, annoyed by this interruption of his alluring description of himself as the sole survivor of a submerged world. 'I'd swim to the highest mountain in the world what there'd be a teeny bit of the top still showin' an' I'd stay there till the rain stopped an' then I'd come down an' walk all over the world in everyone's houses an' shops an' take everything out of all the shops and use everyone's things—'

'Everything'd be *wet*' objected Ginger.

'It'd soon dry,' said William optimistically. 'I'd dry it. I'd light fires.'

'You couldn't. The coal'd be all wet,' said Ginger.

'Oh, shut *up* – what are we going to do now?' said Henry again.

'Let's have a newspaper,' said Douglas suddenly.

They looked at him with interest.

'A newspaper?' said William slowly, as though he were weighing the idea judicially.

'Yes,' said Douglas eagerly. 'Write one, you know an' someone be editor. The editor's a sort of chief man—'

'I'll be that,' put in William hastily.

'An' each write somethin' for it jus' like a real newspaper.'

'An' what about printin'?' said Henry the practical.

'Oh, we can settle all that later,' said Douglas vaguely. 'It's gotter be *wrote* first.'

Henry looked somewhat sombrely round the barn with its bare walls and sodden floor and dripping roof. Its only furniture consisted of a few old packing-cases, which the Outlaws generally utilised for their games on wet days, and an old coil of rope.

'Doesn't look much to write a newspaper *with*,' he said gloomily.

'Well, we c'd easily *get* things,' said the newly-appointed editor, with an air of stern and frowning leadership. ''F you keep findin' *'bjections* we shan't ever get *anything* done.'

''*Bjections!*' said Henry staring. 'I like that! Me findin' *'bjections* when I only *jus'* said there wasn't anythin' to write a paper *with*. Well, look for yourself. *Is* there anything to write a newspaper with?'

William looked round at the packing-cases, the leaking roof and the coil of rope.

'Seems all right to start on,' he said optimistically.

'Anyway, we only want jus' a bit of paper an' a few pencils jus' at first.'

'Well, we haven't gottem have we?' said Henry simply.

'No, but you can eas'ly run an' gettem,' said William.

'Oh, I can, can I?' said Henry indignantly. 'Oh, an' what about me getting all wet out in the rain?'

'Don't suppose it'll do you any harm,' said William callously.

'No, an' I don't suppose it'd do *you* any harm,' retorted Henry with spirit.

'No, but I'm going to be busy gettin' things ready here,' said William.

'So'm I,' said Henry firmly.

It was finally agreed, however, that both Henry and William should go in search of material for the newspaper. The expedition was rendered more interesting by a realistic pretence that the Outlaws were a besieged army and that Henry and William were two heroes who had volunteered to creep through the enemy's lines in search of provender for their starving comrades.

Ginger, writhing about the floor of the barn, simulated to his own entire satisfaction the agonies of one suffering from the pangs of extreme hunger. No one took much notice of him, but he did not mind. He was thoroughly enjoying his own performance.

Douglas set up a rival show by making a pretence of eating one of the packing-cases which he said was a dead horse.

William and Henry with great ostentation of secrecy crept through the hedge that represented the enemy's lines and across the field to the road, where they separated.

William swung along the road. It was still raining. His gait alternated between swagger and caution, according as the rôle of world famous editor or creeper through an enemy's lines in search of provender for his starving comrades, was uppermost in his mind.

It was still raining. He looked up with a certain apprehension, not unmixed with interest, at the smoking chimneys of the Hall as he passed it. At the Hall lived Mr Bott of Bott's Sauce, with his wife and daughter. Mr and Mrs Bott were negligible in William's eyes. Not so the daughter. Violet Elizabeth Bott was a maiden of six years, with a lisp, an angelic face and a will of iron.

She cultivated and used for her own purpose a scream that would have put a factory siren to shame and which was guaranteed to reduce anyone within ten yards of it to quite an expensive nervous break-down. It had never yet been known to fail. William dreaded and respected Violet Elizabeth Bott. She had been away on a holiday with her family for the last month, but William knew that they had returned yesterday.

He hoped that she would leave them in peace for that day at least. She cherished an affection for the Outlaws which was not reciprocated though they were helpless against her weapons. Then William remembered that he was editor of a world-famous newspaper, and throwing a contemptuous laugh in the direction of the Hall chimneys, swaggered on scornfully down the road.

As he neared his house he met a young man with curly hair and a nice mouth walking slowly and despondently down the road with a fishing rod in his hand. He gave William a pleasant smile.

William's stern countenance did not soften. He knew all about that young man and all about that smile. That young man was an undergraduate of Cambridge, who was staying at the village inn for a week's fishing.

For the first few days the fishing had given him complete satisfaction. On the third day he had seen William's pretty nineteen-year-old sister Ethel, and, after that, he had spent most of his time hanging about the road that led past the Browns' house, trying to make friends with William (who did not respond) or taking unauthorised snapshots of Ethel whenever she passed him on the road.

Today the young man looked excited, despite the rain. He had yesterday, by a master stroke of tact and persistence, made friends with the Vicar and had been invited to a party at the Vicarage which was to take place that afternoon.

He was now anxious to know whether Ethel would be there.

'Good afternoon,' said the young man effusively to William.

'G'afternoon,' said William without enthusiasm and without stopping.

William had a hearty contempt for all Ethel's admirers. As he frequently and bitterly remarked, he couldn't see what people 'saw in' Ethel.

'I say – wait a minute,' said the young man desperately.

William, still scowling, slowed down ungraciously.

'Is – I say – is your sister going to the Vicarage party this afternoon?' said the young man blushing.

As he spoke his hand stole to his pocket.

William stopped and his scowl faded. A hand stealing to a pocket put quite a different complexion on the matter.

'Uh-huh?' said William with his eye on the hand.

'I say, is your sister coming to the Vicarage party this afternoon?' said the young man.

William had enough knowledge of the young man's

94

state of mind to realise that in this case an affirmative answer would be better paid than a negative one.

'Yuh,' he said.

'You mean she is?' said the young man.

'Yuh,' said William.

The young man brought out a half-crown and pressed it rapturously into William's hand.

William, clasping it firmly, retreated into the house.

William's task was to collect pencils. Henry's was to supply the paper. William collected pencils, and in collecting pencils as in everything else he was very thorough. He seemed to attract pencils like a magnet. They left their hiding-places of bureaus and davenports and attaché cases and pockets and boxes and flocked into his possession. For days afterwards the adult members of the Brown family were indignantly accusing each other of having taken each other's pencils, nor was peace restored till Mr Brown brought back a large supply of fresh pencils from the City.

In the drawing-room William found Ethel reading a novel.

'I say, Ethel!' said William, 'you are goin' to the Vicarage party this afternoon, aren't you?'

'No,' said Ethel.

'I thought you were,' said William.

'Well, I'm not. I said I'd got another engagement. I

don't want to go to a beastly dull Vicarage party. And, anyway,' with sisterly ungraciousness, 'what's it got to do with you?'

'Oh, nothin',' said William airily, looking round the room to make sure that it concealed no more pencils.

Then, with a reassuring 'All right, I won't,' to his mother, whose voice was now heard entreating him plaintively from upstairs not to get wet, he went out into the rain once more, his 'bag' of pencils concealed in his pockets.

The young man was still in the lane, but with his back to him. William had an uneasy suspicion that a course of absolute probity demanded a report of the fact that Ethel would not be at the party and a return (or, at any rate, an offer of the return) of the half-crown which had obviously been obtained under false pretences.

William, however, remembered suddenly and with relief that he was a disguised spy bringing aid to a beleaguered army through the lines of the enemy (one of whom, of course, was the young man with curly hair) and crouching low in the shadow of the hedge, he managed to pass the young man without attracting his attention.

Henry was at the barn with his 'bag' of paper when William reached it. Henry, too, had done well. He had brought an unused drawing book that belonged by rights to his younger sister, the four middle pages from all his school exercise books (more than four invites comment and demands for explanations), all the envelopes and foolscap he could find, and a piece of very elegant mauve note-paper stamped with his address that he had found on his mother's bureau.

William had brought, as well as his pencils, a false moustache and a wig, chiefly consisting of baldness, which belonged to his elder brother Robert. These were meant to shed lustre on his editorial rôle. He donned them immediately on entering the barn. Then, with an air of businesslike concentration, he dealt out paper and pencil. The editorial staff (late Outlaws) fought each other for the best packing-cases and the dryest spots on the floor of the barn, and finally took their places and what remained of the paper and pencils after the fight.

'Well,' said Henry rather gloomily, 'how're we goin' to *start?*'

'Gotter think of a name first, I s'pose.'

There was silence while the Outlaws thought.

'*Outlaws' Daily Times*,' said Ginger at last.

'That means doin' it every day whether it rains or not!' jeered Douglas. 'Not likely.'

'*Outlaws' Weekly Times*, then,' said Ginger.

'*Not* every week, neither,' said Douglas very firmly.

'Why not *Outlaws' Telegraph?*' said Henry.

''Cause it's *not* a telegraph, silly,' said William, 'it's a *newspaper*.'

'Well, why not have *Outlaws' and District Times?*' said Douglas, 'same as the one we take in at home?'

This title met with no objection. The name *Outlaws' and District Times* was adopted.

'Now we've gotter write news,' said William cheerfully. William sat, moustached and wigged, at the biggest packing-case.

'But there *isn't* any news,' objected Henry, 'nothin's happened 'cept rain.'

'Well, say it's been rainin' then,' said Douglas encouragingly.

'You can't fill a newspaper with sayin' it's rainin',' said Henry.

'Newspapers don' only say news,' contributed Ginger with an air of deep wisdom, 'they – they sort of say what they sort of – think of things.'

'What sort of things?' said Henry.

'They sort of write about things they don't like,' said Ginger rather vaguely, 'an' about people doin' things they don't like.'

William brightened.

'We could easy do that,' he said. Then after a slight deliberation, pencil on insecurely moustached lip and head on one side: 'Well, let's all start writin' about people doin' things we don't like, and start now straight off.'

The Outlaws signified their assent.

There was silence – a silence broken only by the sound of the rain dripping on and through the roof of the old barn, and the groans of the Outlaws in mental travail.

Then suddenly through the silence came a shrill voice.

'Hello, William, darling.'

He looked up with a groan.

Violet Elizabeth, gum-booted, macintoshed, sou'-westered, stood smiling happily in the doorway.

'I made them let me come,' she explained. 'I wanted to find you all an' play with you, tho I thcreamed an' thcreamed an' *thcreamed* till they let me.'

She beamed around triumphantly.

'What you doing?'

'We're writing a newspaper an' we don't – want – girls,' said William firmly.

'But I want to write a newthpaper, too,' pleaded Violet Elizabeth.

William scowled so fiercely that his moustache fell off. He picked it up and carefully adjusted it again.

'Well, you're not *going* to,' he said, with an air of finality.

Violet Elizabeth's blue eyes filled with tears. That

was her first weapon. William, though he had no hopes of final victory, did not mean to be worsted by her first weapon.

'I c' write, too, I can,' said Violet Elizabeth plaintively. 'I c' write newthpaperth, too, I can. I'm a *good* writer, I am. I can thpell, too, I can.'

'Well, you're not going to *thpell* here,' mimicked William heartlessly.

Violet Elizabeth dried her tears. She saw that they were useless and she did not believe in wasting her effects.

'All right,' she said calmly, 'I'll thcream then. I'll thcream, an' thcream, an' thcream till I'm thick.'

More than once William had seen the small but redoubtable lady fulfil this threat quite literally. He watched her with fearsome awe. Violet Elizabeth with a look of fiendish determination upon her angelic face opened her small mouth.

''Sall right,' said William brokenly. 'Come on – write if you want to.'

Violet Elizabeth came on. She wanted to. She found on the floor a piece of grimy paper and a pencil with a broken point, both of which had been discarded as unfit for use by the others, and sat down beaming ecstatically on the ground by William. Violet Elizabeth adored William. She smiled around on them all.

'What thall I write?' she demanded happily.

'Write anything,' snapped William.

'I'll make up a croth-word puthle,' she said brightly.

William threw her a glance over his unstable moustache. In spite of her general objectionableness she certainly had ideas.

'What you doin', William?' she said sweetly.

'I'm writing a serial,' said William with a superior air.

He stooped to pick up his moustache and then tried to affix it again, but it seemed to have exhausted its adhesive powers, and after a few unsuccessful attempts, he slipped it surreptitiously into his pocket.

'Dothn't it thtick any more?' said Violet Elizabeth sympathetically, 'I'm tho thorry.'

He disdained to answer.

'You writing a therial, William?' she said. 'How nithe!'

'People,' said William ferociously, 'what write newspapers aren't allowed to talk.'

'All right,' said Violet Elizabeth sweetly. 'I don't mind.'

Again there was silence. All the Outlaws were working hard, with frowning brows, bitten pencils, dishevelled hair, agonised, grimy countenances.

'I've finished my croth-word puthle,' piped Violet Elizabeth.

'You can't have,' said William in indignant surprise.

'Well, I have, tho there!' said Violet Elizabeth with spirit.

'Let me look at it,' he said sternly.

She passed it to him.

1 down – Wot you hav dropps of.

1 acros – Oppossit of cat.

William looked at this sternly for a long time.

'Well, what is it?' he said at last.

'Can't you gueth it, William?' said Violet Elizabeth with triumph in her voice, 'ith cough an' dog. C-O-F – Cough.'

'You don't have drops of cough,' said William scornfully.

'Yeth, you do, William,' said Violet Elizabeth. 'You have cough dropth. I've had them. I've had cough dropth, I have.'

'You don't spellem like that, anyway,' said William.

'Well, how *do* you thpellem?' said Violet Elizabeth.

William, who was rather hazy on the point, quickly changed the subject.

'Well, what's the opposite of a cat?'

'Dog, William.'

'Dog isn't the opposite of cat.'

'Yeth it ith, William,' said Violet Elizabeth sweetly, ''cauth I *know* it ith.'

'It's a rotten puzzle,' said William with contempt.

'Ith not, William,' said Violet Elizabeth unperturbed, 'ith a nithe one. You ought to give a prithe of a hundred poundth for guething it like they do in newthpaperth.'

'Well, I'm not *going* to,' said William firmly.

'Wish you two'd shut *up*,' growled Ginger who was pulling his hair and chewing his pencil. 'I can't think.'

'Shut up,' said William to Violet Elizabeth.

'All right, William,' said Violet Elizabeth meekly. 'I don't mind.' Violet Elizabeth, having gained her main object, could be disarmingly meek.

For some minutes there was silence broken only by the sighs and groans of the editorial staff.

The silence was finally broken by Violet Elizabeth who raised her voice again shrill and unabashed.

'I don't thee what good a newthpaper ith without any crimeth.'

They looked at her. She met their gaze unflinchingly and repeated her statement.

'I don't thee what good a newthpaper ith without any crimeth.'

'I wish you'd stop int'ruptin' an' int'ruptin' an' *int'ruptin*',' said William. 'How d'you think we're goin' to get any work done with you int'ruptin' an' *int'ruptin*'?' But he added, because her words had really intrigued him, 'What d'you mean sayin' that a newspaper isn't any good without crimes?'

'Thereth alwayth crimeth in newthpaperth,' said Violet Elizabeth, with that air of superior knowledge which the Outlaws always found so maddening in one of her extreme youth. 'Thereth crimeth and polithe an' people goin' to prithon. If you're goin' to have a real newthpaper, thomebody ought to do a crime.'

'All right,' said William, nettled by this terrible child's invasion of his editorial province. 'All right. Go an' do one then!'

Violet Elizabeth leapt to her feet.

'Yeth, I will, William,' she said sweetly. 'I don't mind.'

A sigh of relief went up as the small form disappeared into the rain. And again there was silence in the barn.

It was evident at last that most of the Outlaws had finished their tasks or, at any rate, that the first fine careless rapture of inspiration was failing. Ginger began to throw mud pellets at Douglas while Henry began to direct, by means of various dams, the course

'IF YOU'RE GOING TO HAVE A REAL NEWTHPAPER,' LISPED
VIOLET ELIZABETH, 'THOMEBODY OUGHT TO DO A
CRIME.'

of a small rivulet that was trickling down the barn
floor, so that it should reach William.

They all scuffled exuberantly for a few minutes,
then William said:

'Well, let's c'lect the papers now an' make up the
newspaper.'

'How much're you goin' to sell it for, William?' said Ginger optimistically.

'Who'd buy it, anyway?' said Henry.

'I bet anyone'd be *glad* to buy it,' said William indignantly, '*a jolly* good newspaper like this!'

William collected the papers, perched himself upon the most important-looking packing-case, made a last unsuccessful attempt to put on his moustache, pulled up his wig (which was too big for him), and began to read. It is perhaps unnecessary to remark that on all the Outlaws' school reports on spelling, the comment 'Poor' occurred with monotonous regularity.

This was Henry's contribution:

'SWEETS.'

'Something ought to be don about sweets. Even the cheepest sorts are too deer fancy paing a penny an ounce for quite ornery sweets when you only get tuppence a week and an ounce lars no time. They ought to be made harder to so as they'd lars longer. Wot we all say is that somethin ought to be don about sweets fancy people letting this stat of things go on and on and not doing something about it. The guvment ought to do something about it, they ought to give a subciddy to it like what they do to mins fancy them not doing wot we all says is—'

Here, apparently, Henry's inspiration had entirely given out.

Henry listened to William's reading of his contribution with a blush of pride.

'That's *jolly* good,' commented William.

'Yes, that's jolly good,' the others agreed feelingly. The modest author's blush deepened. 'Yes, we'll put that first.'

The next was Ginger's. Ginger's spelling was, perhaps, slightly above the Outlaw average, but his literary genius scorned such artificial aids as punctuation.

'HOMEWORK.'

'There ought not to be any homework in school and anyway what there is is too much just think of poor boys coming home from school eggsausted and weery and then having to do homework latin and sums and french and gography and gomatry and a lot more just think of it and think what a lot old Maskie sets look at our fathers and grone-up brothers they don't have to do homework when they come home from work eggsausted and weery why should we its getting our brains abslutly wore out homework ought to be put a stop to by law and schoolmasters what set it ought to be put in prissen and hung it ought to count same as cruelty thats what I think about homework.'

This effort was received by the Outlaws with enthusiasm.

William then took up Douglas's composition. It was headed 'Washing.'

'When we considder washing,' read William, 'the question is one of – I can't read this word.'

'V-i-t-l,' spelt Douglas, slightly annoyed. 'Vitl.'

'Vitl?' said William. 'What's vitl? I've never heard of it.'

'Well, I *have*,' said Douglas, 'an' if you keep stoppin' jus' because you've never heard of ornery English words I – I jus' won't write any more.'

'All right,' said William, unmoved by this threat, 'don't then.' He proceeded with the article – 'is one of vitl – if there *is* such a word,' he added doubtfully in parenthesis, 'importence. Peple nowadays wash to much Mothers and Fathers think nothing of sending pore boys to wash both before and after meels sevverel times a day it wares away the face and hands and if boys wasn't made to wash sevverel times a day both before and after meals peple would be more helthy We know that – can't read this.' This part of the article, in fact, had received the full impact of one of Ginger's mud pellets. Douglas snatched the paper from him with a sigh of exasperation.

''Squite easy to read,' he said sternly, 'an' you're spoilin' it all with not bein' able to read ornery writin'' and understand ornery words. People can't keep what its about in their heads when you keep not bein' able to read ornery writin', I understand ornery words.'

He peered at the mud-encrusted paper on which his article was inscribed. 'This is what it says. Savvidges don't wash, and everyone knows that savvidges are helthy and if only pore boys were not made to wash sevverel times a day both before and after meels they'd be as helthy as what savvidges are it would be nice if everyone in the world was blacks because then peple culdn't see when you were dirty and if blacks—'

Here interposed a hole where one of Ginger's mud bullets had gone right through the paper – 'if blacks – I can't read what comes next,' ended Douglas thoughtlessly.

'Yah!' said William triumphantly.

''Tisn't my writing I can't read,' said Douglas with spirit, 'it's the hole what Ginger made what I can't read.'

'Oh, is it?' said William sarcastically. 'Oh, no, it's not your writing you can't read, is it? Oh, no.'

They fell upon each other in furious combat, peace was not restored till they had both rolled into a puddle. Then, just as if nothing had happened, they returned to the editorial packing-case.

'That's all,' said William, ''cept her silly crossword puzzle that we won't have in, and,' with an air of mingled modesty and importance – 'my serial. Shall I read my serial now?'

The Outlaws assented half-heartedly by means of grunts.

'All right,' said William with the air of one yielding reluctantly to overwhelming pressure. 'All right – I don't mind readin' you a bit of it, anyway. It's called 'The Black Death Gang.'"

He paused impressively.

'Dun't sound very excitin',' said Douglas. Douglas considered that William's editorship had entirely murdered his own contribution.

William ignored him.

'I'll read the first chapter,' he said. 'It starts like this.' William cleared his throat very elaborately and lowering his voice to what he fondly imagined was a thrilling whisper but which in reality was a hoarse croak, began:

'It was a pitch black dark night, the black harted villun John Smith was creepin' along the shore with his pockets full of smuggeled beer and such like.'

'Such like what?' said Douglas.

'Shut up,' said William raising his voice from its hoarse croak to a note of stern threatening; then, sinking it again to its hoarse croak, 'But in the cleer light of the moon the brave gallunt manly hero Dick Jones saw the villun at his dedly work.'

'Thought you said it was a pitch-dark night,' said Douglas, rather unkindly. William, for the time being, ignored him and continued to read.

'Ho, villun,' said Dick Jones walking up to him in his brave manly gallunt heroick way. 'Ho, villun, I know that you're a sneeky meen deceetful crul pig. What dush thou here?'

'Why, was he dushing the beer or something?' said Douglas.

William continued to ignore him.

'He held out his gun as he spoke, holding it pointing strate at John Smith's meen wicked branes but alas he had not notised that the villun carried a pistol in his mouth and at once with a clever but villunus movement of his teeth the villun fired it strate at Dick Jones manly gallunt hart. Fortunately it missed his manly gallunt hart but it struck his rist that was holding the gun strate at the villun's branes. The gun fel and the hero mooning and stagering said brokenly through his teeth—'

'Who'd broken his teeth?' said Douglas.

Once more William ignored him.

'Said brokenly through his teeth – to be continued in our next.'

'What'd he say that for?' said Ginger quite innocently.

Douglas uttered a loud and jeering laugh. William

flung his masterpiece upon the ground and the second and long overdue combat took place. All joined in. It was still taking place when Violet Elizabeth's shrill young voice sounded from the distance, 'Come an' thee what *I've* done!'

A sudden silence fell upon the Outlaws. William and Douglas sat up and loosed their hold on each other. William dragged his tie round from somewhere at the back of his neck and Douglas wiped the mud out of his eye with an unrecognisable handkerchief.

'Oh, *crumbs*!' they groaned simultaneously.

Violet Elizabeth had trotted happily down across the field over the stile and into the main road, intent upon a career of crime. In the road she found the young man with curly hair. He was on his way to the Vicarage party. Beneath his macintosh he was dressed with scrupulous care. His heart was singing at the thought of meeting his adored. In his pocket-book reposed those snapshots of Ethel which he had managed to take without her knowledge. He did not like to be parted from them for one second.

In fact, every now and then he stopped, opened the pocket case and threw a surreptitious glance at them. They made his heart flutter afresh each time. Of course, if they got *really* friendly this afternoon, he'd show them to her and then she'd *guess*. He walked rather slowly. He had a suspicion that he was far too early and though be did not want to miss one possible minute of his beloved's company, still he did not want to disgrace himself by appearing ignorant of the requirements of social etiquette. She might think that he was ill-bred if he arrived too early. She might think that he was the sort of person who doesn't know how to do the right thing. And the very idea of that turned him hot and cold. Dante and Beatrice – the two cases were curiously alike, only Dante's love for Beatrice was a pale and commonplace thing compared with his love for the beautiful unknown. Perhaps if they got *really* friendly this afternoon, he'd just murmur, 'Beatrice!' to her, and perhaps she'd understand.

A small child in gum-boots, macintosh and sou'wester was coming down the road. She seemed to be looking about her expectantly. She was rather an engaging-looking child. The young man smiled at her.

The young man liked children, chiefly because he had not met many. The little girl looked up at him with a confiding smile. The young man slowed down. The church clock struck half-past three, and the Vicarage was only a few minutes' walk away. Oh, most decidedly too early to go out to tea anywhere as yet.

'Hello,' said the little girl with a bright smile.

'Hello,' he replied.

He'd while away a few minutes with this friendly

child. In about ten minutes he might go on walking very slowly. Quarter-to-four would be all right.

'Pleath thit on the thtile with me,' said the little girl.

He was rather flattered. There must be something about him that appealed to children, and everyone said that children were good judges of character. He wished that *she* could see this little child turning to him with such flattering friendliness and confidence.

'All right,' he said. 'Let's.'

The stile was very wet but they both wore mac-intoshes. They perched there side by side in the rain.

The child did not speak. The young man felt that he ought to say something. He'd always had a vague idea that he was 'good with children' though he'd as yet met few children to try it on. He felt that this silence didn't do him credit.

'It's very wet today, isn't it?' he said brightly.

'Yeth,' said the child simply.

It had not been, he felt, a happy remark. It was the sort of remark that anyone might have made to anyone. It was not a remark that if *she* had overheard it would have riveted her attention on to him and remained for ever in her heart, a precious memory. With vague recollections of *Helen's Babies* in his mind, he took out his watch.

'Would you like to see the wheels go round?' he said.

He could not help having an uneasy suspicion that though slightly better than 'It's a very wet day, isn't it?' still it lacked originality. The bright child, however, said, 'Yeth, pleath,' and seemed quite pleased. Perhaps it had not read *Helen's Babies*.

He took out his watch and opened the back of it.

'The wheelth aren't going round,' said the child dispassionately.

He made an exclamation of annoyance. Of course – he forgot he'd broken the mainspring of the beastly thing last night. He put it back in his pocket.

'Thow me your money,' said the child imperiously.

The young man obligingly took out his pocket-book. He was rather glad of the excuse. It was quite five minutes since he had looked at the most engaging snapshot of *her* – three-quarter back view, just as she was turning out of her garden gate into the road. He looked at it now.

'There's my money,' he said kindly, 'these are one-pound notes, and these are ten-shilling notes, and this is a five-pound note, and these,' blushing, 'are photographs of a most beautiful—'

He grabbed at the stile, nearly overbalancing. The small child had seized his pocket-book and was already disappearing round the bend of the road. Hastily reconstructing his ideas of innocent childhood, the young man followed in swift pursuit.

He caught her up at the end of the road and held her arm.

'Give me that back,' he said sternly.

She uttered a scream that turned the young man's blood cold. Then she stopped screaming and said quite composedly:

'I'll thcream again if you don't let go'f my arm!'

Broken in spirit by that terrible scream, the young man let go of her arm. He knew that another scream like that would have shattered his nerve completely.

Besides, anyone hearing it would think that he was murdering the poor child. Suppose – the perspiration stood out on his brow at the thought – suppose *she* came along and heard the child scream like that and saw him holding her arm. She'd think – Heavens! she'd think he was hurting her.

Then he saw that as he was standing motionless in the grip of that nightmare thought, the child, still firmly clasping his precious pocket-book, was wriggling her small form through a very inadequate gap in the hedge and was now practically in the field beyond it.

One glance at the gap told the young man that it would not admit his more solid person, so he doubled quickly round to the stile. The small child was running up the field towards an old tumble-down barn at the further end. The young man followed, not daring again to lay hands on her, but keeping his pocket-book anxiously in view.

'Come an' thee what *I've done*,' shrilled the young person.

He followed her into the old barn. Four boys in various stages of dishevelment were engaged in a rough-and-tumble fight on the muddy floor. One of the boys wore a badly fitting and rather mangy wig hanging over one ear. The young man recognised him with a leap of his heart as *her* brother. Pieces of paper, evidently laboriously written upon, were trodden into the mud around the battlefield. The four boys sat up and gaped at the two intruders. The small child waved aloft the pocket-book triumphantly.

'I've thtolen it,' she said, 'I'm a crim'nal.'

Proudly she laid it in the hands of the boy with the ill-fitting wig.

'Tell him I thtole it,' she said to the young man.

The young man rubbed his eyes.

'Am I mad?' he said, 'or am I dreaming?'

The small child had taken affairs into her own hands.

'You've got to be the judge,' she said to William, 'and you,' to the young man: 'Tellem how I thtole your purth an' put me in prithon an' put all about it in the newthpaper an' my photograph. You *muth* have my photograph in the newthpaper, cauth they alwayth do with crim'nals.'

Calmly she surveyed them. They gaped at her.

She laid down the pocket-book on the largest packing-case and opened it. The photograph of Ethel fell out.

Suddenly someone appeared in the doorway.

To the young man it was as if a radiant goddess had stepped down from Olympus. The barn was full of heavenly light. He went purple to the roots of his ears.

To William it was as if a sister whom he considered to be elderly and disagreeable and entirely devoid of all personal charm had appeared. He groaned.

'Oh, William, you are an *awful* boy,' said Ethel, 'I've been looking for you everywhere. Mother says have you been out in all this rain and if you have, go *straight* in and change.'

'Well, I haven't,' said William. 'I've been shelt'rin' here.'

'You do look *awful*,' said Ethel, gazing at him despairingly.

Then her glance fell upon the open pocket-book, upon the packing-case and upon her photographs.

'Who – who took these?' she said in quite a different tone.

'I – I did,' stammered the young man, who was now a dull petunia shade.

'But – why?' said Ethel in a very sweet voice.

Really, she did not need to ask why. The soulful look of the young man's eye and the petunia shade of the young man's face told her why.

'I say, it's stopped raining,' said Ginger joyously from the doorway. 'Let's go out.'

'Why?' said Ethel demurely, with curling lashes lowered over peachlike cheek, 'why did you only take me side and back view? I look nicer from the front.'

The young man gulped. Emotion gave him the appearance of one about to have an apoplectic fit.

'M-m-m-may I take you from the front?' he said.

Ethel took up the snapshots again.

'I think you'd better,' she said, 'to make a complete set. We'd have to find a suitable background, of course.'

The young man conquered his embarrassment and took a bold plunge.

'The background I'd like,' he said, 'is Fairy Glen. We'd pass the Inn on the way and I'd call for my camera. It's stopped raining and the sun's coming out. Will you?'

Fairy Glen was at least two miles away.

Ethel's blue eyes danced and her pretty lips quivered.

'Why not?' she said.

The *Outlaws' and District Times* lay trampled in the

SUDDENLY SOMEONE APPEARED IN THE DOORWAY.
WILLIAM GROANED.

mud of the floor of the empty barn. The Outlaws were being Red Indians in the neighbouring wood. They had completely forgotten the *Outlaws' and District Times*. It had whiled away a wet afternoon and for the Outlaws it had served its purpose.

Ethel and the young man were on the road which led to the Fairy Glen. They were getting on very well, indeed. They, too, had completely forgotten the *Outlaws' and District Times*. For them, too, it had served its purpose.

'OH WILLIAM, YOU ARE AN AWFUL BOY!' SAID ETHEL.

121

CHAPTER 5

WILLIAM'S MAMMOTH CIRCUS

JOAN was coming home, Joan of the demure dimples and dark curls, Joan who was William's best and earliest love.

She had been away for a very long time, and William, who was loyal to old loves and old friends, felt that her return needed some more than ordinary celebration. The other Outlaws, who had always approved of Joan, agreed with him. So they met in the old barn to consider what form the celebration should take. Ginger was in favour of a play, but his suggestion was not received with enthusiasm by the others. The Outlaws had got up plays before, but they had not been successful. Something had always gone wrong with them somewhere, though nobody ever knew exactly where. Moreover, a play demanded a certain amount of learning by heart which in the eyes of the Outlaws savoured unpleasantly of school. True, in the last play which they had acted they had decided not to learn anything beforehand and to speak as the spirit should move them, but even the Outlaws – optimists though they were – had had to admit that it had not been a success. The spirit had either failed to move them at all or had moved them in the wrong direction and the plot which they had decided upon beforehand had not even been approached.

Henry suggested a firework display, but though the idea of this kindled the Outlaws' imagination, they reluctantly abandoned it owing to total absence of funds.

William's suggestion of a circus was received with acclamation till Douglas temporarily damped their ardour by remarking, 'Yes 'n where shall we get any an'mals for it? What's the use of a circus without an'mals?'

But William waved aside the objection.

'We can easy *get* an'mals,' he said. 'Why you c' hardly walk down the road without meeting an'mals. There's an'mals simply all over the world.'

'Yes, but they aren't *ours*,' said Henry, virtuously.

'Anyway,' said William, not pressing this point, 'we've *got* an'mals, haven't we? I've got Jumble an' Whitey, an' I c' easy collect some insects an' teach 'em tricks an' – an' there's Ginger's family's cat, an'—'

'An' my aunt's got a parrot,' put in Douglas.

'An' there's a pig in the field nex' our garden,' said Ginger eagerly. 'I bet I dress it up an' learn to ride it.'

Quite suddenly the circus seemed to be approaching the realms of possibility.

'An' we'll want a few clothes to dress up in,' said William.

To William no function was complete that did not include dressing up, preferably in a top hat and a long, trailing dressing-gown. This costume represented, in William's eyes, any character from Moses to Napoleon.

It was Douglas who raised the next point.

'Where shall we have it, anyway?' he said gloomily. 'I guess *this* isn't much of a place.'

The old barn was certainly a ramshackle affair. The roof leaked; the floor was generally three or four inches deep in mud; the windows were broken and the walls consisted chiefly of ventilation. The place was dear to the Outlaws' hearts, but they felt that as a show place it was hardly worthy of them. They felt that it might both figuratively and literally have a damping effect upon a circus.

A gloomy silence fell after this remark.

'Why not one of our gardens or tool sheds?' suggested Henry brightly.

This suggestion was treated with the contempt it deserved. Only Henry would have suggested arranging a circus on grown-up territory and practically under grown-up eyes.

'Oh, yes,' said William with heavy sarcasm. 'Oh, yes, let 'em all see us with Douglas's aunt's parrot an' – an' dressed up in their clothes. Oh, yes, they'll like it, won't they? They won't come out an' stop us, will they? Oh, no!'

'All right,' said Henry sulkily. 'You s'gest some- where then.'

There was a silence. They looked at William. William's position as leader seemed for a moment to tremble in the balance. But William was not their leader for nothing.

'Why not Rose Mount School?' he said. 'It'll be empty. It's holidays.'

Rose Mount School was a large girls' school that had settled about a year ago in the vicinity of William's home. The ordinary attitude of the Outlaws to this establishment was one of indifference bordering on contempt. William had not thought of it as the scene of his Celebration till he saw Ginger's and Henry's and Douglas's eyes fixed expectantly upon him. Then in a flash of inspiration the idea had come. It was the Rose Mount School holidays. The place would be empty. There would be a caretaker of course. The caretaker might possibly be the fly in the ointment, but the care- taker would, after all, only lend to the situation that element of danger and excitement without which, to the Outlaws, life was so barren.

The Outlaws looked at William with admiration in their eyes.

Ginger voiced the general sentiment.

'Crumbs!' he said, 'what *fun*. Yes, *let's*.'

Joan was to arrive on the Tuesday. The Outlaws decided to hold a few rehearsals beforehand in the old barn, and not to brave the caretaker of Rose Mount School till the day of the actual performance.

The first few days were spent in collecting the artistes. The next-door pig refused to be bridled and sat upon by Ginger, and refused with such gusto that Ginger, limping slightly and sucking one finger, retired from the unequal contest remarking bitterly that if he'd known pigs could carry on like that he'd've jolly well left 'em alone. The parrot could not be procured for rehearsals, though Douglas assured them that he would bring it for the actual day.

'Honest I will,' he said earnestly, ''cause my aunt's going away then. I know an' I can jus' borrow it an' if her ole maid finds out she can – well, she can jus' find out – an' it talks; it says 'Stop it' an' 'Oh my hair!' an' things like that.'

William announced that he was teaching Whitey a trick. Whitey was William's white rat, and the 'trick' consisted in running up William's coat to a biscuit balanced on his shoulder. William was inordinately proud of this.

''Straordinarily clever, isn't it?' he said, looking at his pet fondly.

It was decided finally not to include William's dog Jumble in the 'circus.' Jumble cherished a deep suspicion and dislike of all creatures that moved on four legs except himself and his kind, and it was felt that if Jumble figured in the circus, then Whitey and Rameses (Ginger's family's cat) would not figure in it – for more, that is, than a fleeting moment. Jumble, despite his mongrelhood, had a proud and warlike spirit.

Henry felt that he was not contributing his due share to the 'circus,' but brightened considerably on remembering that his little sister had been presented with a new clockwork monkey only a week ago. It was a realistic monkey, and on being wound up walked across the room in a realistic manner. It was called Monk.

He explained this to the other Outlaws.

'It looks jus' same as a real monkey doin' tricks,' he said eagerly. 'She won't guess it isn't – not if we do it a good way off, anyway. It *looks* like a real monkey.'

'She'll see you windin' it up,' objected William.

'No, she won't. I'll turn my back while I wind it up.'

'She'll hear the noise.'

'No, she won't – well, she'll jus' think it's the monkey coughin' if she does.'

This seemed to satisfy them.

'Well,' said William summing up their resources, 'there'll be my rat an' Ginger's cat an' Douglas's aunt's parrot an' Henry's sister's monkey. *That*,' he ended in a tone of satisfaction, 'oughter be a *jolly* good show.'

William was notoriously optimistic.

It was decided that William should be ring-master. He made a whip that satisfied the deepest cravings of his soul by tying a long leather bootlace on to the end of a stick. He persisted that he could 'crack' it, though the others denied that the 'crack' was audible. It was only when they tired of standing in silence while William flourished his leather bootlace about in an endeavour to produce what they would admit to be an audible crack, that Ginger said: 'All right, *p'raps* it does make a noise. *P'raps* we're all deaf.'

And William had to be content with that.

As regards the costume of ring-master, William insisted on a top hat. His own father's top hat was inaccessible. Mr Brown, whose top hat had been utilised by his son on more than one occasion and had suffered in the process, had learnt wisdom and now kept that article of adornment under lock and key. Ginger's father, however, was of a less suspicious nature and Ginger thought that if he chose his time carefully he could easily 'borrow' (the word in the Outlaws' vocabulary had a very wide application) his father's top hat, and convey it to Rose Mount School under cover of darkness in time for the performance.

Next William, as ring-master, insisted on some robe of office, preferably of an all-enveloping and flowing character. And here Douglas came to his help. Douglas thought that he could bring a dressing-gown of his mother's which she only wore on special occasions, and, therefore, would not miss.

The actual rehearsal in the barn was not an unqualified success, owing chiefly to the absence of most of the properties and some of the performers.

Whitey was there, and at first performed very creditably. On being released from his box, he ran up to William's shoulder and ate his biscuit in his very best style. That, however, was the end of his good behaviour. Having consumed his biscuit, he showed base ingratitude by making an unprovoked and unprincipled effort to escape, and on being captured by Ginger, he bit his finger and then chewed a button off his coat.

'Nice sorter *rat*,' said Ginger bitterly as he sucked his finger, 'more like a mowin' machine.'

''S as good as your ole family's cat,' said William indignantly, as he placed his pet in its box, 'an' he didn't mean to hurt you. It was only his fun.'

'Fun!' said Ginger, with a short, ironic laugh. 'Fun! All right, 'f he starts bein' funny with me again, I'll start bein' funny with him.'

At this moment Rameses escaped from his basket, and unless Whitey had been transferred at once to his box, the worst (from Whitey's point of view) would have happened. Rameses had not wished to come. Rameses did not wish to take part in the 'circus,' at all. He made a spring at the disappearing Whitey, missed him by a claw, flung himself at Henry and scratched his cheek, spat at William, hissed at Douglas, and after an exciting chase was finally cornered by Ginger and put back into his basket.

'Well!' said Ginger, mopping his brow with a grimy handkerchief, with which he then proceeded to bind up his scratches, 'Talk about *gratitude* – I took no end of trouble finding a basket that'd fit him an' then he carries on like this.'

'Well, we've not done many *tricks* 'cept scratchin' an' bitin' an' such like,' said William, summing up proceedings. 'Not much to make a *circus* of so far's I can see.'

'Well, what about you?' said Douglas with spirit, 'what about those insecks you were goin' to teach tricks to?'

'I haven't c'lected 'em yet,' said William with dignity. 'I – I,' with a sudden flash of inspiration, 'I don't want 'em getting' *stale* before the day.'

They turned on to Henry next. 'Where's that walkin' monkey you said you was goin' to bring?'

'Well,' said Henry, 'I've got to be jolly careful how I take her things. She makes enough fuss about it.'

'Thought she couldn't talk yet,' said William.

'No, but she can yell an' scream an' carry on somethin' awful if I jus' *touch* any of her things. It's goin' to be jolly awful when she can talk as well,' he ended gloomily. 'I'll have to wait till she's asleep the night before an' get it an' even then she'll make enough fuss when she wakes up an' finds it gone.'

William looked round at the box containing Whitey and the basket containing the still scratching, spitting, swearing, but now invisible Rameses, and sighed. Then his unfailing optimism came to his aid.

'Well, I daresay it'll turn out all right on the day,' he said.

The Outlaws were walking stealthily down the road towards Rose Mount School. It was the evening before the day of the performance. Joan was expected to arrive in the morning and was to be escorted to Rose Mount School for the Celebration in the afternoon. Joan did not know this (the Outlaws did not shine as letter writers) but they trusted Joan to come at all costs when she was told that they expected her. Joan was like that.

Douglas triumphantly carried the parrot, scolding angrily, in his cage beneath its baize cover.

William carried his box of insects and Whitey in his box.

Ginger, whose face and hands were by this time a maze of scratches, still carried with true British determination the still furious Rameses.

Henry carried beneath his coat the clockwork monkey which he had taken from his little sister's toy box after her departure to bed. As regards tomorrow he was hoping for the best. Perhaps she wouldn't remember it. He might be able to replace it in her toy box before she thought of it. Not that he had much real hope. She had a notoriously awkward memory.

Jumble followed jauntily behind. Jumble seemed to think that he was to take part in the show, though he had been sent home six or seven times. When Jumble was sent home he retired to the ditch till the Outlaws had proceeded some way and, he hoped, forgotten about him (Jumble was as great an optimist as his master), then he emerged from the ditch and followed again, keeping a discreet distance.

He had smelt Whitey, and was anxious that the acquaintance should not end with the sense of smell.

He had heard Rameses, and at the sound his heart had kindled with the lust of battle.

He had seen Monk, and though Monk lacked smell and sound to stir his appetite, still the sight of Monk had intrigued him, and he meant at the earliest opportunity to investigate Monk further. Jumble quivered to the tip of his nondescript tail with expectation.

Douglas carried his mother's dressing-gown over his arm. It had proved more frilly than William thought compatible with his dignity, but it was better than nothing. Ginger carried his father's top hat on his head.

They entered the gate of Rose Mount School very cautiously and made their way under cover of the bushes towards the kitchen window. William peeped through the kitchen window while the others stood in the shadow and watched him. A very old woman was asleep in a chair by the fire. Fate had favoured the Outlaws. The caretaker and his wife had gone away for a short holiday, leaving the caretaker's wife's mother in charge. She was a very cheering sight as she sat there sleeping by the fire. She looked stout and well established and as though she would sleep for a long time yet. She looked, too, as though she'd be rather deaf when she did wake up. She looked a satisfactory sort of caretaker altogether.

Immensely cheered by the sight of her the Outlaws walked round to the front of the house. Opening the drawing-room window with the help of Ginger's pen-knife, they entered as silently as they could and began to dispose their circus performers about the room.

Douglas's aunt's parrot called out, 'Stop it!' in a loud voice, and then uttered a harsh ironic laugh. Rameses was silent for the time being. He had either fallen asleep or was quietly planning some devilry. Whitey was audibly employed in trying to eat a way through his box. Jumble sat down on the hearth-rug and began to scratch himself. Henry thoughtlessly put Monk down in his immediate vicinity and Jumble stopped scratching himself, seized Monk by one ear, and sent him hurtling across the room into the glass door of a bookcase, then sat down wagging his tail. He looked upon himself obviously at that moment as a super-dog, a cave-dog, a hero, a conqueror. At this shock Monk's works began to function with a little growling sound, and Jumble flung himself to the attack once more. William caught him just in time and Henry rescued Monk from the debris of the glass door of the bookcase.

'Wish you'd keep your dog a bit quieter,' said Henry with indignation.

'Well, I *like* that,' rejoined William with equal indignation. 'You go sticking that thing down next to a brave dog like Jumble an' expect him not to fight it. I bet *some* dogs would be frightened of it, too – an ugly-looking thing with a face like that. I bet *some* dogs would've jus' ran off as fast as they could. I bet not *many* dogs would've gone for it like that. I bet Jumble's about the *bravest* dog in the world. You all oughter be *proud* of knowin' a dog like Jumble—'

Jumble endorsed these sentiments by a short sharp bark.

'Oh, stop it, stop it, *stop* it!' said the parrot irascibly beneath his cover.

'Well, hadn't we better start *doin'* somethin'?' said Douglas mildly.

'All right,' said William, still holding Jumble. Jumble was watching with a gleaming eye the excrescence in Henry's coat that represented the vanished Monk.

'All right. 'Sno good having a rehearsal because prob'ly someone'd go makin' a noise an' wake her. An' we don' *need* a rehearsal. We've had a sort of rehearsal an' it's no use rehearsin' an' rehearsin' an' *rehearsin'* an' gettin' everyone tired before we start. I votes we jus' hide the things away somewhere so's we can find 'em again for the circus tomorrow, 'cause if we take 'em all home again I bet we'll lose 'em or someone'll take 'em off us or *somethin'll* happen. Seems to me it's safer to leave 'em here now we've got 'em here. Hide 'em somewhere safe, you know, where *she* won't find 'em.

'I bet *she's* woke up already what with all the noise you've all been makin',' said Douglas severely.

William opened the door very silently and listened.

No sound came from the kitchen regions except a faint snore. The caretaker's mother-in-law still slept.

''S all right!' he hissed as he returned and closed the door.

'Well, where shall we hide 'em?' said Henry, looking round the drawing-room. 'Doesn't look to me as if there *was* much place to hide 'em – not where she wun't find 'em – dustin' an' such like an' she'll chuck 'em away or else stick to 'em an' *then* where'll our circus be?'

'Oh, my hair!' chuckled the parrot derisively.

'I've got an idea,' said Douglas suddenly.

They looked at him expectantly. Jumble had been put down upon the ground again, and, temporarily forgetting the elusive Monk, was occupied in tearing bits off the hearthrug and eating them.

'I votes,' said Douglas solemnly, 'that we hide one thing in each room an' then even s'pose she finds one she's not likely to find 'em all.'

The deep, almost Machiavelli-like cunning of this suggestion won the admiration of the Outlaws.

'*Jolly* good,' said William approvingly. 'Yes, we'll do that. Let's start with this room. What'll we hide here?'

'Let's hide your insects,' said Ginger.

They approached the box which William had inadvertently left open. It was empty.

'They've hid themselves,' said William, as though pleased at the sign of the intelligence from his exhibits. ''S 'all right. I can find 'em again tomorrow. Or, anyway, I can c'lect some more. What shall we hide next? I bet we won't find it easy to hide that ole parrrot. It takes up such a lot of room. She's sure to find it wherever we put it – specially if it keeps on talkin' and carryin' on the way it does.'

'Well, you *wanted* a talkin' one, didn't you?' said Douglas with spirit. 'What's the good of one that can't talk for a circus? You *wanted* a talkin' one an' then you grumble 'cause it talks.'

'I'm not grumblin',' said William distantly. 'I'm only statin' a fact. I'm only sayin' that it's a pity it can't talk when it's in a circus an' not when it's not.'

The parrot sniggered and murmured, 'Oh, my hair! Stop it!'

'I b'lieve,' said Henry impressively, 'that there's a cellar. Well, if we put him in a cellar she prob'ly won't hear him when he talks an' she prob'ly won't find him 'cause she prob'ly won't go down into the cellar, so it'll prob'ly be all right.'

This idea appealed to the Outlaws chiefly because of the opportunity it afforded of investigating the cellars. The Outlaws loved cellars.

'All right,' they said, 'let's go 'n' see.'

On tiptoe, led by William, they crept into the hall.

William held Jumble under his coat and the box containing Whitey under his arm. Henry held Monk under his coat. Ginger carried the still quiescent Rameses in his basket and wore his father's hat on his head, and Douglas carried the cage containing the parrot and his mother's dressing-gown over his other arm.

There was a door under the stairs. They opened it. There were steps. Yes, most certainly cellars. Very cautiously the little procession crept down. Glorious cellars, enormous cellars, heavenly vistas of cellars opening out of each other. They explored blissfully for some time for sheer love of exploration. Then William recalled them sternly to the business of the day.

'Let's find a nice dark corner for the parrot,' he said, 'so's he'll go to sleep an' not start talkin' all over the place.'

They found a nice dark corner. Douglas had brought a plentiful supply of parrot food in his pocket and he poured this into the parrot's dish. The parrot gave a deep sigh and then burst into a peal of high-pitched ironic laughter. Douglas surveyed his mother's wrap.

'Might as well leave this here, too,' he said, throwing it upon a derelict clothes horse that stood near. It hung down in graceful folds.

'Looks almost 's good 's a ghost,' said William, admiring the effect. 'Put the hat on it too.'

But Ginger was enjoying wearing the hat and did not wish to give it up just yet. He rather fancied himself in it. He wished that he were to wear it instead of William.

'No,' he said firmly, 'we don't want to put too many things in one place. We want to have *some* things left if she starts nosing round down here. Let's go an' have a look round upstairs.'

Leaving the parrot, who was still laughing sardonically to himself, the Outlaws, considerably lightened of their burdens, crept up to the hall again. The caretaker's wife's mother's snores still reverberated gently through the house.

'Upstairs!' hissed William. His eye gleamed with the light of the explorer. To William life was one long glorious Romance. Upstairs, however, proved, on the whole, disappointing. It seemed to consist solely of dormitories and mistresses' bedrooms. The only excitement was half a dozen Italian stamps on the window-sill of one of the dormitories. They turned out, however, to be 'pricked' and useless for collections.

'Well, anyway,' said Henry, putting them on one side with disgust, 'we can leave Monk here.'

'Let's see him walk,' said Ginger with sudden interest.

William buttoned Jumble firmly up inside his coat

(a proceeding to which Jumble objected, but to which he was quite accustomed), and Henry turned the key which wound up the works of Monk. To the Outlaws' great delight Monk walked across the room till he came to a chair which barred his progress. He then perforce stopped, but was obviously willing and anxious to continue as soon as the chair was removed.

Henry was just going to remove it when Jumble, who had caught sight of his enemy through a button-hole, made a spasmodic effort to escape, and bursting asunder William's one remaining button, flung himself from William's grasp. He was captured in the nick of time by Ginger and returned to William's bosom barking furiously and making frenzied efforts to escape.

William, smothering Jumble's outburst as best he could, took him from the room, followed by the other Outlaws, leaving Monk still embracing the obstructing chair. Jumble, who really knew quite well that they were uninvited guests in the house and that he ought to be silent, but had been temporarily overcome by his feelings, nuzzled his head apologetically under William's shoulder. They leant over the balusters listening fearfully. No sound came from below but the faint ghostlike echoes of distant snores.

'Better not go back to that room,' whispered Henry, 'we'll leave Monk there. I bet it's quite a good hiding place. I bet she won't go lookin' there. What's that room?'

Ginger opened the door cautiously.

'It's a box-room,' he said. 'I'll leave this ole hat here. It's a good hiding place for it.'

Douglas had followed him. William and Henry were investigating a room at the other end of the landing.

Douglas looked round the room critically. His gaze wandered round floor and wall and ceiling, and rested finally on the top of the door. He chuckled.

'I bet I could do a trick there,' he said. 'You go out a minute and don't look and come in when I tell you.'

Ginger went out.

'Come on!' said Douglas in a hoarse whisper after a few minutes. Ginger returned to the door. It was open a few inches. He opened it further. The top hat dropped upon him from above, appearing to extinguish him. Douglas gave an exultant chuckle at the result of his trick.

'It balances jus' above the door,' he explained, 'let's do it on ole William.'

He climbed on to a box, balanced the hat again, then, managing to squeeze himself through the narrow aperture, went with Ginger to look for William.

William was in a linen cupboard making perilous

experiments with a lift that evidently descended to the kitchen regions. In the excitement of this Douglas and Ginger forgot the hat. It was only fear of waking the sleeping woman below that prevented William from essaying the descent into the nether regions in person. Instead, they sent Rameses and Whitey in their respective receptacles half-way up and down the lift till sudden movements in Rameses' basket showed that he had awakened again to a sense of his grievances.

'P'raps we'd better be goin',' said William reluctantly, and they took box and basket under their arms again and crept downstairs. They went into a large study at the bottom of the stairs. The walls were lined with books. William looked around him without enthusiasm.

'Dull-looking place,' he commented. Then his eye fell upon a large wooden box upon the desk in the window. He opened it. It contained a few papers.

'It's a nice place for Whitey,' he said, 'plenty of room an' a nice big keyhole for air. We'll make it nice an' comfy for him an' he'll be all right till tomorrow.'

He spread his handkerchief at the bottom in an attempt to ensure Whitey's comfort in his place of confinement. The other Outlaws added theirs. Finally Whitey was laid on the top of this, and after biting William's finger during the process, settled down to an ungrateful but wholesale destruction of his bedding.

They could hear the muffled tearing of handkerchiefs as they shut the box.

'Well, that's a nice way to carry on,' said Ginger indignantly, 'when we were jus' tryin' to make him comfortable.'

'He prob'ly thought we *meant* him to eat 'em,' explained William, ever loyal to his pets. 'I think it's jolly clever of him.'

'Well, there's only Rameses left,' said Douglas.

Rameses was quite awake by now. He was quietly swearing and tearing at his basket-work.

'He'll have to go back home,' said Ginger, 'they'd miss him an' he'd have the whole place down before morning 'f we kept him here – I say, I believe I heard someone moving—'

They listened. Someone was moving. Someone was opening the kitchen door and coming down the hall.

Like lightning the Outlaws streaked out of the window, and, still carrying Rameses in his basket, disappeared in the distance.

It was the next morning. Joan had returned – more adorable than ever. The Outlaws had assembled at her back gate in a little sheepish crowd to wait till she came out. They had intended to pay her a state call and ring boldly at the front-door bell, but their courage had failed them, their swagger had dropped from them, and instead they hung sheepishly about her back gate, casting furtive glances at her window and pretending a sudden violent interest in the hedge and the ditch at that point of the road. But Joan saw them and ran out to them at once with no pretence of indifference, with none of that quality known to the Outlaws and their contemporaries as 'swank.'

'Oh!' she exclaimed with shining eyes, 'how *lovely* to see you all again!'

William swallowed and blinked. He had always suspected Joan of being the supreme product of her sex and now he was sure of it.

'What you doin' this afternoon?' he said, with an attempt at his old superior nonchalance.

'I'm going out to tea,' said Joan. 'Oh, but it *is* so nice to see you all again.'

'We'd got a sort of show for you, that's all,' said William indifferently, 'but's all right if you're goin' out to tea.'

Joan clasped her hands. 'Oh, of *course* I'll come, William. Of *course* I'll come. I won't go out to tea. I jus' simply won't. And how *nice* of you to do it. And how *nice* of you to come round here to see me.'

William slashed carelessly at the grass around him with his ash switch (William always carried an ash switch for the purpose of slashing at the grass and fences and hedges around him).

'Oh, we jus' happened to be passing,' he said with elaborate unconcern. 'You – you'll come then?'

'Oh, *yes*, William – what time?'

''Bout three. We'll fetch you.'

'HOW LOVELY TO SEE YOU ALL AGAIN!' EXCLAIMED JOAN.

'Oh, William, how *lovely*.'
So *that* was all right.

The Outlaws approached Rose Mount School stealthily in single file. They wanted to spy out first the
movements and position of their enemy, the caretaker,
and to make sure that the properties and artistes were
as they had left them. They peeped cautiously through
the kitchen window. The kitchen was empty. So far, so
good. They went round to the other side of the house.
And there they received their first shock. The drawing-
room, so gloriously empty last night, was full now of
females standing about and talking excitedly in
groups. One of them caught sight of the Outlaws,
flung up the window and called:

'Go away, boys, at once! Do you hear? Shoo! Go
away at once or I'll send for the police.'

The Outlaws, speechless with astonishment and
dismay, faded into the bushes.

'Well!' said Ginger eloquently.

'Crumbs!' said William.

'My eye!' said Douglas.

'Where've they come from?' said Henry.

'Let's try the other side,' said William recovering
from his stupor of astonishment.

They tried the other side. The Library also seemed
bewilderingly full of females. Ginger, venturing

incautiously near the window, his eyes agog with amazement and horror, was spied by one of them. She strode to the window and flung it open.

'Go away at once, you naughty little boys,' she said. 'Don't you know that this is private property? Go away at once, I say!'

Again the Outlaws faded into the bushes.

'*Well*,' said Douglas, 'what we goin' to do now—'

'An' my father's hat's there,' said Ginger.

'An' my sister's monkey's there,' said Henry.

'An' what we goin' to do for this afternoon?'

'An' who *are* they?'

'Well, we've gotta do *somethin*',' said William firmly.

'All right. S'pose you go an' ring at the front door an' ask for our things,' said Ginger.

'Yes, an' s'pose *you* do,' said William.

'Well, I'm not afraid.'

'An' *I'm* not afraid.'

'All right, go then.'

'All right, I will,' said William. 'I'll go now. I'm not afraid. I'm not afraid of anyone in the whole world.'

Determined to justify this summary of his character, the intrepid hero emerged from the bushes and walked up to the front door. He rang the bell with unnecessary violence in order to demonstrate to all within that he wasn't afraid of anyone in the whole world. A small fat female in horn-rimmed spectacles came to the door.

'What do you want, boy?' she said severely.

'Please,' said William hoarsely, with a mixture of defiance and humility in his bearing (defiance to prove that he feared no foe in horn-rimmed spectacles or anything else, and humility to propitiate the severity which shone from the lady's every feature). 'Please can we jus' come in an' fetch a few things—'

'Go away at once,' said the lady angrily. 'You're the little boys I saw hanging round here a few minutes ago. And if you don't go away at *once*, I'll send for the police.'

'Please,' said William, dropping his defiance and becoming abjectly humble, 'please, there's jus' a few of our things here—'

'There are *none* of your things here, you naughty little boy! How *dare* you tell such stories. I'll ring up for the police this *instant* if you don't—'

William faded again into the bushes.

''S no good,' he said despondently to his companions, 'they won't let us in.'

'Yes, an' what about my aunt's parrot,' said Douglas indignantly, 'starvin' to death in the cellar. An' I specks they've found out he's gone now at my aunt's an' they'll be makin' no end of a fuss. An' there he'll be for months an' months starvin' to death.'

'Yes, an' what about my father's hat?' said Ginger, 'an' he's goin' to a wedding next week.'

'And what about Monk?' said Henry, 'she'd forgot him jus' at first, but she was lookin' round for somethin' when I came out an' I bet it was Monk. Well, an' if he has to stay here for months an' months there'll be a nice fuss.'

'Let's try the kitchen window,' said Douglas. 'There wasn't anyone in the kitchen when we came in an' I bet we can get down into the cellar from the kitchen.'

This suggestion was considered and approved of, and Douglas, as the author of it, was entrusted with the delicate mission of scouting in the region of the kitchen to make sure that the coast was clear. He departed with an ostentatious elaboration of secrecy that would have done credit to a cinema villain.

He returned looking crestfallen.

'I say,' he said in an awed whisper, 'the kitchen's full of 'em now. They're messin' about with eggs an' cookery books an' things.'

Blank dejection descended upon the Outlaws.

'Well,' said Douglas pathetically, 'jus' *think* of my poor ole parrot starvin' to death in a dark cellar.'

'Oh, do shut up about your ole parrot. It'd got enough stuff to keep it alive for years an' years. What about my father's hat an' Henry's sister's Monk? I bet we'll catch it hotter from our fathers than you will from an ole aunt.'

This suggestion of inferiority of retribution touched Douglas's honour to the quick.

'I bet you won't, then,' he said indignantly, ''cause she'll tell my father an' I bet I'll get it 's hot as *anyone*.'

'I say – *look*!' said Ginger excitedly.

He was peering over the bushes towards a little rose garden that lay secluded in the grounds of Rose Mount School. In it stood a lady of uncertain years, leaning against a sundial, obviously engaged in trying to decipher the inscription.

'I say,' whispered William, 'she looks – she looks sort of soft. I vote someone goes an' talks to her an' tries to find out how long they'll all be here.'

It was decided that Ginger should do this. Ginger, though of villainous appearance, was supposed by his contemporaries to have a winning way with members of the fair sex.

So Ginger, assuming an ingratiating smile and watched closely by his friends through the bushes, approached the lady by the sundial.

'G'mornin',' he said, raising his cap with a flourish.

It was easier to raise his hat with a flourish than to replace it with a flourish. As a result of innumerable wettings his cap had shrunk to about half the size of the lining and so sat unevenly upon his bullet head.

'Good morning,' said the lady quite pleasantly.

Ginger's spirits rose. Evidently life had not yet inspired her with that dislike of small boys with which it seemed to have inspired the majority of her sex.

'Please,' continued Ginger with nauseating but well-meaning politeness, 'could you tell me, tell me – er – what all these people's doin' here?'

'It's a retreat, little boy,' said the lady kindly.

Ginger brightened.

'A retreat?' he said. 'Why, is there a war goin' on somewhere?'

'No, dear,' explained the lady still kindly. 'We're the Society for the Study of Psychical Philosophy.'

'Oh,' said Ginger.

'And we're meeting here for a course of lectures and discussions. We're going to do *everything* ourselves. We've sent the caretaker home because the spirits have told us that it is degrading to ask any other human being to perform personal service for another. Tolstoy, of course, held the same tenets, did he not?'

'Uh,' said Ginger blankly. Then, after a slight pause, 'You goin' to be here long?'

'For some weeks, we hope. You learn Latin, little boy, do you not? I wonder if you can translate this motto for me.'

But Ginger had disappeared. He was returning with his gloomy tidings to his friends.

'*Weeks!*' gasped Douglas. 'An' the poor ole parrot down there in the cellar starvin' to death.'

'An' my father goin' to a wedding next week,' groaned Ginger.

'An' they'll be *sure* to blame me for Monk,' said Henry. 'They blame me for *everything*.'

But again Ginger's watchful eye had spied something.

'Look,' he said in an awed voice, 'they're all goin' into that room an' sitting down. One of 'em's goin' to make a speech.'

Impelled by curiosity the Outlaws drew near the window. The window was open. They crouched beneath it and listened. A very tall female dressed in a green sweater began to speak.

'Friends,' she said, 'I have summoned this meeting for a very special – a very serious – reason. We have agreed that no useful work can be done

THE OUTLAWS CROUCHED
BENEATH THE WINDOW
AND LISTENED.

in a house where the spirits of the house are unfriendly to us. Friends,' she made a dramatic pause, 'the spirits of this house are unfriendly to us. It is with deep grief but not without due consideration that I say it. The spirits of this house are unfriendly to us. We all know what valuable psychic powers Mrs Heron possesses. Mrs Heron's psychic powers have been of the greatest assistance to us in our researches. Mrs Heron says that never has she had so clear, so unmistakable a revelation as she had last night. Mrs Heron will describe it to you herself.'

'FRIENDS,' SAID THE WOMAN IN THE GREEN SWEATER, 'I HAVE SUMMONED THIS MEETING FOR A VERY SERIOUS REASON.'

The lady in the green sweater sat down. A small intense-looking lady with a squint and a dramatic manner arose.

'Friends,' she said in a deep thrilling voice, 'last night I went to bed as usual,' dramatic pause. 'I went to sleep,' dramatic pause. 'I awoke to hear a voice – very faint and in the distance, it seemed to summon me' – dramatic pause. 'I arose. It led me down, down, down, growing louder and clearer at every step.

'I found myself in an underground place,' dramatic pause. 'Probably the cellars of this building. There' – long, super-dramatic pause – 'there I saw – saw more distinctly than I have ever seen a psychic revelation before, saw with my eyes as plainly as I see you all now – a long white figure,' she was too much worked up now for dramatic pauses – 'there I heard a voice – heard it more distinctly than I have ever heard a psychic revelation in my life – heard it as plainly as I hear my own voice now.

'The voice said, 'Stop.' I turned in terror. I admit I was terrified. The voice pursued me up the stairs. It said, 'Oh, beware!' I fled upstairs in terror and there pursued me the sound of sinister menacing spirit laughter. Friends, I feel that the spirits of this house are actively hostile to us. I feel that some terrible calamity may result from our sojourn in this house – I – but before I continue let me ask whether anyone else had any psychic experience in the night.'

A woman with an indeterminate nose and a lugubrious expression arose.

'I did,' she said, also in a deep thrilling voice. 'I thought I heard some disturbance in the night. It may, of course, have been our friend, Mrs Heron, descending the stairs. I came out upon the landing. A door opposite mine was partly open. I opened it and at once something was violently flung into my face. I picked it up. It was a man's top hat. I looked around the room. It was quite empty. The hat lay now at my feet. The room was a box-room. Obviously the hat had formed part of the collection of articles which I saw piled up about the room. But the important thing is that by *no human agency* but, friends, by spirit hands that hat had been hurled violently into my face with obviously hostile intent when I opened the door.'

She sat down. The audience looked pale and tense. In a trembling voice the chairman continued:

'I think that the evidence you have heard is clear and irrefutable. Before I proceed, has anyone else any psychic experience to recount?'

A small lady with a pale round face and quite circular eyes arose.

'I have,' she said proudly, 'though I must admit that it was terrifying at the time, still I cannot help feeling a certain pride as it is the first time that any psychic revelation has been vouchsafed to me – Like our two friends, I thought that I heard a sound in the night. I arose and went on to the landing. There was a closed door opposite. I opened it. The room was empty. I could see every corner of it. I gazed around. Then – I had done nothing except move a chair that stood in my way as I entered – I suddenly saw a – Thing – advancing towards me over the floor.'

'What sort of a thing?' said an hysterical voice.

'I cannot describe it,' said the speaker with a shudder. 'You would have said at first sight that it was a small animal, but it was unlike any animal I have ever seen. The sight of it filled me with horror. It was coming towards me. I flung myself from the room and shut the door. Just in time. I heard it hurl itself against the closed door with a sickening thud – If I had not been in time I am convinced, friends, that I should not be here speaking to you now. One glance at the creature told me that it was something not of this world.'

She sat down amidst a flutter of excitement. The chairman rose again.

'I think,' she said, 'that you have heard enough to prove to you that we cannot with safety remain here. You know that we were offered The Limes in Lofton for our retreat and conference, and I propose that I write to say that we will go on there tomorrow. I will write to the headmistress, who so kindly lent us this school, to explain to her that the psychic conditions are not favourable. I will say no more than that to her. I have all the papers relating to the offer of The Limes in the box which I brought here yesterday when I came to look at the place and make final arrangements. It is, I think, on the table in the Library.'

The lady of the sundial, looking pale with fright, but still amiable, kindly rose to fetch the box. She returned with it in a few minutes and put it upon the chairman's desk. The chairman opened it.

Whitey was rather annoyed by his long captivity. He had finished the Outlaws' handkerchiefs last night and was feeling hungry again. He remembered the trick that always earned a biscuit. There was a button upon the chairman's shoulder and it looked to Whitey just like a biscuit. He streaked up her dress to her shoulder, clawed at the button, found it was a button and not a biscuit, bit her ear in a burst of quite justifiable annoyance, became suddenly scared by the uproar on all sides, streaked down again and disappeared as suddenly as he had appeared.

The unconscious form of the chairman was carried to the front door in order that she might revive the more quickly in the open air, and the meeting proceeded without her. The lady with the indeterminate nose arose again.

'After what we have seen with our own eyes—' she began in a trembling voice.

'Oh, b-b-b-b-b-but,' said the hysterical voice, 'it was only an ordinary white rat.'

'It was *something*,' corrected the first speaker darkly and mysteriously, '*something* in the temporary form of a white rat.'

'Oh, you don't think—?' panted the hysterical voice.

'I do,' said the speaker in the low thrilling voice, 'and I propose that we leave this roof now at once as soon as we can pack up our things and escape while yet we can. We will go to Lofton and if necessary stay in the village till The Limes is ready. I think that we have received warnings it would be foolhardy to disregard.'

There was a general bustle and flurry as the members of the Society for the Study of Psychical Philosophy arose to pack and escape while yet they could.

It was the afternoon. The Society for the Study of Psychical Philosophy had departed. The caretaker had been summoned but could not return till late at night. Rose Mount School stood gloriously empty. But not quite empty. The Outlaws were there on the lawn before the house. They had retrieved the parrot (apparently highly amused by the whole proceedings) and the dressing-gown from the cellar. They had taken Whitey, scratching and biting, from beneath the bureau and assuaged his proud spirit with biscuits and cheese. They had fetched Monk and the top hat from the rooms where they had wrought such havoc on the nerves of the Students of Psychical Philosophy last night.

Ginger had brought Rameses (still in a misanthropic frame of mind). Jumble had come on his own accord, and was at present engaged in chasing a wasp round a tree.

William had made a fresh collection of insects and taught them tricks (William's insects found it very easy to learn 'tricks.' Any movement of any sort on their part was explained by William as a 'trick'). And William was gloriously dressed in the top hat and dressing-gown.

Joan was there, sitting in a drawing-room chair which William had brought out for her, Joan who had made good her promise to come at all costs, Joan who gazed at William with bright adoring eyes and said 'Oh, *William*, isn't it all lovely!'

William stood in front. The other Outlaws stood behind, each holding an exhibit. William 'cracked' his whip, got it caught inextricably in a neighbouring laurel bush and after a brief inglorious struggle relinquished it.

'Ladies an' gentlemen,' said William, 'you are now goin' to see the one and only performin' rat in the world.'

With that, resplendent in top hat and dressing-gown, glorious, irresistible, monarch of his kingdom, William, the Pirate, the Smuggler, the Red Indian, the Robber Chief, the Ring-master, William the Victorious, William the Ever-Come-Out-On-Top swaggered across the lawn for Whitey.

CHAPTER 6

THE MAGIC MONKEY

ROSE Mount School was really responsible for the whole thing. Rose Mount School was a girls' school situated near the Outlaws' native village, and as a girls' school it was, of course, worthy of only scorn and derision. Yet the sight of the Rose Mount girls dashing about a field in hot pursuit of a ball, armed with curiously shaped sticks, attracted the Outlaws despite themselves, and they would frequently wander round by way of Rose Mount School playing-fields on their way to afternoon school.

Not that they admitted the slightest interest in Rose Mount hockey. Far from it. They only went that way because they happened to have set out for school rather early, or because they wanted to get some conkers from the wood on the hill, or because they wanted to have a look at Farmer Luton's pig or – or anything but that despite their manly and heroic natures they were beginning to take an interest in what was in their eyes essentially a girls' school game. The Outlaws did not yield to this weakness without a struggle. Hockey was not a game played in any self-respecting boys' school. It was confined to girls' schools. It was a game suited to inferior beings with inferior powers and an inferior outlook on life. It was unworthy of even a glance from the Outlaws' manly eyes. And yet – and yet it seemed an interesting sort of game.

It drew the Outlaws again and again to the road over the hill where from a large gap in the hedge they could furtively watch its progress. Furtively, of course. They still pretended to take no interest in the maidenly sport. But in time they found the attitude of aloof indifference difficult to maintain, and it was a relief to all of them when Ginger announced one afternoon: 'I say, *men* play hockey. My cousin told me. They have matches an' play it same as football.'

The game having been thus raised to a manly status, they began to discuss openly and eagerly the rules and the procedure of it. They argued fiercely over the capacity of each individual member of the Rose Mount School eleven. In fact, the game became the staple subject of their conversation and the absorbing interest of their lives.

They would stand crouching together at the gap in the hedge and cheer on the players lustily till an irate mistress came to send them away. Then they found a gate from which they could watch and cheer equally well and when sent away from there would reappear at the gap in the hedge. The irate mistress finally grew tired of sending them away from one place only to see them reappear at another, and, though still irate, began to leave them alone. Hence the dishevelled figures of the four Outlaws, shouting encouragement, cheering excitedly, became a familiar and even gratifying sight to the Rose Mount hockey eleven.

But it was not likely that merely watching other people play a game would for long satisfy the deeper needs of the Outlaws' souls. It was while they were discussing the exact nature of 'offside' that Ginger said suddenly:

'Their sticks are only sort of walking-sticks upside down an' – an' there *needn't* be so many of 'em playin'. *Any* number'd do.'

That was the last time that Rose Mount eleven had their Outlaw audience, and more than one of them missed the applause that a good shot would win from those four young ruffians crouching together in the gap in the hedge or suspending themselves recklessly over the gate.

Douglas's father and Ginger's father, meeting by accident the next Sunday afternoon, confided to each other that on taking their walking-sticks from the hat-stand they had found the handles deeply encrusted with mud and the varnish entirely worn away. They agreed that it was a curious coincidence.

The scene where the Outlaws began to practise their new game was the field behind the Old Barn. The game as played by the Outlaws did not conform to the rules of any County Hockey Club, but it appealed to the Outlaws far more than the more conventional game would have done. Caps or coats represented the goals. They 'bullied' in correct style as learnt from Rose Mount School, then the real game began.

They leapt and yelled and brandished their sticks, and hurled themselves upon the ball and tripped each other up and kicked the ball and each other indiscriminately. There were practically no rules. To an impartial observer it was more suggestive of a permanent Rugger scrimmage than anything else, but it was – the Outlaws agreed emphatically – a jolly good game. They played it on every possible occasion. They met early before school to play it, they played it between school, they played it after school.

Now the Outlaws, whatever they did, were watched and if possible emulated by their schoolmates. Though in the eyes of the grown-up world the Outlaws were the very dregs of boyhood, in the boy world the Outlaws were aristocrats. So by the end of a week innumerable little groups of boys were playing 'hockey' with their fathers' walking-sticks – yelling and leaping and brandishing their sticks, and tripping each other up after the manner of the Outlaws. Gradually these groups began to coalesce.

The Outlaws found that a game of hockey with six was more exciting than a game of hockey with four, and that a game of hockey with eight was even more exciting than a game of hockey with six. So the Outlaws accepted any kindred souls to swell their 'team'. Fathers in the locality were mystified that week by an epidemic of mutilation or complete disappearance among walking-sticks.

The only people whom the Outlaws refused to admit to their team were the Hubert Laneites. Hubert Lane was an enemy of William's, and the friends of Hubert Lane were enemies of the friends of William. It was an ancient enmity, and no one knew in what it had originated. Hubert Lane was fat and pale, easily moved to tears, slow to endanger his personal safety, given to complaining to his parents and masters when annoyed. 'I'll tell my father of you,' was Hubert's invariable answer to any verbal or bodily insult. And Mr Lane was in every way worthy of his son, and that is all that need be said about *him*.

But, strange to say, Hubert had his following. Hubert had endless pecuniary resources. Hubert's pockets were always full of sweets, and his larder at home was always full of rich and unhealthy-looking pastries. And there were boys who were willing to swallow Hubert, so to speak, for the sake of these things.

So by the end of the week the various small hockey groups had resolved themselves into two large rival teams – William's and Hubert's. Hubert's hockey was of a less violent nature than William's, but the Hubert Laneites were unexpectedly keen. They played in the field behind Hubert's house. Occasionally they hung over the stile leading to the Outlaws' field and hurled insults and abuse at the Outlaws, turning to flee to the near and safe refuge of the Lane homestead when the Outlaws started in pursuit.

Yet nothing might have happened if it hadn't been for Mrs Lane. Mrs Lane was notoriously lacking in any sort of sense. Mrs Lane had always refused to acknowledge the existence of the Outlaws v. Laneites feud. She was always meeting William's mother and saying: 'Our little boys are *such* friends, Mrs Brown, you *must* come in and have tea with me sometime.' Or she would meet William in the village and pat his head and say: 'You're one of my little boy's school friends, dear, aren't you?' She was fat and smiling and placid and incredibly stupid. So it was really Mrs Lane who brought about the whole thing by stopping Mrs Brown in the village and saying smilingly: 'Our little boys are *such* friends, aren't they? And they're both *so* keen on this wonderful new game, aren't they? And they've both got teams, haven't they? Don't you think it would be a *sweet* idea for their teams to have a match against each other?'

Mrs Brown didn't, but she didn't say so.

'And you *must* come in and have tea with me sometime,' went on Mrs Lane, 'because our little boys are *such* friends.'

And even then nothing might have come of it, but Mr Lane happened to come along at that moment, and his wife said: 'I've just been saying to Mrs Brown that it would be such a *sweet* idea if Huby's and Willie's hockey teams could have a *match* against each other.'

Now, Mr Lane, as I have said, was only a more odious edition of his son. But he imagined himself a fine sporting fellow whom all boys adore, and he happened to be in a good temper. So he rubbed his hands and gave a great booming laugh and said, '*Splendid!* A top-hole idea! Huby shall write the challenge tonight.'

And Huby did. Or rather, Huby's father did.

The Outlaws received the challenge with mixed feelings. They welcomed the thought of a scrap with the Laneites. But not a scrap organised and presided over by Mr Lane, who would be sure to write letters of complaint to all their fathers if they happened to lay hands upon Hubert's sacred person, except with the utmost tenderness and respect.

William, with the help of the other Outlaws, answered the challenge.

'DEAR SIR

'We have reseeved your letter, and will be very glad to play a hocky match against you on Satday, and we bet you anything you like we will beet you.

'Yours truely,

'WILLIAM BROWN and others.'

Mr Lane (whose good temper still continued) was delighted with this. 'Ha, ha!' he said, 'a most unconventional answer to a challenge, to be sure. Our good William's composition and orthography are no great credit to him. I must speak to his schoolmaster about them when I meet *him*.'

But Mrs Lane was getting quite worked up about it.

'You shall have a lovely tea afterwards, Huby, darling, like they do after *real* matches. I'll give you a *lovely* tea for both teams – for both your team and Willie's in the shed. You'll like that, won't you?'

Hubert mumbled ungraciously that it would be 'all right.' It always broke Hubert's heart to have to give of his larder's treasures, of his cakes with glorious icing and cream insides, to any but his very boonest of companions, and the thought of the Outlaws consuming these treasured delicacies was gall and wormwood to him.

The Outlaws practised hard for the match. They decided to make the best of the brief hour of contest and to ignore entirely the presence of Mr Lane. He might, they decided, write to their fathers as much as he liked afterwards. They were going to make the most of it while it lasted. They were going to jolly well lick the Hubert Laneites to a fizzle.

Rumours, too, of the glorious tea to be provided by Mrs Lane had reached them and still further exalted their spirits. The Outlaws were not proud. They would not refuse iced cakes because they came from the (metaphorically) gilded larder of the opulent Lanes. Rather would they consume them with might and main in order that fewer might fall to the Laneites' share.

And now Henry's sister's walking toy monkey comes into the story again.

Henry's sister loved the monkey very dearly (out of pure contrariness, Henry considered), and wept bitterly whenever she was deprived of it. And she had been deprived of it last week, when, without asking her or anyone's permission, Henry had taken Monk to form part of a circus organised by William. Henry had been sternly reprimanded by his father for this offence, and on the very day before the hockey match he committed it again.

William was giving a repeat performance of his circus, and Monk as one of the star turns simply had to be present, so Henry had taken Monk again, hoping that his small and tyrannical sister would not notice its absence. But the small and tyrannical sister *had* noticed Monk's absence and had sobbed bitterly all the afternoon. . . .

Henry's mother's tender heart had been touched by the small sister's grief and hardened against Henry. Henry's mother was really very nice, but she took her duty as Henry's mother rather too seriously. She had read that afternoon an article on the upbringing of children which said that the punishment should fit the crime. The writer said: 'If a child has taken some article which he has been forbidden to take, then he must be made to carry the article about with him for a whole day, or more, whatever he is doing and however embarrassing its presence may prove.'

Henry's mother wasn't *quite* sure that it was a rule that would work, but she thought that perhaps it was worth trying, especially as the small sister had transferred her affections to a teddy bear, and Monk, owing to his desertion, was temporarily out of favour.

'Henry,' she said, 'you've taken Monk again when you were told not to, so you must carry him about with you all day – or, if you'd rather, I'll tell your father when he comes home tonight and he can deal with it.'

Henry wouldn't rather. Henry didn't like his father's methods of 'dealing' with things at all.

'All right,' he said obligingly. 'I'll take Monk round with me tomorrow.'

Henry thought that he could easily conceal Monk beneath his coat, and that, even were Monk's presence discovered, Monk's accomplishmeats would prove an asset rather than a liability. And so it came about that Henry set off for the great hockey match with Monk buttoned up under his coat. He was feeling now more apprehensive about Monk than he had done at first because halfway through the morning Monk's works had suddenly refused to function. Monk would not walk now, however much you wound him up. Monk was therefore no longer a performing animal. He was openly and unashamedly a toy monkey, and as such derogatory to Henry's dignity.

Henry was aware that should the Laneites spy Monk they would make the most of him. They would use him as a handle against Henry and the other Outlaws. They would jeer at him openly and unmercifully. They would make themselves a nuisance about it for weeks.

But Henry was a sportsman. Having undertaken to carry Monk about with him for the whole day, he was going to do it.

The Outlaws met together very early before the match. They had been considerably cheered that morning by the information that both Mr and Mrs Lane would be away from home. Mr Lane had tired of the whole idea and gone off to play golf and Mrs Lane had gone to visit a sick friend.

All the Outlaws carried walking-sticks, and Henry carried Monk buttoned closely under his coat. The Outlaws, who knew the story of Monk, tactfully refrained from any allusion to it. The Hubert Laneites had not yet appeared.

'I say,' said Ginger, slashing carelessly on all sides with his stick, 'they say she's giving a *scrummy* tea.'

'I saw 'em,' corroborated Douglas eagerly, 'carryin' trays of things down to the shed from the house. It looked *jolly* fine, I can tell you.'

'What'll we do till they come?' said Henry, trying to compress the excrescence that was Monk into a less noticeable shape beneath his coat.

'Practise,' said Ginger, still slashing wildly and with evident enjoyment.

'We've not got a ball,' said Douglas, '*they're* bringing the ball.'

'Well, I tell you what I'm goin' to do,' said William.

'I'm goin' to go down to their shed an' have a look at what they've got for tea.'

'An' we'll all come, too,' sang Ginger with a joyous slash.

'No, you'd better not,' said William, 'they'd see us if a lot of us went. An' you'd better stay here 'case they come.'

The Outlaws accepted William's decision as final. Douglas found a suitably-sized stone, and he and Ginger fell upon it with their sticks and an engrossing game of hockey for two ensued. Henry was still wrestling with Monk.

William cautiously approached the wall which surrounded the Lane back garden.

He hoisted himself up, dropped silently into the garden and remained for a moment crouching behind a bush. Then he raised his head and looked around him. The coast was clear. The garden was empty. The shed stood only a few yards from him. There was a small window high up in the back of it. He cautiously advanced, hoisted himself up into a tree and looked through the window.

It was a fairly large shed. A table had been laid in the middle of it. The sight of the table made William's mouth water. Cakes – sugar cakes, cream cakes, meringues, eclairs, glorious cakes, the very poetry of cakes, plate upon plate of them. Hubert's mother had,

HE HOISTED HIMSELF UP INTO A TREE AND LOOKED
DOWN THROUGH THE WINDOW. THE SIGHT MADE
WILLIAM'S MOUTH WATER.

indeed, provided with a generous hand. She evidently
gauged everyone's appetite by Hubert's.

There were plates of plainer cakes, too, of

wholesome-looking buns and scones, but they were ordinary cakes, cakes one can have at home any day, the very prose of cakes. They failed to thrill. William guessed that the majority of them would be left after the feast. At one end of the table stood glasses and innumerable bottles of ginger-beer – a noble profusion of bottles. There were a few old packing-cases in one corner of the shed and some old plant pots at the other. Otherwise the shed was empty of furniture. But it was not empty of human beings.

Hubert Lane himself, rather paler than ever, stood by the table and with him his faithful friend and lieutenant Bertie Franks. Like Hubert, Bertie Franks ate too much and cried when hurt and was very careful of his clothes and told his father whenever anyone annoyed him. They were looking greedily and gloatingly at the plates of cake. A corner of the window frame was broken and through it William could hear what they said.

'An' they'll gobble 'em all up,' Hubert was saying plaintively, 'an' there'll be *nothin'* left afterwards.'

'Greedy pigs!' agreed Bertie mournfully, 'jus' think of *them* eating up all our nice cakes—' then he brightened, 'I say, Huby, your father an' mother's not coming after all, are they?'

'No,' said Hubert.

'Well – *well*, I've got an idea.'

'What?' said Hubert still gloomily.

'Well, let's hide 'em – all the nice ones. Let's jus' leave the buns an' scones. There'll be enough an' they'll never know an' we can have them afterwards.'

A light broke over Hubert's mournful face. He beamed. He smiled from ear to ear.

'I say, what a jolly good idea, Bertie. Where shall we put 'em? We can't carry 'em back to the house.'

'No.' Bertie frowned and looked about him. His eye fell upon the packing-case.

'In here,' he said, 'we can turn 'em over sideways an' put the stuff in an' no one'll know and then afterwards,' his little eyes gleamed, 'we can have a *jolly* good tuck in – jus' you an' me.'

They carried the platefuls of cakes from the table to the packing-case, putting the top of the packing-case to the side and finally moving it close to the wall of the shed. Upon the table was left only a few plates of plain buns and scones. 'Quite enough for 'em, too,' said Hubert scornfully.

'Quite,' agreed Bertie. Then his glance fell upon the bottles of ginger-beer. 'An' jus' think of 'em guzzlin' down those too.' Then once more he brightened. 'I say, we can hide those, too – you're *sure* your mother an' father won't be here, Huby?'

'Yes.'

'Well, we'll jus' go an' fetch some water for them

from the house an' that'll do all right for 'em. Then we'll hide the bottles in the *other* packing-case an' have 'em with the cakes – jus' you an' me – when all the others've gone home.'

Again Hubert's small eyes gleamed.

'*Jolly* good idea, Bertie,' he said. 'Let's move 'em quick.'

They put the bottles into the other packing-case, and moved it too against the wall. Then Hubert went to the house and returned with a large jug of water which he put upon the table. The feast had now assumed a Spartan appearance. Then William suddenly noticed two small objects in the middle of the table upon a piece of paper. Bertie and Hubert also were gazing at these. By craning his neck, William discovered that they were a penknife of an exceptionally magnificent kind and a magnifying glass, and that upon the paper was written: 'For the Captain of the Winning Team.'

'Did your mother put that there?' said Bertie.

Hubert nodded gloomily, then said bitterly, 'Can't think what she wants with givin' *two* presents for, anyway. Nice thing if *they* get 'em, won't it be?'

'An' they prob'ly *will* get 'em,' said Bertie still more gloomily, 'they're so *rough*.'

Then a light dawned through the gloom of his expression.

'Well, look here, they won't know. None of 'em knows. Slip the penknife into your pocket, Huby, and I'll have the glass thing. See? Much better than *them* gettin' 'em, isn't it, and your mother'll never know.'

He seized the paper and tore it into tiny pieces and Hubert obediently slipped the penknife into his pocket while Bertie slipped the glass into his. There was a smile, fatuous and admiring, upon Hubert's face.

'I say, Bertie,' he said, 'you *are* clever – shall we tell the others what we've done – *our* side, I mean?'

'Gosh, no,' said Bertie, 'don't tell *anyone* – all the more for us two.' Then he looked round at the table with its plain and wholesome fare and began to chuckle. 'I say,' he gasped, 'if they *knew* – if they only *knew*.'

The joke of this appealed to Hubert. He began to chuckle. It grew on them more and more as they looked round the table with its plain buns and water. They stood laughing helplessly, holding their sides.

William slipped down silently from his hiding place, crept back to the wall, climbed it, and ran quickly back to the field.

Most of the Hubert Laneites and Outlaws had now assembled and were employed in carrying on unofficial preliminary contests. Several sticks had already been broken, and the only ball had been accidentally hit into the pond at the end of the field where it had sunk. A salvage party surrounded the pond, standing with the water well over their boots, fishing vainly for the vanished ball. The player who was responsible for its loss stood by, torn between compunction at having thus lost the most necessary part of the whole proceedings, and pride at the length of the shot which had caused its disappearance.

Cheers were raised by the Hubert Laneites at the sight of Hubert Lane and Bertie Franks coming on to the field arm-in-arm. The question of the missing ball was discussed at some length. One small boy's offer to go home and fetch a coconut (which he said he'd bought yesterday and hadn't opened and would do just *ripping* for a ball) was refused.

The problem was solved by William, who filled his handkerchief with grass and stones and tied it firmly together to form a ball. The next question was the choice of the side of field. No one had brought a coin, so William decided that the two captains should throw stones and the one who could throw the farther should be said to have won the toss. William's throw easily outdistanced Hubert's. Hubert's stone quite by accident hit one of his own supporters, who burst into tears and went home roaring with pain and anger to tell his father.

The actual game does not come into the story. As a matter of fact the actual game demands a story of itself (only it can't have one). It was a glorious game. It was a game famous in the annals of the village. Bits of broken walking-sticks remained to mark the field for months afterwards. The only important fact as regards this story was the fact that the Outlaws won gloriously by twenty goals to nil.

The match was over.

They stood panting, purple-faced, black as to the eyes and bruised as to the shins and wild as to the hair, covered with mud, and put on their coats again. Henry had managed unostentatiously to slip Monk off with his coat. Now he was trying equally unostentatiously to slip Monk on with his coat. William was standing in front of him to hide his movements from the Hubert Laneites.

Hubert Lane and Bertie Franks came up to them. Hubert Lane still pale and noticeably thinner since his exertion of the afternoon (as a matter of fact he'd kept well away from the ball and out of the danger zone) approached with an oily smile.

'Will you all come to our shed an' have some tea?' he said. He winked at Bertie Franks as he spoke and Bertie Franks sniggered.

The whole party moved off in the direction of the Lanes' garden. When they entered the shed and beheld the table of plain buns and water, some faces which had expected a far, far better sight might have been

observed to drop. But not William's. William, standing loyally by the Monk-encumbered Henry, wore his
most sphinx-like expression. They all gathered round
the table. Buns were passed. Water was poured out.
Bertie Franks and Hubert Lane were sniggering
together in a corner.

Suddenly at an unguarded movement of Henry's,
his coat burst open and Monk fell out. The Hubert
Laneites (sore both in mind and body as a result of the
match) burst into a triumphant outburst of jeering.
'Oh, look at Henry's toy monkey.' 'Yah! he's brought
his toy monkey.' 'Oh, Baby.' 'Diddums have to bring
his ickle monkey, then?'

For a minute the Outlaws were at a loss. Dimly they
felt that an onslaught upon the Hubert Laneites over a
table full of food (however disappointing in quality)
provided by Hubert's mother would be a proceeding
lacking in seemliness. And the Hubert Laneites, seeing
their predicament, grew more bold and insulting every
minute.

'Yah, Baby.' 'Where's his milk bottle?'

The Outlaws looked to William for guidance and
even as they looked there flickered over William's
heated, mud-speckled countenance that light which
betokened to those who knew him that inspiration had
visited him once again. It passed almost at once,
leaving it sombre and inscrutable as ever. He took

Monk from Henry, and holding it up addressed the Hubert Laneites.

'If you *knew* what this was,' he said very slowly, 'you'd be *jolly* careful how you carried on talkin' about it.'

Despite themselves the Hubert Laneites were impressed. William's tone, William's eyes, William's scowl, impressed them. William, they knew, was not a boy to be taken lightly.

'Well, what *is* it?' said Bertie Franks, jeeringly.

'It's magic,' said William, in a deep voice, ignoring Bertie Franks and addressing the others. They tried to jeer again, but the fixity of William's eye and the earnestness of William's voice had its effect upon them. Although outwardly they scoffed at magic, still they were not far removed from the age when the idea of magic was as natural to them as nursery fairy tales could make it, and not a few of them still believed in it secretly. William uttered a short, mirthless laugh.

'If only you *knew*—' he said, and then was silent, as if afraid of betraying secrets.

'All right,' challenged Hubert Lane, 'if it's magic let it *do* some magic then.'

'Cert'nly,' said William. He addressed the others. 'You see that ole packing-case standin' by the wall there?'

All eyes turned towards the packing-case.

'That's jus' an ole empty packing-case, isn't it, Hubert?' said William.

Hubert paled slightly and blinked his small eyes.

'Er – yes,' he stammered. 'Yes – 'course it is.'

William made Monk describe a circle with its arm. They all watched with interest, eyes staring, mouths still mechanically masticating bun.

'Well,' said William, 'now Monk's bewitched it so's it's full of lovely cakes. Jus' you look and see.'

There was a rush to the packing-case. There were screams of surprise and excitement as the treasure-trove was discovered. There was a general scrimmage for the cakes. Someone rescued them from the general scrimmage and carried them to the table where they were handed round.

Hubert Lane and Bertie Franks watched in silence, their mouths hanging open in dismay, their eyes almost dropping out with surprise and horror. Gradually the clamour subsided. Everyone looked at William and at Monk with deep though mystified respect.

'I *say*,' said a small boy as distinctly as he could through a large mouthful of cream bun. 'I say, can it do anythin' else?'

''Course it can,' said William. 'Look at that other packing-case over there.'

In silence they all turned to look at the other

packing-case. There was a thrill of tense expectancy about them. The only movement was the movement of lips and the mechanical journeys of laden hands to mouths, for not once did the late combatants cease in their hearty consumption of the newly discovered treasure. The plates of buns stood scorned and neg-

WILLIAM MADE MONK DESCRIBE A CIRCLE WITH ITS ARM. 'NOW,' SAID WILLIAM, 'MONK'S BEWITCHED THAT CASE SO'S IT'S FULL OF LOVELY CAKES.'

lected. One had even been knocked on to the floor and no one had troubled to pick them up.

'That's jus' an' ole empty box, isn't it, Hubert?' said William.

Hubert gulped.

'Y-y-y-y-y-yes,' he spluttered. William made Monk wave his other arm.

'Well,' he announced, 'now he's bewitched it so's it's full of lovely bottles of ginger-beer.'

There was a rush to the box and cries of excitement as the guests discovered the secret hoard. They cheered loudly. They grabbed at the bottles. They drank from them without troubling to fetch their glasses. There were bottles for all

THEY ALL WATCHED WITH INTEREST, EYES STARING, MOUTHS STILL MECHANICALLY EATING BUN.

and to spare. They wallowed gloriously in heavenly ginger-beer. Hubert and Bertie watched in silence. They had turned rather yellow and their eyes were still starting out of their heads. They didn't know what to make of it all.

Again the clamour gradually subsided and everyone looked at William and Monk.

They were replete with sugar cakes and lemonade. They were gloriously happy. They were eager for more.

'What else can he do, William?' they said.

'He can do *anythin*' I tell him to,' said William.

'Tell him to do somethin' else.'

'All right,' said William obligingly. 'Who'd like a nice new penknife?'

'*I* would,' yelled a dozen voices excitedly.

'Well, you've not got one in your pocket to give to anybody, have you, Hubert?' said William.

Hubert went from yellow to green.

'No, I've *not*,' he spat out viciously.

'No,' said William to the others, 'he's not got one in his pocket. Now, who'd like a nice new magnifying glass?'

'I would,' screamed the entire company.

'Bertie hasn't got one in his pocket now, have you, Bertie?'

'N-n-n-no,' said Bertie, glaring round at them all fiercely, 'I tell you I *haven't*.'

William made Monk describe circles in the air with both his arms.

'He says,' said William solemnly, 'that though they haven't got them in their pockets *now* – if you take them and dip their heads three times in the rain tub – Hubert's and Bertie's – you'll find 'em in their pockets when you've finished – a penknife in Hubert's and a magnifying glass in Bertie's, but you mustn't look first, and you *must* duck 'em three times, or you won't find them.'

With a yell of terror Hubert turned and ran from the shed. He was followed closely by Bertie, who was followed closely by a yelling, excited crowd consisting of both Hubert Laneites and Outlaw supporters who had forgotten even the remains of the cakes and ginger-beer in their frenzied thirst for penknives and magnifying glasses.

They caught Hubert and Bertie most conveniently just at the rain tub.

The four Outlaws walked happily homewards. They still bore the dust and wounds of the afternoon's conflict, but they were gloriously happy. They were surfeited with cakes and ginger-beer and triumph over their enemies. Over the fence that bordered the Lane mansion they could see that excitement and turmoil still reigned. The boy who first ducked Hubert had found in his pocket the prophesied penknife. The boy who first ducked Bertie had found in his pocket the prophesied magnifying glass. And every other boy was struggling for a chance to duck Bertie or Hubert in hopes that the magic process would produce yet more penknives and magnifying glasses in their pockets. Bertie and Hubert were being ducked and ducked again.

Belief in Monk's powers and lust for penknives and magnifying glasses had temporarily overshadowed all more humane feelings. The yells of Hubert Lane and Bertie Franks rose unavailing to the heavens. Evidently the Lane domestic staff had decided to turn a deaf ear to all that went on that afternoon.

The Outlaws had with commendable foresight withdrawn before any crisis should arise (for example, the return of the parent Lanes) in which Monk's vaunted magical powers should prove useless.

They walked jauntily. Henry carried the magic Monk openly and in triumph upon his shoulder. They munched cream cakes (of which they had taken a large supply before making their unostentatious exit). Occasionally, one of them would chuckle – deep, mirthful, reminiscent chuckles – as he thought over the events of the afternoon.

'I say, William,' said Henry at length, 'what made you think of it?'

The Magic Monkey

William dug his unspeakably dirty hands into his pockets and elevated his unspeakably snub nose. 'Oh jus' nat'ral cleverness,' he said with a swagger.

CHAPTER 7

WILLIAM AMONG THE POETS

THE Outlaws were crouching behind a bush in the wood, watching Robert, William's seventeen-year-old brother.

Robert was evidently unaware of his audience. He held a book in his hand from which as he walked he read aloud in an impassioned tone of voice, gesticulating eloquently with his free arm. Often he stood still in order to read and gesticulate to better effect. 'Oh, Love,' he said in a deep, thrilling voice, striking an attitude before an oak tree.

'Oh Love,
Oh, Life,
Oh, all the world to me,
My heart beats to thy beats—'

Still reading, he began to walk on, with long fierce strides.

'Oh, soul of mine—'

He tripped over a bramble and fell ungracefully to the ground. An irrepressible snigger arose from the bush behind which the Outlaws were concealed.

Robert picked himself up and looked around suspiciously. But the Outlaws had withdrawn just in time. No human being was in sight and Robert, reassured, strode on again. For one dreadful moment he had thought that those little wretches were following him. Meanwhile the 'little wretches' were creeping in his wake from bush to bush, watching his every movement.

Robert, as the result of a short attack of influenza, during which he had been thrown on his own resources, had 'discovered' poetry. He had finished all the available novels of adventure and so was thrown back upon a book of poetry, lent to him by his sister Ethel, and had been surprised and delighted by its possibilities. It was glorious to read out aloud and he thought must be fairly easy to write. At present he was confining himself to the reading of it.

As soon as he recovered from the attack of influenza he began to take long solitary walks in the woods, reading aloud as he went with appropriate gestures. At least, he thought that they were solitary walks.

He did not know that the Outlaws, always curious as to Robert's activities, had begun to follow him on his poetic expeditions, and found the spectacle of absorbing interest.

Yesterday had been especially interesting. Yesterday

Robert, feeling a sudden misgiving as to his appearance (he certainly looked extremely healthy, despite the influenza, and not over intellectual) had 'borrowed' a pair of his father's horn-rimmed spectacles. He was intensely pleased with the air of intelligence they imparted to his countenance, but this advantage was counterbalanced by the fact that they were a little too big and he had to hold them on all the time. The Outlaws, however, thoroughly enjoyed it. The sight of Robert holding out a book with one hand, holding on his spectacles with the other, reading aloud as he walked and stumbling over briars at intervals had been a diverting one.

Robert was turning round. The Outlaws promptly dodged behind their bush. Robert, after colliding with a tree, turned on his tracks and came past them, still reading.

'My bleeding heart,' he read, 'is racked with pains untold—'

The Outlaws' heads, popping up from their place of concealment as soon as he had passed, gazed after him with interest. They 'scouted' him to the end of the wood. Nothing particularly thrilling happened, except that, with eyes still fixed on his book, he walked through a stream that he evidently hadn't meant to walk through, because he said: 'Thy face is like a star to me – Oh, *damn*!' and the

'Oh, damn!' presumably wasn't part of the poem.

At the edge of the wood he put the book into his pocket, shed his air of poetic intensity, and set off to walk home in a normal fashion.

When his figure had finally disappeared, the Outlaws emerged from behind the bush.

'He was quite good today, wasn't he?' said William, with the air of one who has staged the show.

As a matter of fact it was William who had introduced the Outlaws to the highly-diverting entertainment of Robert Reading Poetry to Himself in the Wood.

'All right,' said Ginger critically, 'but not so funny as when he had the specs.'

'Well, p'raps he'll bring 'em again tomorrow,' said William hopefully.

But Robert didn't. He didn't go to the woods at all the next day. The Outlaws hung about the Brown homestead ready and eager for their daily entertainment, but Robert seemed disinclined to provide it. Robert, instead of pocketing his little book of poetry and sallying forth to the woods, sat by the morning-room fire reading the newspaper, unaware of the four anxious faces watching him covertly through the window.

Finally William said: 'Well, he's not goin' to go out actin' funny today – so let's go'n play Red Indians.'

So they went and played Red Indians.

But somehow the zest was gone out of Red Indians. Instead of being Red Indians they kept wondering what Robert was doing and whether they were missing anything. Finally, William, throwing away the single hen's feather that represented his status as Chief of a Thousand Braves, said: 'I wonder if he's jus' goin' out later or if he's doin' it in a diff'rent place?'

And Ginger said gloomily: 'F'r all we know, he's carryin' on funnier than ever an' we're missin' it all.'

So the Outlaws stopped being Red Indians and returned to the pursuit of Robert.

They peeped in cautiously through the morning-room window, where they had last seen Robert, but Robert was not there.

'*Told* you so!' said Ginger, gloomily. 'He's gone off bein' funny somewhere without us.'

At this minute Mrs Brown came into the room. She saw her son and her son's friends clustered round the open window, and said mildly to William:

'What do you want, dear?'

'We're looking for Robert,' said William.

'What do you want him for, dear?' said Mrs Brown.

Mrs Brown was always pleased to see any sign of friendship between her two sons. Sometimes she thought that dear William did not admire and respect his elder brother as he should, and that dear Robert did not love and cherish his little brother as he should. Still, Mrs Brown always hoped for the best.

'What do you want him for, dear?' she said again.

William was silent a minute. He couldn't tell his mother that he wanted to watch Robert's moments of poetic ecstasy with unholy glee. So he said:

'I – I-er-I thought I'd sort of like to have a talk with him.'

Mrs Brown beamed. She'd always *known* that sooner or later dear Robert would inspire that love and admiration in William that an elder brother should inspire in a younger one.

'He's just gone to see one of his friends – Hector, I think it was, dear,' she said. 'Go there after him. I'm sure he'd be *so* glad to have a little talk with you.'

Even Mrs Brown didn't really, in her heart of hearts, believe this last statement, but as I have said, Mrs Brown lived in a permanent state of hoping for the best.

The Outlaws set off together for Hector's house. Ginger, who was Hector's younger brother, led the way.

'He can't be carryin' on funny there,' said Ginger, gloomily. 'He'll only be talkin' or playin' tennis or doin' somethin' ordinary.'

But the Outlaws wanted to make quite sure. They

had stalked and enjoyed Robert the Poet for so many days that they were loth to let him go. They wanted to make quite sure that he had relinquished his career of (involuntary) public entertainer. A cautious reconnoitring of the outside of the house revealed no trace of either Robert or Hector.

Their four bullet heads peered furtively over the window sill of each downstairs window; but drawing-room, dining-room, morning-room, were empty.

Then Henry said: 'I b'lieve I can hear someone talkin' in the summer-house.'

So the Outlaws crept in single file to the back of the summer-house, where there was a convenient window.

Robert and Hector were in the summer-house, but they were not alone. With them were Douglas's brother George, Jameson Jameson (a faithful satellite of Robert's), and – Oswald Franks. The eyes of the Outlaws dilated with horror when they fell upon Oswald Franks. Oswald Franks was the elder brother of Bertie Franks, and Bertie Franks was one of the Outlaws' sworn foes.

Oswald, beneath a very superior manner, was quite as bad as Bertie. He, too, was fat and pale, and cowardly and greedy. But he talked very well, chiefly on art and literature, and William had had a horrible suspicion for some time that Robert admired him. That a brother of his should admire – *admire* – a brother of Bertie Franks! William ground his teeth at the thought. And now Oswald Franks sat with Robert and his friends, as one of them. William glared furiously at the unconscious Robert. The only redeeming feature of the situation was that quite evidently Robert and not Oswald was directing proceedings. He was standing up and making what appeared to be quite an impassioned speech.

The Outlaws strained their ears to catch Robert's words.

'And so I think,' Robert was saying, 'that we ought to form a Society, a – er – a sort of Society to study it an' to write it – poetry, I mean. For all we know, some of us may turn out to be famous poets. It's all a – a sort of matter of practice – just like motor-driving. What I mean to say is that when you're sort of beginning to drive it all seems very difficult – changing the gears and steering and that sort of thing – but when you've done it a few times it sort of comes easier till you can drive as well as anyone – well,' added Robert, remembering an unpremeditated meeting between his runabout and a lamp-post the week before, 'well, *nearly* as well.

'Well, what I mean is that it's probably the same with poetry. If we make a rule that each member of the Society's got to make up a poem every week, well, it'll begin to come easier an' easier, just like driving a motor does, till we're all just as good at it as anyone could be and – and probably some of us'll turn out to be famous poets. If you're interested, that is, and I don't see how anyone can help being interested in poetry. It's so – noble. It makes you sort of feel you want to live a better life.

'I've been reading a lot lately and that's what it did to me. I feel I'm quite a different sort of man now to what I was before I began to read poetry. Of course we all did poetry for exams at school, but it didn't have that effect upon us because we were too young to want to be noble – or else it was the wrong sort of poetry. The right sort of poetry's uplifting. It sort of uplifts you. Well, what I'm trying to say is that I propose that we young (I don't mean *really* young of course), that us—'

Robert stopped for a moment, frowning. He was searching desperately for a word. Then his brow cleared; he had found it: 'We devotees of poetry should form a band of poets like Keats and Shelley and Wordsworth and Shakespeare and the others – and meet to read poetry and write poetry.'

He sat down blushing, suddenly overwhelmed by the force of his own eloquence.

The others were obviously impressed.

'I don't mind poetry,' admitted Jameson Jameson. 'I'd just as soon do poetry as anything, because it's such rotten weather and one gets tired of hanging round the house. I once,' he ended modestly, 'nearly got a prize for a limerick.'

Then Oswald Franks arose and began to hold forth on the Art of Poetry in a manner that completely eclipsed both Robert and Jameson Jameson. Certainly Oswald could talk. Not even his bitterest enemy could deny that. He could have talked both hind legs off the proverbial donkey. He held forth glibly on Poetry in all its branches. Nothing that he said was very original, but he possessed the supreme gift of saying it with an air. He ended by saying that they ought to do the thing in a proper sort of way and make a sort of society of it and as Robert had thought of it, Robert ought to be President. He added that he himself would be quite willing to combine the offices of Secretary, Treasurer and Vice-President. The others, he added, would be the members of the Society. Though as I have remarked before, Oswald had nothing startlingly novel to say, still his way of saying it was rather effective. He spoke with an air of weighty knowledge.

Before the others quite realised what they were doing they had elected Robert as President and Oswald Franks as Secretary and Treasurer and Vice-President, and themselves as members of the Society.

'I now propose,' went on Oswald, who was carrying all before him, 'that we have a meeting this time next week and each write a poem before that and meet somewhere and read our poems and decide which is the best, and that we give a sort of prize to the one who writes the best one.'

'What sort of a prize?' said Robert, with an expression of frowning business-like presidential importance. He had an uncomfortable feeling that Oswald was getting a little too important.

'A sort of medal or a badge,' said Oswald, 'which we wear the week our poem's the best and the next week hand on to whoever's is the best that week, or if ours is the best again, keep. Do you see what I mean?' he added. 'I'm the Treasurer, so if you'll all hand over a small sum – say a shilling – to me, I'll see about getting the badge. Do you all agree to that?'

'Is everyone unanimous?' said Robert in his most Presidential manner.

'I think,' objected George slowly, 'that a shilling each is rather a lot. I think that we could get a sort of badge for less than five shillings.'

Oswald Franks flicked a speck of dust off his trousers with a contemptuous gesture (borrowed from a famous actor whom he had seen at a matinée the week before) and smiled.

'We surely don't want to cheapen the affair, do we?'

They hastily agreed that they didn't want to cheapen the affair. Robert, feeling that some remark was due from him at this point, said:

'Is everyone unanimous that we don't want to cheapen the affair?'

There was a subdued murmur of acquiescence. George was temporarily discredited by trying to cheapen the affair, but he was unashamed. 'Well, five *shillings*,' he murmured doggedly, 'just for a badge. I bet you could get one for sixpence.'

'Would you like me to resign my position in your favour?' said Oswald with a sarcastic smile.

'Yes,' said George simply.

This answer was unexpected and Oswald looked slightly taken aback.

But he quickly recovered.

'Does the meeting wish to pass a vote of lack of confidence in me?' he said, regaining his debonair and slightly scornful smile.

The meeting murmured that it didn't, and glared at George.

'Is everyone quite unanimous on the point?' said Robert, trying to win back a little of the limelight from the all-conquering Oswald.

'The next thing is,' said Robert, with a flash of inspiration, 'to decide where we can meet.'

'We must find some place,' said Oswald, 'where those little wretches aren't likely to find us out.'

By 'those little wretches,' as his audience both seen and unseen knew well, he meant those younger brothers and friends of the younger brothers who were, unknown to the Poets, watching through the window. The Poets groaned at the allusion.

'Little beasts!' said Hector passionately. 'I *know* he's ruined my bicycle, though he swears he never touched it. He's had it out and had a fall on it. I know. The pedals are all jammed and I can't ride it at all. I'd like to wring the little beast's neck!'

'They're all the same,' said Robert gloomily. 'Apple pie beds and cheeking you and taking your things – all over the place.'

The unseen watchers grinned.

'Well, we've not fixed up where we'll meet,' said Hector mildly, ''cept that it must be where those little beasts can't find us. We jolly well don't want them to suspect *anything*. You know what they are.'

The Poets sighed. They knew indeed what they were.

'My carpentering shed's nice and big,' said George, 'we could easily meet there. And no one would disturb us.'

'All right,' said Oswald, 'that's settled, then.'

Robert was beginning to resent bitterly Oswald's invasion of the presidential province.

'That's settled, then,' he said in a tone of aggressive authority; 'is everyone unanimous?'

Apparently everyone was.

'Well, there isn't anything else to decide, is there?' added Robert.

'We haven't fixed on a name yet,' said Oswald with his slightly superior drawl.

Robert felt annoyed with himself for not thinking of that. To make up for this he suggested: 'What about Society of Poets?'

'Too ordinary,' said Oswald, repeating the gesture of flicking dust from his trousers.

Robert ground his teeth.

'What about the Society for the Propagation of Poetry?' said Hector.

'In foreign parts,' murmured George absently.

'I propose,' said Oswald, 'the Society of Twentieth Century Poets. Has anyone any objection?'

No one had. Everyone, Robert hastened to ascertain, was unanimous.

'Well, as there's nothing more to decide,' said Robert, 'I propose that I – you read a little poetry now for a few minutes.' He said this with triumph. He felt that by this he was consolidating his position as President. He'd got in the suggestion before Oswald had had time to think of it, anyway.

He took a book from his pocket, coughed deprecatingly, struck an attitude and began:

'It shall not me dismay
That I've grown old and grey,
Nor tell-tale glass I chide
That will not wrinkles hide.'

He felt rather nervous – far more nervous than when he recited to nature alone (and, all unconsciously, to the Outlaws concealed in nature). He stopped, gave another deprecating cough and was just about to continue when Oswald stretched out his hand for the book.

'Your throat seems rather bad, Robert,' he said sympathetically. 'I'll go on, shall I?'

He took the book and at once began to read in a low dramatic voice. Robert blinked. The Outlaws crept away.

For the next few days the Outlaws curtailed all their usual pursuits in order to keep the Twentieth Century Poets under observation. Certainly the Twentieth Century Poets repaid the trouble.

They adopted the conventional poetic appearance and behaviour. Led by Oswald they gradually exchanged the necktie for the neck bow. By some mysterious means known only to themselves, they managed to make their collars look much lower than they really were. They refrained from having their hair cut.

Ethel, Robert's sister, possessed a black velvet jacket, and this Robert used to take and wear furtively when he was sure that she was out and not likely to return. When wearing it he felt so entirely and satisfactorily the President of the Society of the Twentieth Century Poets. He felt Byronesque. He even affected a slight limp.

He posed in front of his looking-glass. He stripped his room of all but bare necessities in order to make it look more garret-like. He strode up and down reading poetry. He sat with a damp towel round his lengthening hair, thinking out themes for poems. He walked in the woods and communed with nature. He bought a rhyming dictionary.

William all this time seemed to the outward eye to be immersed as usual in his own affairs. Robert would have been amazed and aghast to learn that there was not a single movement of his which William did not watch.

William's unblinking eye was glued to the keyhole while Robert donned his damp towel and paced or postured in Ethel's velvet coat. William followed him out into the woods on his communing expeditions with nature. William, when Robert was safely out of the way, went into his bedroom and read his poetry with a critical frown upon his freckled face.

It was with very great difficulty that the Outlaws

obtained (unofficial) access to the next meeting of the Twentieth Century Poets. Fortunately, George's carpentering shed was rather an elaborate affair (George himself was passionately proud of it), and it possessed a loft. It was about as small as a loft can well be, and the Outlaws were such a tight fit for it that they were

WILLIAM'S UNBLINKING EYE WAS GLUED TO THE KEYHOLE WHILE ROBERT DONNED HIS DAMP TOWEL AND POSTURED IN ETHEL'S VELVET COAT.

stiff all the next day, and Ginger complained that he could taste William's hair for a week.

Accessible by means of a precarious ladder, it possessed a crack in its floor through which the Outlaws – wedged into a solid mass – could catch a fleeting glimpse of proceedings below by the simple expedient of pushing each other's heads out of the way. They had to get into position a good half-hour before proceedings began.

The Twentieth Century Poets arrived very

THE LOFT HAD A CRACK IN ITS FLOOR THROUGH WHICH
THE OUTLAWS COULD CATCH A FLEETING GLIMPSE OF
THE PROCEEDINGS BELOW.

promptly. Robert, as President, was given the carpenter's bench for his seat. Hector sat on a bracket that George had spent the entire morning over, and broke it. George, on the whole, bore it very well. Jameson sat on the floor and Oswald took the stool. He took it with an air that somehow made the stool a far more important seat than the carpenter's bench where Robert sat.

Robert had very much wanted to come in the velvet jacket, but Ethel happened to be at home that afternoon so he couldn't. He wore, however, an enormous black bow (Oswald's was orange, and, Robert considered, rather loud) and had brushed his hair straight down over his forehead to make it look as long as possible.

The President opened proceedings by saying: 'Well, we're all here, so let's start off, shall we?'

'We'd better read the minutes of the last meeting,' drawled Oswald.

This rather startled Robert. Robert was not familiar with the procedure of a public meeting.

'Uh?' he said uncertainly. Oswald smiled.

'Shall we take them as read, then?' he said kindly.

'Oh – er – yes. Yes, of course,' said Robert, looking very nervous and very fierce.

'Let's read our poems next, then, and then vote on whose is the best. Suppose George begins.'

George, it appeared, though with the best intentions in the world, had not been able to write a poem that week. His fountain pen had run out and he'd lost the bottle of fountain pen ink and he didn't want to spoil his pen by filling it with any old ink, and he thought that writing in pencil was, perhaps, against the rules.

Robert looked rather stern at this.

'Yes,' he said, 'but that wouldn't have stopped you from making one up, would it? Why didn't you make one up, then you could have recited it?'

'I did,' said George, unblushingly, 'at least I think I did. I know I meant to. But with not having my pen filled and not being able to write it down, I forgot it.'

Robert passed on to Jameson Jameson. Jameson Jameson rose with alacrity to read his poem. It was very long and very morbid. It dealt with a crossing sweeper who died of starvation. It was written in the convention of the old-fashioned school but taking great liberties with metre and rhyme. It seemed, to the listeners, never-ending.

The Twentieth Century Poets gazed morosely in front of them while the crossing sweeper's inmost feelings when in the act of dying of starvation were portrayed in verse after verse. Jameson Jameson himself was obviously deeply moved by it. There was one terrible moment when they thought that he was going to begin on the funeral but it passed.

Jameson Jameson sat down full of mingled pride in his performance, and emotion at the fate of the crossing sweeper. There was a long silence.

Robert coughed, and made a mental note that some rule must be made dealing with the length of the poems in future.

George went on furtively planing a piece of wood. George was deeply devoted to his hobby of carpentering and did not want to waste time. He was making a very ornamental rabbit hutch for an attractive female cousin whom he admired.

Fortunately, Jameson Jameson took the silence with which his poem was received as a tribute to its eloquence. He imagined his silent audience as deeply moved as he was.

It was Hector's turn next. Hector had written a poem. He assured them almost passionately that he had written a poem but he had lost it. He thought that someone must have thrown it away thinking it was rubbish. No, he couldn't recite it. He remembered that it was something about an iceberg, but that was all. He remembered that because he'd had such an awful time trying to find something to rhyme with iceberg. He hadn't found anything in the end. He'd had to leave a blank.

Robert rather sternly proposed a fine of sixpence for anyone who should fail to produce a poem. All notified their assent except George, who was not listening. George was beginning to have horrible misgivings about his rabbit hutch. After all he'd never seen a hutch quite so freely ornamented with fretwork. Handsome it might be, but was it practicable? Would the rabbits like it? Would the cousin like it? Though it would be nice and cool in the summer, it would certainly be draughty in the winter.

'Do you agree, George?' said Robert, sternly.

George tore his thoughts from his rabbit hutch problem.

'Oh – er – yes,' he said, hastily. He might, of course, make a felt covering for the winter.

It was Robert's turn now. Robert took a paper from his pocket and arose. He looked very earnest and very much embarrassed.

'Good old Robert!' whispered William, from above.

'Mine's – er – very short,' said Robert. 'It's – er – an Ode to a Snowdrop. The first verse is in *vers libre*. *Vers libre*,' he explained kindly, 'is the French for "without any rhymes".' Then he began to read:

'A snowdrop,
The first sign of Spring
Called snowdrop because it's like a drop of snow.
A snowdrop,

Emblem of purity
And high endeavour.'

Robert stopped, blushing furiously. 'Of course,' he said modestly, 'that sort of poetry's quite easy to write because there aren't any rules. It's looked upon as quite good poetry nowadays, though. Walt Whitman wrote it and a lot of the best poets write that sort of poetry just because it's so easy to write and there aren't any rules. But I've written the other verse in the other way, I mean with rules and rhymes and that sort of thing. This is the second verse.

'Oh snowdrop, who above the snow
Dost raise thy beauteous head.
Thou tellest us with thy silent voice
That the grim winter is dead.'

'To make it scan,' explained Robert, still blushing, you have to put the emphasis on the last syllable of winter. But you can. It's all right. You can do anything like that. It's called poetic licence—'

The others were obviously impressed by this.

'Good old Robert!' again whispered William encouragingly from his lofty eyrie.

'Sh!' said the other Outlaws.

Then Oswald arose. Oswald's face had worn a

smile of mingled amusement and contempt as Robert read his poem. He now took a piece of paper out of his pocket. Oswald's mother's poetical library contained a copy of Mrs Browning's poems and Oswald had ascertained that Robert's poetical library (which he rightly took to represent the whole of Robert's poetical knowledge) did not.

'A Poet,' he announced as his title, and then began to read.

> 'Ha, a poet! know him by
> The ecstasy – dilated eye,
> Not uncharged with tears that ran
> Upward from his heart of man;
> By the cheek from hour to hour
> Kindled bright or sunken wan
> With a sense of lonely power,
> By the brow, uplifted higher
> Than others, for more low declining;
> By the lip which words of fire
> Overboiling have burned white,
> While they gave the nations light!
> Ay, in every time and place
> Ye may know the poet's face
> By the shade, or shining.'

Oswald stopped. There was a gasp of amazed

surprise. Even George's mind was drawn from its gloomy mental contemplation of the drawbacks of a fretworked rabbit hutch. There was a dead silence. The Twentieth Century Poets sat and gazed at Oswald in stunned reverence. Like the Queen of Sheba there was no more spirit in them. Oswald smiled his superior smile at them.

Of course the voting was a mere farce. Everyone, as Robert, gathering together his stupefied faculties with an effort ascertained, was absolutely unanimous. There was no doubt at all that Oswald was a great poet. Oswald produced an ornate badge and handed it to Robert, who then solemnly presented it to Oswald.

And that was the end of the first meeting of the Twentieth Century Poets.

The next day Bertie Franks, fat and pale and unpleasant-looking as ever, met the Outlaws with a whoop of exultant scorn.

'Yah! My brother c' write better po'try than yours. Yah! My brother got the badge 'n yours didn't. Yah!'

He did not stay to receive their onslaught. He sped as fast as his fat legs would carry him to the refuge of his front gate. Then, leaning over it, he continued his pæon of triumph.

'Yah. Your brothers think they c' write po'try, an'

they can't. Who won the badge? Yah! To a Snowdrop! Yah! Yes, an' *your* ole brother,' to William, 'thinks he's President, don't he? Yes, a fine President, in't he? Can't write po'try for nuts, can't—'

Disdaining the rights of public property, the Outlaws charged in at the gate, but already Bertie's fat, short figure was entering the refuge of his front door. They retired in baffled fury, pretending not to see Bertie's pale face grimacing at them derisively from the drawing-room window.

This incident depressed the Outlaws. The Twentieth Century Poets had, they felt, considerably lowered their prestige.

And Bertie revelled in it. He swaggered, he swanked, he preened himself, he plumed himself, he put on side, he jeered, he taunted them, he collected his friends around him (Hubert Lane and other kindred spirits) and they all exulted over the Outlaws. 'Yah! Whose brothers think they c'n write po'try? Yah!'

The Outlaws' pride suffered indescribably during all this. The Outlaws were used to triumphing over their enemies. They were not used to being triumphed over. They felt aggrievedly that Robert and the others might have made a better show. And Oswald swanked about wearing his badge and his superior smile.

But the spirits of the Outlaws rose as the day of the next meeting of the Twentieth Century Poets approached, Surely, they thought, Oswald's poem would not be the best again. Surely the others would have made a special effort. Surely they would not be exposed again to the laughter of their enemies—

They concealed themselves in the loft in good time. They looked very anxious. If Oswald won the badge again today they felt that life would not be endurable.

The Twentieth Century Poets assembled by degrees. They also looked rather anxious. They also recognised the solemnity of the occasion. They also did not wish the all-conquering Oswald to conquer yet again. Robert looked especially nervous, as though wrought up to do or die. He had spent all the previous night over his poem. Oswald came in last, wearing the badge and smiling. He took the conduct of affairs from Robert's hands entirely. He evidently considered himself President now as well as Treasurer and Secretary and Vice-President.

George read his poem first. George was feeling gloomy. He had had to begin the rabbit hutch all over again. The attractive female cousin had scornfully refused the fretwork. She said her rabbits would catch their deaths and did he think he was being funny or what?

So he had written a poem about a blighted lover who ended his life by hanging himself from the top of a tall pine tree and whose bleached bones were found dangling there by the maiden in the morning. He received Hector's comment, 'He'd bleached and skeletoned pretty quick' in dignified silence and sat down, staring moodily in front of him.

Either the threat of the sixpence fine or the intolerably superior mien of Oswald had had effect upon the Twentieth Century Poets. All had brought a contribution. They read their efforts nervously, one eye fixed the while upon Oswald to see if his superior smile should fade at all as he listened. It did not.

Their gloom increased except in the case of George. A sudden brilliant idea had occurred to George; he'd turn the abortive rabbit hutch into a work-box for the attractive female cousin. Line it with red satin or something. She'd like that, surely. His spirits rose considerably.

Robert was reading his poem. It was entitled 'To Spring' and, though it contained many time-honoured and therefore doubtless true sentiments, it somehow did not read as well as Robert had hoped it would when he had sat composing it through the midnight hours. It was better than the others, but it quite evidently did not cause the superior Oswald one moment's uneasiness.

Then came Oswald's turn. Oswald, this time, had rather a narrow squeak. Relying rather too confidently upon his readers' poetic ignorance he had borrowed a poem of Lord Byron's and was just beginning to read in stirring tones:

> 'Oh, snatched away in beauty's bloom,
> On thee shall press no ponderous tomb;'

when Jameson Jameson interrupted.

'I say,' he said, frowning thoughtfully, 'I'm almost *sure* I learnt that at school – something awfully like it, anyway.'

Oswald, however, had made preparations for this contingency. He looked at the paper more closely, then smiled:

'Of *course*!' he said. 'I've made a mistake. This is a poem of Byron's I'd brought to read to you after the meeting.' He put it away and took another paper from his pocket. The second paper was a sonnet of Matthew Arnold's with which he was more fortunate. The only poem of Matthew Arnold's with which the poets were familiar was the 'Forsaken Merman,' which they had all learnt at their Preparatory schools. They listened in a gloomy silence; at the end every one of them, as Robert morosely ascertained, was unanimous. Oswald again solemnly handed the badge to Robert and Robert solemnly handed it back to Oswald.

The meeting, however, did not end in a reading of poetry by Oswald, though Oswald was evidently quite willing that it should. Oswald was enjoying his glorious career of badge-winning and poetry reading. But Hector had a suggestion. Hector had come across a paper for young people called *The Young Crusader*, which was making its appearance. The first number had only just been published, and a prize was to be given for the best poem, and he proposed that they should all compete and see whether any of them won the prize.

The secret hope of Hector's was not that any of them should win the prize, but rather that Oswald should not win it. He thought that Oswald was finding things too easy. He suspected that in a large newspaper competition the great Oswald might find himself among the also rans. Oswald himself, apparently, had the same suspicions.

'I don't know,' he said, 'but what it wouldn't be best to *wait* a bit before we start going in for outside competitions.'

But rather to his surprise the others did not agree with him. They were beginning to find the proceedings of the Society of the Twentieth Century Poets a little monotonous. An outside competition might vary that monotony.

Oswald yielded with his superior smile.

'Very well,' he said in a kind and condescending tone of voice, 'if it gives you any pleasure—'

'I put the matter to the vote,' said Robert, who, in a noble effort to save the rags of the dignity of his Presidential position, had taken a book called *The Conduct of Public Meetings* out of the library, and had been studying it in secret.

The matter was put to the vote and duly carried.

Hector had brought a copy of the paper, and Robert began to read out the rules of the Poetry Competition. Only began – for once more, when Robert who still found his position as President glorious but embarrassing, stopped for his nervous cough, Oswald again expressed concern for his throat, took the paper from him and finished reading it.

The poem was to be a sonnet. It could be on any subject (Oswald's smile may have been seen to widen at this news), and it must be the unaided work of the competitor. The poets listened with interest. They made little notes on the backs of envelopes.

'What is a sonnet, anyway?' asked George.

The others affected not to hear him. Robert decided to go to the library at once after the meeting before the others should have time and get out some sort of a book that would explain to him the exact nature of a sonnet.

The Outlaws walked home in a gloomy silence.

'Well, he got it again,' said Ginger at last in a tone

that voiced the general feeling of despondency.

'They'll be worse than ever,' said Douglas.

'Yes,' said Henry, 'an' he'll go an' get the big prize an' *then* there'll be no doin' anythin' with them.'

'It isn't as if they'd have a proper fight,' said William.

'An' *him* goin' about wearing the old badge all day,' groaned Ginger.

'Well, I think,' said William sternly, voicing the inevitable resentment of the backer against the unsuccessful backed, 'I think they might *try* a bit harder. Why, I could write po'try better than some of them write it. An' anyway, I think Robert's po'try *jolly* good, an' if I was one of 'em I'd vote for it. 'S only 'cause they can't understand that Oswald's po'try an' so it sounds sort of grand to them. That's all. I *bet* Robert could do it as well if he wanted to. Pers'n'ly,' with dogged loyalty, 'I like Robert's sort of po'try better'n *his*.'

'Why shou'n't *we* make a Po'try Society?' suggested Ginger.

As a matter of fact, William had already thought of this.

'We *could*,' he said stoutly, 'an' I bet we'd make up better po'try than *any* of 'em. But – well, we can't jus' yet. Not while Bertie Franks an' the others are carryin' on like this. We've got to go on watchin' Robert's Society an' perhaps we can *help* them sometime. I bet

I could help Robert to make up a reely *fine* poem, but,' sadly, 'I know he wun't let me. I c' make up pages an' *pages* of po'try.'

'Well, we c' *practise* makin' po'try,' said Ginger.

They agreed that they could.

'I c' make up *all* sorts of po'try,' said William with a swagger. 'I can make up the nachur sort, like—

'The day is bright to see,
An' lots of leaves are growin' on the tree—

'An' the adventure sort, like—

'He bashed him dead
An' blood came pourin' out of his head—

'an' – an' – *any* sort straight off like that without stoppin' to think – rhymes an' all. I bet,' darkly, 'that if I b'longed to their ole society that ole fat Oswald wun't carry off the badge every time like what he does.'

But their way led past the Franks' house and silence fell upon them as they approached. Yes – Oswald had evidently reached home with his badge.

A little crowd of triumphantly yelling, jeering boys stood at the gate. Bertie Franks and his friends were awaiting them. Their taunts were not marked by any great originality.

'*Yah!* Whose brothers can't write po'try? *Yah!* They thought they'd get it this time, then, didn't they?

'*Yah!* An' they didn't – they can't write po'try for nuts. We've got the badge again,' they chanted. 'We've got the badge again. WE'VE GOT THE BADGE AGAIN."

The Outlaws' onslaught was too late. Bertie Franks & Co. reached the safety of the side door just in time. The side door was fortunately near the front gate. Overcome by their feelings, the Outlaws once more charged up after them to the side door, but were indignantly repelled by a large and muscular gardener, and their ignominious retreat watched gleefully by Bertie Franks & Co. from the window. They walked away seething with fury.

'We've gotter *do* somethin' about this,' said William grimly.

The Outlaws lay in the field near the old barn. They were still gloomy. They had been very busy lately carrying out the self-appointed task of guardian angels to the Twentieth Century Poets. William had visited Robert's bedroom daily in secret to inspect the progress of his sonnet. It was, William pronounced condescendingly, in conclave with the Outlaws, going on quite nicely, though he gave them to understand that he could have improved on it considerably had

Robert been wise enough to ask his help. He still went about uttering extempore poems. The habit was beginning to annoy the Outlaws. They lay at their ease eating grass and brooding over the problems of the Twentieth Century Poets.

It appeared that no one had been able to ascertain anything about Oswald's sonnet, but as Oswald still wore his superior smile they assumed that Oswald himself at any rate was satisfied with it.

Bertie Franks & Co. felt no doubts on the subject.

'Yah!' they had yelled only the day before from a safe refuge. 'Yah! Who's goin' to get the Magazine prize? I bet you think your ole Robert is! Well, he's *not*! *Oswald* is. Poor ole Robert – poor ole Robert – thinks he can write po'try – Yah!'

'If only they'd let us get prop'ly near them,' said William longingly, for the hundredth time.

'Well, let's plan somethin' to *do*,' said Henry impatiently.

Ginger interrupted.

'There's some teeny little mushrooms jus' where I'm lyin',' he said with interest.

They abandoned the immediate discussion to examine them.

'They're toadstools!' they jeered derisively.

Ginger paled.

'I've been eatin' 'em,' he said faintly.

'Well, I bet you anything you like you'll be dead tomorrow,' said William, with the air of one who makes a sporting offer.

'How many 've you eaten, Ginger?' said Henry with interest.

'About four,' said Ginger.

'Poor ole Ginger,' said William cheerfully, 'you're sure to die. I bet I can make up a piece of po'try about it,' he went on, with a burst of inspiration.

> 'Ole Ginger is dead,
> He ate toadstools instead
> Of mushrooms—'

'Oh, shut *up*,' said Ginger. 'I bet if it was *you* what was goin' to die—'

But here Douglas provided a diversion. He had found a copy of *The Young Crusader* lying about at home, and had quietly appropriated it. The Outlaws bent over it eagerly, studying the rules, all except Ginger, who sat staring morosely in front of him, evidently contemplating mentally his immediate dissolution, and murmuring ''S all very well for *you*—'

'The man what writes the paper,' said William excitedly, 'he's called Mr Boston, an' there's a Mr Boston comin' to give a speech at the village hall nex' week on somethin' called Prortional Representation.'

'He's the same one,' said Douglas, 'he goes about speakin' on politics as well as writin' the paper. I heard George say so.'

'He's comin' *here*?' said William slowly, 'the man wot's goin' to judge their pomes?'

'Yes,' said Douglas.

'Crumbs!' said William, impressed, and again after a pause, 'Crumbs.' They looked at him expectantly. Even Ginger lost his toadstool complex, and said, 'Yes? – well?'

'Well,' said William slowly, 'we oughter be able to do *somethin*'.'

Mr Eugene Boston, editor of *The Young Crusader* and amateur politician, arrived by a train about an hour before the one by which he was expected, and set off for a brisk walk. He met no one, arrived at the village hall just very shortly after the time he was expected, gave an interesting lecture on Proportional Representation and then went home.

It was for Mr Eugene Boston quite a pleasant and uneventful evening.

When the time came for the arrival of the train by which Mr Eugene Boston was expected, William crept furtively on to the station. His frowning, freckled face wore a look of tense resolve.

He watched the train with a ferocious scowl as it

slid to a standstill, and scanned the passengers who alighted with the air of a detective on the lookout for criminals. Finally his eye rested on one of them. He certainly might be a lecturer. He was a precise-looking man who wore a beard and an air of intellect and carried a leather bag. And curiously enough, though he was not Mr Eugene Boston, he was a lecturer.

He was a Mr Farqueson, mis-named by his parents Augustus, and he had come to lecture on Central Asia at a village a few miles farther on which did not possess a station. He had said in his letter to the Vicar that he would walk, but he was half-expecting someone to meet him. He looked around. He was a very amiable, mild, short-sighted man. William approached him.

'You the lecturer?' said William, with stern, unsmiling countenance.'

'Er – yes, my little boy. Yes, certainly.'

He was rather taken aback by the ferocity of William's expression.

'You – er – you've come to meet me?' he went on pleasantly.

'Yes,' said William.

The whole thing seemed to be simpler than William had thought it would be.

'I thought it might be rather nice to walk,' said Mr Augustus Farqueson tentatively, 'but if you have some conveyance with you—'

'No,' said William, 'I haven't got anything like that with me.'

'Well, come along,' said Mr Augustus Farqueson brightly, 'let us set off.'

They set off.

William had counted on the lecturer's not knowing his way, and in this he was right. They set off together down the high road in the direction leading away from the village hall. Mr Augustus Farqueson conversed about Central Asia, but William did not respond.

William led the way over a stile, Mr Augustus Farqueson followed less nimbly.

'A short cut, I presume?' he said rather breathlessly, and then returned to Central Asia.

William, still silent, led him over the field up the hill.

Mr Augustus Farqueson's breathlessness increased, but with true British determination he continued to talk about Central Asia. He asked if William were interested in Central Asia. William, it seemed, was not. Mr Augustus Farqueson could hardly believe his ears. Despite his breathlessness he began to do his utmost to interest William in Central Asia. They came to another stile. It was rather a difficult stile and it led into a ploughed field. Mr Augustus Farqueson, from the top rung of the stile, looked at it in dismay. Then he looked down at his little twinkling, highly-polished boots.

'It's – er – rather muddy, is it not?' he said.

There was a right of way and, generally, a path through that field, but it happened that the farmer had just finished ploughing, and it was for the public now to claim its right of way and make its own footpath over the loosened, furrowed earth. It happened that William and Mr Augustus Farqueson were pioneers. The farmer had only finished ploughing that afternoon, and no one else had as yet appeared to claim the right of way.

'It's all right,' said William, leaping down into the loose muddy earth.

Mr Augustus Farqueson followed more slowly. He was beginning to feel a horrible misgiving about the boy and another about the ploughed field and another about whether he really *was* on the right road to the Church Hall at Bassenton. There was something – something rather *peculiar* about the boy. Very gingerly he lowered a small shining boot into the loose clayey soil. 'I think,' he said pleadingly, 'that – that perhaps we're trespassing. Perhaps it would be wiser to return to the main road.'

But William didn't think so. William hastened on ahead through the mud. Mr Augustus Farqueson floundered unhappily behind. He didn't talk about Central Asia any more. For the time being he'd lost all interest in Central Asia. The loose earth was ploughed

'I THINK,' SAID MR FARQUESON, 'THAT PERHAPS WE'RE
TRESPASSING. PERHAPS IT WOULD BE WISER TO RETURN
TO THE MAIN ROAD.

into little hillocks over which Mr Augustus Farqueson
kept stumbling. He had clay and mud on his nice dark
suit. His nice shiny little boots and the bottoms of his

WILLIAM HASTENED ON AHEAD THROUGH THE MUD

trouser legs were caked with clay and mud. Dusk was falling.

He began to feel very unhappy.

Yet he stumbled desperately on in the wake of the strange boy. It was just like a nightmare. Instead of being in a nice warm, brightly lit room, talking about Central Asia to a nice, interested audience he was struggling over hills and dales of clay and mud behind a boy he was beginning to detest.

He ought never to have come with this boy. He was beginning to believe that this boy hadn't really been sent to meet him. He'd noticed something strange about the boy from the very first. He ought to have been on his guard against him. Why, the boy hadn't even been interested in Central Asia. He ought to have guessed then that there was something wrong with him. And suddenly the boy stopped and waited for him with a look of determination on his frowning face. Little Mr Augustus Farqueson advanced slowly, feeling more apprehensive than ever.

'You've gotter give it to Robert,' said the boy fiercely.

'Er – give what to Robert?' said Mr Augustus Farqueson faintly.

'The prize, the po'try prize, that ole Oswald – I tell you he's no good, he isn't – it's only 'cause he makes 'em sound sort of grand, an' so they think they're better than Robert's but they're *not*.'

'Er – what?' said Mr Augustus Farqueson still more faintly.

'You know,' said William impatiently. 'You know – they've made a Society, it's jus' like drivin' a motor – an' it's so noble – an' it made Robert feel quite diff'rent an' that's why he made the Society, the young – young devotions of poetry – because it's so uplifting – jus' like drivin' a motor car. But Robert, he sits and works *reely* hard – findin' out rhymes an' that sort of thing an' I don't see why Oswald should have it jus' because he makes them sound sort of *grand*. They aren't any *better* than Robert's. They aren't as *good* as Robert's.'

'Of – of course not,' said Mr Augustus Farqueson.

He spoke very, very faintly. The nightmare was growing more terrible every minute. The boy was mad. That was the explanation of the whole thing. Of course, he ought to have known from the strange beginning. Why, he'd noticed something strange about him even on the railway station.

He didn't know where he was. It was getting late. He was probably miles away from the Church hall where he ought to be lecturing. He was alone in a ploughed field in the gathering dusk with a mad boy. It was terrible.

'Will you promise to give it to Robert?' said William.

Of course it was only a boy, but it was well known that a madman's strength is ten times that of an ordinary man's. This mad boy's, therefore, would probably be at least five times.

'Er – certainly I'll give it to Robert,' he said again soothingly.

'You promise on your honour?' said William.

'Yes, I promise. And now, my dear kind little boy' (one ought always to humour them. He remembered hearing that) 'and now, my *dear* kind little boy, will you *kindly* take me back to—'

'What's it going to be?' said William.

Mr Augustus Farqueson took out his handkerchief and furtively mopped his brow.

'Er – what's what going to be, dear little boy?' he said, with a ghastly smile.

'The prize,' said William, 'what's it goin' to be?'

Mr Farqueson's smile grew more ghastly still.

'We – we must wait and see, mustn't we?' he said with an unconvincing playfulness, mopping his brow again.

'Then you won't give it to Oswald?' said William.

'Oh, no,' Mr Augustus Farqueson assured him with another mirthless smile. 'Oh, no, most certainly I won't give it to Oswald.'

'Thanks,' said William, then 'Well, let's get on.'

So they got on. They proceeded over the hills and dales of loose earth till they reached the further stile. This led to a large field in which was an old barn. The boy was evidently leading him to the barn. Mr Augustus Farqueson followed simply because he was too much bewildered to do anything else. The boy stopped at the door and Mr Augustus Farqueson peered curiously over his shoulder.

There were three other boys there.

'He's here,' said his leader triumphantly, 'and he's

promised to give the prize to Robert and not to Oswald.'

The three boys cheered. Mr Augustus Farqueson stood blinking with horror in the doorway. Four of them – all mad – all as mad as hatters. There must be some sort of Asylum for the Young near from which they'd escaped. It was awful – four mad boys each with the strength of five men. He did a hasty sum of mental arithmetic in his head.

Yes, it would be like fighting with twenty men. He must escape while he had time.

He turned and fled into the gathering darkness. He ran faster than he had run since his far-distant school-days. He emerged at last, breathless and panting, into a main road. He ran along the main road. There was a lighted building and people standing at the doorway looking up and down the road. It was his audience watching out for him. Fate had kindly led him straight to the Church hall, Bassenton.

When Robert returned from Mr Boston's lecture that evening, William was waiting for him. William's face wore its most sphinx-like look.

'Was it nice, Robert?' he said innocently.

'Yes,' said Robert.

'Did he – did he speak to you?'

'Of course not,' said Robert again.

'Was he late?' said William.

'A little,' said Robert. 'Why?'

William smiled to himself.

The fact that Robert actually did win the prize needs some explanation. Both paper and circulation were in its infancy. There were only twelve entries for the competition.

Of these only one reached any poetic standard at all, and it was disqualified because its author had omitted to give his name and address. Most of the others were disqualified for some reason or other. Some omitted to sign the paper certifying that the poem was their own unaided work. Some had omitted to ascertain what a sonnet was. Oswald signed the paper and sent in a sonnet in perfectly correct form, but, having grown over-confident, he had chosen a fairly well-known sonnet of Shakespeare's, so he, too, was disqualified. That left Robert. Robert's effort was not poetry, but it indubitably conformed to the rules governing the composition of a sonnet, so the editor, somewhat reluctantly, adjudged the prize to Robert.

So he wrote quite a long article about Oswald's sonnet, pointing out how immoral it was of Oswald to sign a paper certifying that he had written one of Shakespeare's sonnets. He held Oswald up to public execration; he poured scorn upon Oswald's superior head, naming him by name.

The prize was a small silver cup which Robert received by registered post the day after the results were published. It was a pleasant ending to the activities of the Twentieth Century Poets. It was the end, of course. The weather had improved; none of the Twentieth Century Poets wanted to be a twentieth century poet any longer. They were immensely proud of Robert and Robert was immensely proud of himself.

But their pride was nothing compared with the pride of the Outlaws.

Only the day before the results were published Bertie Franks & Co. had followed them down the road (at a safe distance) with derisive yells of 'Who's goin' to win the prize? Yah boo! WE'RE goin' to win the prize.' So completely had Bertie Franks & Co. identified themselves with Oswald.

But now it was the Outlaws' turn. Very daringly William 'borrowed' the cup that stood in state in Robert's bedroom, and fastened it on to a long pole. They inscribed a (very) home-made banner with the words, 'WE'VE WON THE PRIZE.' William and Ginger (whose digestion seemed to have been quite untroubled by the toadstools) carried the banner. Douglas carried the pole and the cup. Henry performed inharmoniously on a trumpet. They did not see Oswald. Oswald, after reading the article about himself in *The Young Crusader*, had retired into private life till such time as his unenviable notoriety should have faded. But they met Bertie Franks & Co. They took no notice of them. They marched past them in proud triumph, chanting the legend of the banner and blowing on the trumpet. And they were rewarded by the glorious sight of their enemies slinking off, abject and ashamed.

After this most satisfactory triumphal procession, the Outlaws went home again.

Then William descended to the morning-room where Robert sat reading for the hundredth time his sonnet which was printed on the competition page of *The Young Crusader*. Robert's face was glowing with pride.

He was thinking what a pity it was that he couldn't really take up the calling of a famous Poet – but now that the weather had cleared, what with tennis and the river, and the footer season beginning as soon as the tennis and river season closed, one really hadn't time for it. He'd shown them that he could be a poet if he cared to be and that was the main thing. He didn't know that it was worth the trouble to keep on with it indefinitely. It took up too much of one's time.

The Twentieth Century Poets had had a final

meeting yesterday (Oswald had not attended) at which they had cheered Robert till they were hoarse, solemnly deposed Oswald from all his offices and then dissolved the Society. They'd all agreed that though it had been interesting in a way they'd had quite enough of it.

Robert saw William approaching and hastily turned over the page. He didn't want William to see him reading his own poem. He thought how well they'd managed to keep the Society a secret from those little wretches. Those little wretches had had absolutely no idea of it till they heard that he'd won a prize.

William cleared his throat and drew nearer. He thought that the time had come to tell Robert. Robert ought to know that he owed it all to him. It ought to make Robert so grateful that he'd do anything in the world for him. There were quite a lot of things he'd like Robert to do for him. He'd like, for instance, a much closer acquaintance with the internal organism of Robert's runabout than Robert had so far allowed him.

Then there was that telescope of Robert's and that ukulele of Robert's. He'd like undisputed possession of both those for at least a day. Surely when he told Robert all he owed to him he'd be ready to give him anything. A picture of a life of pleasant intimacy with Robert's possessions arose before his mental vision.

Robert would probably be quite *overcome* with gratitude and would ask him to choose anything he liked. He thought he'd choose the telescope.

He looked over Robert's shoulder at the paper, and by way of opening conversation pointed to a photograph in the middle of the page. It was the photograph of a young and muscular man with a clean-shaven face.

'Who's that, Robert?' he said pleasantly.

'The editor,' said Robert shortly.

William's jaw dropped open. He blinked. By no stretch of imagination could the original of this photograph be the man whom William had led to the barn that night, and from whom he had extorted a promise to give the prize to Robert.

'N – not the man what judged the pomes an' gave the prize, Robert?' he said almost pleadingly.

'Yes, of course,' said Robert impatiently.

'N – not the man what you went to hear lecture?' said William.

'Yes, of course,' said Robert.

'D – did he look *jus'* like that?' said William faintly.

'*Yes*,' said Robert, 'why?'

'N – nothing,' said William.

He walked away looking rather thoughtful.

He decided not to ask Robert for the telescope, after all.

He decided not to ask Robert for anything.

He'd done his best, but—

Anyway, he'd collect the others and they could march past the Franks' house again with the banner and the trumpet.

That part of it was all right, anyway – *jolly* well all right. The other part must have gone wrong somehow, but – Well, after all, everyone made mistakes sometimes. Even Moses and Napoleon and people like that made mistakes sometimes.

William's thoughtful expression died away and a smile of triumph took its place.

Yes, they'd have another procession.

That part was all right.

CHAPTER 8

WILLIAM AT THE GARDEN PARTY

WILLIAM was feeling grateful to Robert. Gratitude to Robert was not a normal emotion of William's. Their ordinary relationship was marked by that deep distrust not unusual between brothers aged eleven and seventeen respectively. William cherished in his breast many, many grievances against Robert, and Robert cherished in his breast many, many grievances against William – but last week, Robert had all unwittingly earned that not unmixed blessing. William's gratitude.

There were those who said that they preferred William's open enmity to William's gratitude. William had a laudable habit of translating feelings into action and when William was openly out to avenge himself upon you the results were as a rule far less devastating than when he was out to help you.

Anyway, Robert, having received a handsome present of five pounds from his godmother, and being in a generous mood, gave William five shillings. This munificent gift happened to extricate William from a difficult financial position. William had taken his air gun to be mended and had subsequently, through a series of unfortunate incidents (including a broken pane in the greenhouse, and damage done to an enemy's school cap, which resulted in parental correspondence and the enforced purchase of a new cap for the enemy by William's father), found himself insolvent.

The air gun was mended, but Mr Beezum, the repairer, showed an uncharitableness that caused William unbounded surprise and pain, and refused to let William have it without payment, and moreover refused to take William's collection of stag beetles as payment, although William explained that they were worth far more than a shilling (the sum total of his debt), because he had 'tamed' them. Mr Beezum did not stop at this ungenerous refusal. He showed a still more unchristian spirit by adding that unless he were paid by the end of the week he would go to see William's father about it. William felt that this would be an undesirable anticlimax.

William had seen quite as much of his father as he wanted to see for the present over the greenhouse pane and the enemy's cap, and he felt, rightly, that his father reciprocated the feeling. A visit from Mr Beezum to William's father, complaining of William's undischarged liabilities was, thought William, to be prevented at all costs. So he strained every nerve to raise the shilling before the end of the week.

He offered his services to his mother at 6d. an hour, and his mother, after a slight hesitation, allowed him to help with the arrangement of the flowers. In ten minutes he had broken two vases, knocked over a pail of water, annihilated a bunch of sweet peas by sitting on them, and left the tap running in the pantry so that the hall was completely flooded. At this point his mother hastily terminated the arrangement, refusing even to pay him for the ten minutes. William then wandered into the garden to brood over the unreasonableness and unkindness of the human beings among whom Fate had cast his lot.

''Straordinary,' he said bitterly to the next door neighbour's cat on the wall, as he absently threw small pebbles at it, ''straordinary – You'd think they'd *like* helpin' folks an' bein' *kind*. You'd think she wouldn't mind jus' a bit of water about the hall – jus' sort of washin' it for her. You'd think – well, anyway, how'd I know the ole glass pane would break when a stone jus' *touched* it – they oughter've been cross with the man who made such bad glass 'stead of with me, an' I bet he'd've threw *my* cap into the pond if I'd given him a chance an' it's a nice thing, isn't it, *me* havin' to pay for *his* ole cap – an' *he's* a mean ole thing not to let me have my air gun back. It's same as stealin', *I* think –

244

keepin' things what don't belong to you – I bet I c'ld have him put in prison if I went an' told a judge about it – an' I bet my beetles is worth pounds an' *pounds* now I've tamed 'em and if he comes up to tell Father, I shall jus' say – I shall jus' say—'

It was while William, with frowning brows, still absently throwing stones at the cat on the fence, who remained quite unperturbed (because it knew that William's stone-throwing was merely a gentle accompaniment to his thoughts), was seeking some brilliant and crushing remark which would overwhelm with shame both his father and Mr Beezum, that Robert came out, his five-pound note in his pocket and a general air of affluence about him, and carelessly presented William with five shillings.

'There you are, kid,' he said airily, and walked off with a slight swagger to treat himself to a very large stone ginger at the village pub.

William gazed after him open-mouthed with gratitude.

'I – I'll *do* something for Robert for this,' he said with husky earnestness.

William had not meant to attend the garden fête at the neighbouring village of West Mellings. He decided, however, at the last moment to accompany his family there, partly because he had heard that there would be roundabouts and coconut shies, and he had two whole shillings out of the five still left, partly because he was still inspired by gratitude towards Robert and a desire to express his gratitude in some tangible form, and he hoped that the fête would give him some opportunity of doing this. He had paid for his air gun with what he fondly imagined to be a crushing air, and though Mr Beezum certainly did not look as small as William thought he ought to look, still William hoped that he had taught him a lesson that would last him the rest of his life. He had purposely refrained from spending any of the remaining money in Mr Beezum's shop in order to enforce the stern lesson he was teaching Mr Beezum.

'I've got another four shillings left,' he said meaningly as he received the mended air gun.

'Well, I hope you won't go spending of it all at once same as you generally do,' said Mr Beezum, taking the wind out of his sails. 'Why don't you save it?'

This suggestion was, of course, beneath contempt, and William walked out of the shop in scornful silence.

His family received the news that he had decided to accompany them to the garden fête without enthusiasm.

'I don't think you'll *enjoy* it, dear,' said his mother doubtfully.

'I bet I will,' said William, cheerfully, 'there's ice

cream an' roundabouts an' coconut shies an' things. I bet I'll enjoy it.'

His mother sighed.

'You'll *try* to keep clean, dear, won't you?' she pleaded, with horrible visions before her eyes of William as he usually appeared at the end of even a few minutes' enjoyment. 'Remember that you'll be coming home with us. You don't want to disgrace us, do you?'

William ignored this question.

'Oh, blow the kid!' said Robert. 'What does he want to come for? He's sure to mess things up.'

Robert had forgotten the five shillings and was fortunately unaware that the consuming passion in William's mind at present was a burning desire to do him service.

'I *might*,' said William mysteriously. 'I *might* be able to *help*. You don't *know* yet how I might be able to help.'

Then he departed with great dignity, leaving Robert staring after him blankly.

The fête afternoon passed off more or less uneventfully. William made first for the ice-cream stall, next for the toffee stall, then bought a stick of rock and a bar of chocolate from an itinerant tray bearer, then went to the coconut shies, where he failed to win a coconut, but succeeded in hitting a passing curate.

The curate, who was a very good young man, took it on the whole quite well.

'You should be more careful, my little man,' he said, rubbing the side of his head and smiling a smile that was meant to express Christian forgiveness and geniality. (It didn't at all. It expressed only an excusable desire to smack William's head, barely held in check by a strong sense of duty and regard for appearances.)

William, who hadn't meant to hit the curate, explained that the sun was in his eyes, and watched the protrusion on the curate's forehead increase to the proportion of a fair-sized egg with proprietary interest. Then he went to the roundabouts and rounded about on a gigantic cockerel in blissful happiness, sucking a large stick of rock, till he had got down to his last sixpence. Then he saw Ethel coming to fetch him to join his family for tea.

He had lost his cap, his hair stood straight on end, the rock and toffee and chocolate and ices had left visible marks of their passing in large circles round his mouth. His efforts at the coconut shy stall had sent his collar and tie round to the region of his left ear, his hands were black and sticky and his knees, where he had fallen when jumping to and fro over the fence at the back of the coconut shy stall, were covered with mud.

Ethel shuddered and winced at the sight. The thought of this object's joining the well-dressed Brown party around the dainty little table in the enclosure was too horrible.

'Do you want any tea, William?' she said.

'Yes,' said William, his mouth full of rock.

Ethel handed him sixpence.

'I'll give you that,' she said, 'not to want any tea.'

William pocketed it.

'Now do you want any tea?' said Ethel.

'No,' said William, trying unsuccessfully to jump over the bran tub (which was left temporarily unattended) and bringing bran tub and himself to the ground. He got up, brushed off a certain amount of bran from his person and hurried away from the scene of disaster.

Reaching the shelter of a large tree, he took out Ethel's sixpence to gaze at it fondly. It did not occur to him to wonder why Ethel did not want him to want any tea. The ways of the grown-up world were so full of mystery that he never even attempted to solve them. He'd got sixpence – that was the main thing – and he could get far nicer things himself with sixpence than you ever got at any old grown-up tea. Whistling discordantly, with his hands in his pockets, he set off to buy another stick of rock, then he bought another bar of chocolate, then he had another ride on the roundabout, then he had another coconut shy.

Ethel returned to the tea enclosure where several elegantly-dressed friends had now joined the Browns. Ethel felt a glow of pride at her diplomacy.

'William doesn't want any tea,' she said.

'Oh *dear*,' said Mrs Brown, much perturbed, 'I do hope he's not going to be ill – Ethel, did he *look* ill?'

'No,' said Ethel.

'But – but he's *always* ready for a meal as a rule,' said Mrs Brown.

'Oh, he's all right,' said Robert.

'I'll take his temperature the minute we get home,' said Mrs Brown, still anxious.

Then they forgot William. There was a very elegant young man among the friends who was much impressed by Ethel, and there was a very pretty girl who was having a nice little flirtation with Robert. And all went merry as a marriage bell till, in the middle of a funny story told by the young man, the smile froze on Ethel's face and her eyes filled with horror. In silence they followed her eyes.

A figure was walking jauntily along on the other side of the rope that separated the tea enclosure from the rest of the fête ground. It had no cap. Its hair stood up on end. A dirty collar (clean only an hour ago) and tie set up on end under one ear. Dark coloured rings, suggestive of toffee and chocolate, surrounded its mouth. Its knees were black; its bootstrings untied, its clothes covered with mud and bran. In one hand it held a stick of rock; in the other an ice-cream horn. It licked them alternately.

Suddenly it caught sight of the elegant party watching it in horror-stricken silence from the other side of the rope. A radiant smile overspread the grimy countenance. The figure was evidently quite unaware of the appearance it presented.

'Hello!' it said cheerfully, 'I'm having a *jolly* good time, are you?'

After tea there were races. Robert went in for the race for those over sixteen. Robert had not the

'HELLO!' SAID WILLIAM CHEERFULLY. 'I'M HAVING A *JOLLY* GOOD TIME, ARE YOU?'

slightest doubt that he would win. He had been distinctly annoyed after tea to observe that he was followed wherever he went by the horrible rock-licking, ice-cream-sucking figure of William. He imagined that William did this to annoy him. He did not know that William was inspired solely by a desire to prove his gratitude. It was certainly embarrassing for Robert to have to explain to the very pretty girl that the terrible object was his brother. He imagined that the pretty girl's manner cooled perceptibly after that disclosure. But he meant to reinstate himself by winning the race.

At the starting place he was next to the Vicar's son, whom he disliked on sight – a ferret-faced boy with protruding teeth and who had also been hanging round the pretty girl, and who had, Robert bitterly reflected, no ghastly brother, like William, to spoil his chances.

William hovered round Robert giving him unasked advice between the alternate sucks of rocks and ice cream.

'Run for all you're worth, Robert,' – suck – 'Yes, bend down like that for startin',' – suck – 'and then *jump* forward,' – suck – 'then run jus' to keep near the front,' – suck – 'an' then, then give a sud'n *sprint* an'—'

'Shut up,' hissed Robert fiercely from his stooping position at the starting line.

William was still feeling grateful for the five shillings.

'All right, Robert,' he said meekly, as he regretfully swallowed the last of his ice-cream horn, and moved hastily across the field to the winning tape. Robert said afterwards that if it hadn't been for the sudden vision of William's horrible figure – rocky and branny and muddy and dishevelled, waving and cheering at the winning tape when he thought he'd left him safely behind at the starting line – he'd have won the race without any doubt at all.

'Well,' said William, crestfallen. 'I *thought* I looked all right. I *thought* I looked same as I looked when we started out. I'd seen myself in the glass then and I looked all right. How was I to know I'd changed? – an' I was only saying, 'Go it, Robert,' – an' 'Good ole Robert,' an' things like that, trying to *help* him!'

'Well, you didn't help me,' said Robert, bitterly.

For the sad truth is that Robert came in neck-and-neck with the Vicar's ferret-faced son. At least it looked to the spectators like a neck-and-neck ending and evidently it also did to the umpire, for he gave it as a draw, and they drew lots and the ferret-faced boy won and was presented with a silver cup and went in friendly confabulation with the pretty girt.

Robert was furious. Moreover he was confident that he had really won the race. He had won it, he claimed, by a fraction of a head. His nose had reached the winning tape before the ferret-faced boy's. And it was William's putting him off so that had prevented his winning by several yards. William suddenly appearing like that and shouting and yelling and waving his arms and looking so *awful* – enough to put anyone off. He went into the Vicarage before he returned home and saw the cup in the Vicar's study.

'There it was,' he said bitterly when he rejoined the others. '*My* cup – there on a bracket in the Vicar's study, and I'd be carryin' it home *now* if everyone had their rights. It'd be on the silver-table in the drawing-room with my other cup now, if everybody had their rights.'

The ferret-faced boy passed him, accompanied by the pretty girl, and Robert ground his teeth. And William, swallowing the last fraction of rock, made a great decision.

The next morning, William gathered together his boon companions – Ginger, Henry and Douglas, known collectively as the Outlaws – and addressed them earnestly.

'We've gotter *help* Robert, 'cause he gave me five shillings last week an' – you remember – I gave all of you sweets out of it – an' it's *his* cup really, but the other boy's got it an' we've gotter get it off the bracket in the Vicar's study and put it on the silver-table in the drawing-room with Robert's other cup – poor ole Robert wot really won it all the time.'

The Outlaws, who had not attended the garden fête, were rather vague as to the meaning of this tirade, but they were used to following William's leadership. What they chiefly demanded of life was excitement, and William seldom failed to supply it in large doses to them.

They walked through the wood and over the hill to West Mellings. 'Walk,' perhaps is not quite the right word, 'Walk,' suggests a decorous, unexciting mode of progression that did not apply to the Outlaws at all. They ran along the ditches, they balanced (or failed to balance) on the top of fences, they scouted each other as Red Indians through the woods, they played leap-frog in the lanes, they climbed trees and they held races and they deliberately walked through every stream they found – but at last, after several hours, and an expenditure of energy that would have taken them at walking pace there and back half-a-dozen times, they arrived at the village of West Mellings.

'What we goin' to do?' said Ginger cheerfully, throwing a stone at a telegraph post and hitting a hen, who fled down the road with loud screams of indignation to her native farm.

William assumed the stern air of a leader of men.

'We've gotter go to the Vicarage.' he said, 'and get back Robert's cup. It's on a bracket in the Vicar's study, 'cause his son took it (though it *b'longs* to Robert), and it's gotter go on to the silver-table in our drawing-room, where Robert's other cup is an' where it *b'longs*.'

The Outlaws cheered lustily. The explanation conveyed little to them, but they understood that an exploit of a more or less unlawful nature was in progress, and they swung joyously up the hill to the Vicarage. They peered through the gate. À gardener came up and threatened them with a hose. 'Run off, ye saucy little 'ounds,' he said.

They put out their tongues at him and retreated farther down the road. There they held a consultation.

'One of us has *gotter* get in to the Vicar's study,' said William, with a frowning air of determination, 'an' take that cup that b'longs to Robert.'

Ginger peered through the hedge.

'I think that ole gardener's gone round to the back,' he said.

They advanced to the gate.

Just as they reached it a woman came up.

'You going in to the Vicarage?' she said.

'Yes,' said William, unblushingly.

'Well, do take a message for me, there's a good little boy. I promised to call, but I'm catching a train and I shall miss it if I stay a *minute*. Tell Mrs Lewes that little Frankie Randall can't come this afternoon after all. He's suffering from *nervous exhaustion*. Will you tell her that?'

'Yes,' said William, greatly cheered by the message. It gave him an excuse for entering the Vicarage doors, anyway.

The lady hurried on, and William turned to his gallant braves.

'You stay here,' he directed, 'an' I'll go inside. If I'm not back in an hour,' he added, in the manner of all the best detectives in fiction, 'come an' look for me.' Then, with an air of desperate courage, he stuck his sixpenny pistol into his belt and boldly entered the Vicarage garden. The gardener came round from the back and again advanced upon him threateningly.

'I've gotter message for the Vicar,' said William, with an impudent grimace.

Still growling threateningly, the gardener retired to the back of the house.

William walked up the steps to the front door. It was open. The hall was empty. There was no one in sight. It was a heaven-sent opportunity. He slipped lightly into the hall and looked round for the study. Two open doors revealed drawing-room and dining-room, and a third a passage leading to a kitchen. Still no one came.

The spirit of adventure descended upon him. He crept upstairs, and there, through a door at the top, was the study. It was empty. He entered. And there, upon a bracket just above the desk, stood a silver cup. William's eyes gleamed as he looked at it. It was rather large to be concealed on William's not very ample person. He could throw it out of the window of course – or—

Just then the Vicar's wife entered. William looked at her apprehensively. But she gave him a radiant smile.

'It's little Frankie Randall, I suppose,' she said, 'they never told me you'd come – so glad to see you, dear! We'll go down at once to the Parish Hall, shall we?'

William hesitated. If he delivered the message and explained that he was not Frankie Randall, he would, of course, be constrained to leave the Vicarage at once, throwing away his glorious chance of taking the cup. On the other hand, were he to pretend to be Frankie Randall – whoever Frankie Randall might be – his visit quite evidently would be prolonged. So he assumed his most expressionless expression, and said:

'Yes – thank you – good afternoon.'

She led him down the stairs through a door into the garden and into a small corrugated iron building at the end of the lawn where what seemed to William an enormous crowd of women was assembled. William looked at them and blinked in amazement. He began to think that perhaps it would have been better to have said at once that he wasn't Frankie Randall.

The Vicar's wife was speaking.

'This is little Master Randall, of whom we have all heard so much. It's a great honour for us to have him here this afternoon. He is staying with his uncle, who, as you all know, lives in East Mellings, and he has very kindly come to entertain us. He only arrived last night, so we are *most* grateful to him.'

William looked around him and met the interested gaze of the assembled women with a blank stare. Secretly he wondered what on earth was expected of him. Suddenly he knew.

The Vicar's wife led him over to a corner of the room where he noticed, for the first time, a piano upon a little platform. She motioned him to the seat.

'We all, of course, know you by repute, my dear little boy,' she said gushingly. 'We have read of your wonderful compositions and your wonderful, wonderful playing. Now what we'd like best of all, my dear little boy, is for you to play us one of your own compositions – that would be a real treat.'

William found himself sitting at an open piano with a tense and silent circle of women around him. And William could not play the piano. William had never

WILLIAM CRASHED BOTH HIS HANDS ON THE KEYS IN A
SUDDEN EAR-SPLITTING DISCORD.

learnt to play the piano. He looked desperately around
– rows and rows of expectant faces turned towards
him – a large woman in a green hat in the front row,
looking at him through lorgnettes.

'We're quite ready, dear,' said the Vicar's wife, in

HIS AUDIENCE LISTENED IN AMAZED SILENCE.

the hushed tone in which one speaks in church.

Then William's familiar spirit of devilry came to his aid.

He crashed both his hands upon the keys in a sudden ear-splitting discord. He ran his fingers up and down the keys. He crossed one hand over the other, he hurled himself wildly at the bass and then at the treble. His audience listened in amazed silence. He kept up a Bacchanalian riot of inharmonious sounds for nearly ten minutes, then he stopped and turned his sphinx-like expressionless face towards his audience.

Now the lady in the green hat was the squire's wife, who prided herself on being *au courant* in matters musical and artistic. She knew really very little about music, but she had read in the paper about Frankie Randall, the infant prodigy, and his wonderful playing and his wonderful compositions, and she was determined to show that she knew what was what.

'Beautiful,' she said after a short interval, during which the horrible echoes of William's nightmare of discord died away, and repeated determinedly, '*most* beautiful.'

The Vicar's wife, not to be outdone, murmured, 'exquisite,' and tried to dispel the expression of agony that William's effort had summoned to her face.

The Mothers' Meeting in general said nothing – only gazed at William in horror and looked round for escape.

'Really beautiful,' said the squire's wife again, 'so modern, so free from convention – such spirit.'

The Vicar's wife, still determined not to be left behind by the squire's wife in musical appreciation, took up the refrain.

'To me,' she said, 'it has been a treat that I shall remember all my life. Never has a quarter of an hour's playing caused me such exquisite pleasure.'

The squire's wife thought that this was rather uppish of the Vicar's wife and attempted once more to secure her position as supreme musical arbiter.

'Your name, little boy,' she said to William, 'is, of course, well known to me, and I have wished to hear you play for a long time. I can only say that it has far exceeded my expectations. Such *verve* – such *execution* – such gallant scorn of convention, such – such *genius*. And you composed it entirely yourself?'

'Yes,' said William with perfect truth.

The mothers were stealing out, still casting glances of silent horror at William.

The Vicar's wife addressed them.

'Now you'll all be able to tell your children,' she said gaily, 'and your children's children that you heard this little boy play.'

They made inarticulate sounds and hastened their flight. One of them was heard to remark that she was going home to take an aspirin and then go straight to bed.

'Now I'm sure,' said the Vicar's wife to William, 'that you'd like a little refreshment after your work. I know what a mental and emotional strain creative work is. I often help the dear Vicar with his sermons and feel *quite* limp after it. Now come to the study and have a nice glass of milk.'

She felt that this disposed of the squire's wife. The

squire's wife took her leave coldly of the Vicar's wife and warmly of William.

'May I kiss you, little boy,' she said, 'then I can tell people that I have kissed one of the world's future great musicians.' She implanted a large kiss in the middle of William's cheek. William winced slightly, but otherwise maintained his sphinx-like calm.

The Vicar's wife led him to the study and left him there alone. William at once seized the silver cup from its bracket and darted to the window. From the window he could see the road where his faithful band of comrades waited for him. They saw him and waved encouragingly. With a great effort he flung the cup through the window and into the road.

'Keep it,' he shouted, 'I'll be down in a sec.'

And then the Vicar's wife entered with a glass of milk and a plate of cakes. William disposed of these with an alacrity that surprised her.

'You – you've quite a good appetite, haven't you, dear?' she said faintly.

'Yes,' agreed William.

Somehow she'd imagined that a genius – a *real* genius – wouldn't eat in *quite* such a hearty manner. It somehow slightly lowered her opinion of *genii* in general.

The Vicar entered as William was inelegantly consuming the last bun.

'This is Frankie Randall, dear,' said his wife, 'the little musical prodigy who's staying with his uncle over at East Mellings, and he's *very* kindly been playing one of his own beautiful compositions to the Mothers' Meeting.'

The Vicar looked at him with a slightly puzzled frown.

'The face,' he said, 'looks vaguely familiar to me.'

He had noted William – tousled, untidy, and covered with rock and bran – with disapproval and distaste at the garden fête.

He could not for the moment recall where he had seen this tousle-headed boy before. All he knew was that the face seemed vaguely familiar.

The Vicar's wife laughed coyly at William.

'Ah,' she said, 'that's the price of fame, isn't it dear?'

William, fearing complications, hastily picked up the currants and bits of icing still remaining on the cake plate, stuffed them into his mouth, and said that it was time for him to go.

The Vicar's wife, who was anxious to write an account of the 'recital' for the local press, and was afraid of forgetting such words as 'verve' and 'execution' if she left it too late, agreed that perhaps it was, and William, replete with cake and success, rejoined his comrades.

In triumph they marched away bearing aloft the silver cup slightly battered from its fall in the road, while the Vicar's wife sat in the Vicar's study writing her little article on William's 'recital' and looking up 'verve' in the dictionary.

At the gate of his home William disbanded his followers and walked into the house carrying the cup. With a great pride and triumph at his heart he placed it in the middle of the silver-table in the drawing-room next to Robert's other cup. It happened fortunately that the drawing-room was empty. Then he went up to perform those violent, though often inadequate ceremonies with sponge and brush known as 'tidying for tea.'

When he came down again his mother and Robert and Ethel were in the drawing-room. Evidently they had not yet discovered the presence of the silver cup on the silver-table. William said nothing. He was beginning to feel that he had been almost too grateful to Robert. After all, the five shillings hadn't lasted long and there was such a thing as taking *too* much trouble. He didn't for a moment think that Robert would realise how much trouble he'd taken over it. He felt that on the whole he was on the credit side now as far as Robert was concerned.

'William dear,' said his mother, 'go and tidy for tea.'

'I have,' said William simply.

'Go and do it again, then,' said Robert, 'you might get another layer or two off if you scrub hard.'

William looked at him coldly.

No – Robert certainly wasn't worth all the trouble he'd taken over him – five shillings or no five shillings – playing the piano and being kissed by awful women and chased by gardeners and all that sort of thing.

Just as he was meditating some crushing retort to Robert the Vicar of West Mellings was announced. William's face froze with horror. He looked round for escape, but there was none. The Vicar's ample form blocked the doorway. The Vicar of West Mellings, who knew Mrs Brown very slightly and the other Browns not at all, had merely called for a subscription to his organ fund to which Mrs Brown had promised to contribute. His eyes fell upon William and he gave a smile of recognition.

'Ah,' he said 'so our little genius is paying *you* a visit, is he?'

Mrs Brown, Ethel and Robert stared at him in amazement. William smiled a ghastly smile and said nothing.

The Vicar was by now convinced that that feeling of familiarity that the sight of William's countenance had roused in him was merely the result of having at some time or other seen the little prodigy's photograph in the newspaper.

'I was sorry to miss the treat myself,' he said, 'but my wife tells me that it was really marvellous. Such *verve* – such – er – such *execution*.'

The Brown family were still gazing in open-mouthed amazement and bewilderment from William to the Vicar, from the Vicar to William. William's set smile was growing sicklier every minute.

'But, perhaps,' said the Vicar, 'I'm not too late. Perhaps I'm just in time for a treat here, am I?'

He placed his hand upon William's unruly head.

'This little boy,' he said sententiously, 'is one of the greatest musicians of our age. That's a wonderful thought, isn't it?'

William, still avoiding his family's eyes, again looked desperately around for escape and found none.

'Do you,' burst out Mrs Brown at last to the Vicar, 'do you feel the heat? W-won't you sit down?'

'Thank you,' said the Vicar, 'but I trust that I shall soon hear this little boy play the piano.'

'He can't play the piano,' said Ethel, 'he's never learnt.'

The Vicar looked at her. It happened that Ethel was sitting next to the silver-table, and on the journey to Ethel the Vicar's eyes passed over the silver-table and there stopped as though fascinated by something. For

'THIS LITTLE BOY,' SAID THE VICAR, 'IS ONE OF THE
GREATEST MUSICIANS OF OUR AGE.'

there, in the middle of the table, was the very silver cup
that he had won for the high jump in his far-off college
days. And William, of course, could not have been
expected to know that the Vicar's son had taken his
cup back to school with him and the Vicar's own cup,

the solitary athletic glory of his youth, had been replaced upon its usual bracket.

The Vicar craned nearer. Yes, there was no doubt about it – he could see his own name distinctly inscribed upon the silver. He pinched himself to make sure that he was awake. First of all these strange people informed him that a boy whom he knew to be a famous musical prodigy could not play the piano, and next he discovered his own precious high jump cup adorning their table – it was most extraordinary and just like a dream.

They followed his eyes and also stared at the silver cup, noticing it for the first time.

'William,' called Mrs Brown, but he had gone.

'William?' said the bewildered cleric, 'but surely that boy who's just gone out is Frankie Randall, the great pianist.'

Mrs Brown sat down weakly. 'No,' she said, 'it's William. Whatever's happened to everybody?'

'B-b-but—' said the Vicar, helplessly, 'he was playing most *wonderfully* at the Parish Hall this morning.'

'He couldn't have been,' said Mrs Brown simply, 'he can't play.'

They stared at each other helplessly.

Robert was examining the cup.

'But I say,' he said, 'where has this come from? It isn't ours.'

'No, it's mine,' said the Vicar. 'I've no idea how it got here.'

'It – it's like a sort of dream, isn't it?' said Mrs Brown in a far-away voice. 'A dream in which *anything* might happen.'

'But *how* could that cup have got here?' said Robert.

'Ask William,' said Ethel drily, 'he's generally at the bottom of everything.'

'Robert, dear,' said Mrs Brown, still faintly, 'go and fetch my smelling salts, will you, from my bedroom, and find William and bring him back with you.'

The Vicar was examining his cup, still bewildered, and murmuring, 'But it *was* the boy – it was the boy who played in our house this morning.'

Robert returned in a few minutes to say that he hadn't been able to find William. He'd looked in the dining-room and morning-room and garden, and William's bedroom, but he hadn't been able to find William.

Robert, of course, had not thought of looking in his own bedroom. But William was there. He was tired of being grateful to Robert. He was making him an apple pie bed.

It was unfortunate that when the whole complicated affair was finally disentangled it was too late to stop the little account which the Vicar's wife had sent to the press. William read it when it appeared, with a certain pride, though he thought, quite excusably, that 'verve' meant 'nerve', and wondered what she meant by talking about his 'execution'.

CHAPTER 9

WILLIAM JOINS THE WAITS

IT was only two days before Christmas and the Outlaws stood in Ginger's back garden discussing its prospects, somewhat pessimistically. All except Henry – for Henry, in a spirit of gloomy resignation to fate, had gone to spend the festival season with relations in the North.

'What're *you* goin' to get?' demanded William of Ginger. The Outlaws generally spent the week before Christmas in ascertaining exactly what were the prospects of that day. It was quite an easy task, owing chiefly to the conservative habits of their relatives in concealing their presents in the same place year after year. The Outlaws knew exactly in which drawer or cupboard to pursue their search, and could always tell by some unerring instinct which of the concealed presents was meant for them.

'Nothin' really *'citin'*,' said Ginger, without enthusiasm, 'but nothin' *awful*, 'cept what Uncle George's giv'n me.'

'What's that?' said William.

'An ole *book*,' said Ginger with withering contempt; 'an ole book called *Kings an' Queens of England*. Huh! An' I shall have to say I like it an' thank him an' all that. An' I shan't be able to sell it even, 'cept for about sixpence, 'cause you never can, an' it cost five shillin's. *Five shillin's!* It's got five shillin's on the back. Well, why can't he give me the five shillin's an' let me buy somethin' sensible?'

He spoke with the bitterness of one who airs a grievance of long standing. 'Goin' wastin' their money on things like *Kings an' Queens of England*, 'stead of giv'n it us to buy somethin' sensible. Think of all the sensible things we could buy with five shillin's – 'stead of stupid things like *Kings an' Queens of England*.'

'Well,' burst out Douglas indignantly. 'S'not so bad as what my Aunt Jane's got for me. She's gotter ole tie. *A tie!*' He spat the word out with disgust. 'I found it when I went to tea with her las' week. A silly ole green tie. Well, I'd rather pretend to be pleased over any ole book than over a silly green tie. An' I can't even sell it, 'cause they'll keep goin' on at me to wear it – a sick'nin' ole green tie!'

William was not to be outdone.

'Well, you don't know what my Uncle Charles is givin' me. I heard him tellin' Mother about it. A silly baby penknife.'

'A penknife!' they echoed, 'well, there's nothin' wrong with a penknife.'

'I'd rather have a penknife than an old *Kings an' Queens of England*,' said Ginger bitterly.

'An' I'd rather have a penknife *or* a *Kings an' Queens of England* than a silly ole green tie,' said Douglas.

'A *Kings an' Queens of England's* worse than a tie,' said Ginger fiercely, as though his honour were involved in any suggestion to the contrary.

''Tisn't!' said Douglas equally fiercely.

''Tis!' said Ginger.

''Tisn't!' said Douglas.

The matter would have been settled one way or the other by physical contest between the protagonists had not William thrust his penknife (metaphorically speaking) again into the discussion.

'Yes,' he said, 'but you don't know what *kind* of a penknife, an' I do. I've got three penknives, an' one's almost as big as a nornery knife, an' got four blades *an'* a thing for taking stones out of horses' hoofs *an'* some things what I haven't found out what they're meant for yet, an' this what he's given me is a baby penknife – it's only got one blade, an' I heard him tellin' mother that I couldn't do any harm with it. Fancy' – his voice quivered with indignation – '*fancy* anyone givin' you a penknife what you can't do any harm with.'

Ginger and Douglas stood equally aghast at this news. The insult of the tie and the *Kings and Queens of England* paled before the deadly insult of a penknife you couldn't do any harm with.

William returned home still burning with fury.

He found his mother in the drawing-room. She looked rather worried.

'William,' she said, 'Mr Solomon's just been here.'

William heard the news without much interest. Mr Solomon was the superintendent of the Sunday School, on which the Outlaws reluctantly shed the light of their presence every Sunday afternoon. Mr Solomon was very young and earnest and well-meaning, and the Outlaws found it generally quite easy to ignore him. He in his official capacity found it less easy to ignore the Outlaws. But he was an ever hopeful man, and never gave up his efforts to reach their better selves, a part of them which had hitherto succeeded in eluding him.

'He's going to take the elder boys out carol singing on Christmas Eve,' went on Mrs Brown uncertainly. 'He came to ask whether I'd rather you didn't go.'

William was silent. The suggestion was entirely unexpected and full of glorious possibilities. But, as he understood well enough the uncertainty in his mother's voice, he received it without any change of expression. The slight disgust, caused by brooding over the ignominy of a penknife he couldn't do any harm with, remained upon his unclassic features.

'Uh-huh?' he said without interest.

'Would you like to go?' said Mrs Brown.

'Wouldn't mind,' said William casually, his expression of disgust giving way to one of mere boredom. Mrs Brown, watching him, thought that Mr Solomon's apprehensions were quite ill-founded.

'If you went, William,' she said, 'you'd be quite quiet and orderly, wouldn't you?'

William's expression was one of amazement. He looked as though he could hardly credit his ears.

'*Me?*' he said indignantly. '*Me?* – why, of *course*!'

He seemed so hurt by the question that his mother hastened to reassure him.

'I thought you would, dear. I told Mr Solomon you would. You – you'd like it, wouldn't you, dear?'

'Uh-huh,' said William, careful not to sound too eager.

'What would you like about it, dear?' asked Mrs Brown, priding herself upon her cunning.

William assumed an unctuous expression.

'Singin' hymns an' – an' psalms,' he said piously, 'an' – an' that sort of thing.'

His mother looked relieved.

'That's right, dear,' she said, 'I think it would be a very beautiful experience for you. I told Mr Solomon so. He seemed afraid that you might go in the wrong spirit, but I told him that I was sure you wouldn't.'

Mrs Brown's unquenchable faith in her younger son was one of the most beautiful and touching things the world has ever known.

'Oh, no,' said William, looking deeply shocked at the notion. 'I won't go in the wrong spirit, I'll go in, you know – what you said – a beautiful experience an' all that sort of spirit.'

'Yes,' agreed Mrs Brown, 'I'd like you to go. It will be the sort of experience you'll remember all your life.'

As a matter of fact it turned out to be the sort of experience that Mr Solomon rather than William remembered all his life.

William met Ginger and Douglas the next morning.

'I'm goin' waitin' Christmas Eve,' he announced proudly.

'So'm I,' said Ginger.

'So'm I,' said Douglas.

It turned out that Mr Solomon had visited their parents too, yesterday, and to their parents, too, had expressed doubt as to the advisability of their sons being allowed to join the party. Though well meaning, he was not a very tactful young man, and had not expressed his doubts in such a way as to placate maternal pride.

'My mother said,' said Ginger, 'why shun't I go same as anyone else, so I'm goin'!'

'So did mine,' said Douglas, 'so so'm I.'

'Yes,' said William indignantly, 'fancy sayin' he thought I'd better not come. Why, I should think I'm 's good at waitin' 's anybody else in the world – why, when I start singin' you c'n hear me at the other end of the village.'

This statement, being unassailable, passed unchallenged.

'Do you know where we're goin'?' continued William.

'He said beginnin' up Well Lane,' said Douglas.

'My Uncle George lives in Well Lane,' said Ginger thoughtfully, 'the one what's givin' me *Kings an' Queens of England*.'

There was a short silence. In that silence the thought came to all three Outlaws that the expedition might have even vaster possibilities than at first they had imagined.

'*Then*, where we goin'?' said William.

'Jus' up the village street,' said Douglas.

'My Uncle Charles,' said William thoughtfully, 'the one what's givin' me the penknife you can't do any harm with, lives right away from the village.'

'So does my Aunt Jane – the one what's givin' me the ole green tie.'

William's face assumed its expression of daring leadership.

'Well,' he said, 'we'll jus' have to do what we can.'

Many, many times before Christmas Eve arrived did Mr Solomon bitterly regret the impulse on which he had suggested his party of waits. He would have liked to cancel the arrangement altogether, but he lacked the courage.

He held several practices in which his party of full-voiced but unmelodious musicians roared 'Good King Wenceslas' and 'The First Noel', making up in volume for what they lacked in tone and technique. During these practices he watched the Outlaws apprehensively. His apprehensions increased as time went on, for the Outlaws were behaving like creatures from another and a higher world.

They were docile and obedient and respectful. And this was not normal in the Outlaws. Normally they would by now have tired of the whole thing. Normally they would be clustered in the back row cracking nuts and throwing the shells at friends or foes. But they were not. They were standing in the front row wearing saintly expressions (as far, that is, as the expressions of the Outlaws could convey the idea of saintliness), singing 'Good King Wenceslas Looked Out' with strident conscientiousness.

Mr Solomon would have been relieved to see them

cracking nuts or deliberately introducing discords into the melody (they introduced discords, it is true, but unconsciously). He began to have a horrible suspicion that they were forming some secret plan.

The prospective waits assembled with Mr Solomon at the end of the village at nightfall. Mr Solomon was intensely nervous. It had taken all his better self to resist the temptation to put the whole thing off on the fictitious excuse of sudden illness. He held a lantern in his hand and a large tin of sweets under his arm. He had bought the large tin of sweets last night on the spur of the moment. He had a vague hope that it might prove useful in some crisis.

He raised the lantern and examined the little crowd of faces around him. He looked as though he were counting them. In reality he was anxiously ascertaining whether the Outlaws were there. He'd been clinging all day to the hope that the Outlaws mightn't be there. After all, he had thought hopefully, there was quite a lot of measles about. Or they might have forgotten. But his heart sank. There they were, standing in the very centre of the group. He sighed. Probably there were hundreds of boys all over the world coming out in rashes at that moment, and yet here were these boys as bloomingly healthy as they'd ever been. Life was full of irony.

'Well, here we are,' he said in that voice of rather painful brightness that he always used with the young. 'Here we all are – All got your best voices, eh? Now we'll go down Well Lane first.'

'Uncle George,' whispered Ginger.

'Go straight down the lane,' said Mr Solomon, 'till you get to the Laurels, and then turn in and we'll begin with "The First Noel".'

Obediently the little troupe set off towards Well Lane. It was as quiet and good and orderly as a Sunday School superintendent's heart could wish, and yet the Sunday School superintendent's heart was not quite light. He could not help remembering the proverbial order of sequence of the calm and the storm.

He'd have felt, of course, quite happy if the Outlaws hadn't been there.

He had, however, taken quite a lot of trouble over the itinerary. He meant only to pay half-a-dozen visits, and to sing only one carol at each. It was not likely that they would receive any encores. The whole thing ought to be over in an hour. He hoped it would be, anyway.

He had already prepared the householders who were to be honoured by a visit from his waits, and though not enthusiastic they were ready to receive the visitants in a Christmas spirit of good will. He meant to risk no unchristian reception by paying unexpected visits. Though he was well-meaning rather than musical still he had a vague suspicion that the performance of his choir left a good deal to be desired.

The Misses Perkins lived at the Laurels, and they had assured Mr Solomon that they would love – simply *love* – *to* hear the dear little boys sing Christmas carols, and so would Muffy. (Muffy was the Misses Perkins' cat.) The visit to the Misses Perkins, anyway, ought to go off nicely. Fortunately, the Misses Perkins were slightly deaf.

Everything seemed to be going off very nicely so far. The waits were walking quietly and sedately down the road, not shouting or fighting as boys so often did. Mr Solomon's spirits rose. It was really after all a very beautiful idea – and they were really after all very nice boys. He could see William and Ginger and Douglas walking decorously and silently together. Marvellous how even such boys as those yielded to the Christmas spirit.

They were walking at the head, leading the little troupe; they were turning obediently in at the gate of the Laurels. The young man took out his tuning fork and followed, smiling proudly.

Then the light of his lantern shone upon the gate as he entered and – it wasn't the Laurels.

They'd made a mistake. It wasn't the Laurels. It was the Cedars.

Mr Solomon, of course, could not know that the Outlaws had passed the Laurels and entered the Cedars deliberately because Ginger's Uncle George lived at the Cedars.

'Come back!' called Mr Solomon's thin voice through the night, 'it's the wrong house! Come back!'

But already the waits had burst violently into 'The First Noel'. It was a pity that they did not wait for the note from Mr Solomon, who had his tuning fork already in his hand.

It was a pity that they did not begin all together, and that having begun each at a separate moment each should cling so tenaciously to his own time and interpretation. It was a great pity that they did not know the words.

It was the greatest pity of all that they possessed the voices they did possess. But there is no denying their zest. There is no denying that each one put all the power and energy he possessed into his rendering of the carol. The resulting sound was diabolical. Diabolical is a strong word, but it is hardly strong enough. The English language does not really possess a word strong enough to describe the effect of these waits' rendering of 'The First Noel'.

After one minute of it, Uncle George's window was flung up and Uncle George's purple face was thrust out.

'Go away, you young devils!' he sputtered. 'How *dare* you come here kicking up that infernal din? Go a-*way*, I say!'

Mr Solomon's voice in the rear kept up its shrill but ineffective plaint.

'Come away, boys – it's the wrong house. I said the Laurels – the Misses Perkins and Muffy will be wondering wherever we are – quietly, boys – don't *shout* so – and you've got the wrong note—'

But nobody heard him. The uproar continued to be deafening. The other waits realised that the Outlaws were for some reason or other determined to make as much noise as possible and gladly gave their assistance. They found the process exhilarating. They began to think that the whole affair was going to be more interesting than they had thought it would be. Joyfully they yelled and yelled and yelled. Above them the purple-faced figure of Uncle George gesticulated and uttered words which were (fortunately, perhaps) drowned by the inferno of sound below.

Then suddenly silence came. Abruptly the Outlaws had stopped singing and the others at once stopped too, waiting developments. It was, of course, Uncle George's chance, and the immediate development was a flood of eloquence from Uncle George, to which the waits listened with joyful interest and at which Mr Solomon grew pale.

'Pardon me, sir,' gasped Mr Solomon, at last recovering, 'Quite a mistake – boys mistook house – visit meant for friends of ours – no offence intended, I assure you.'

But so breathless was he that only the two boys nearest him heard him, and no one heeded him. For to the amazement of all of them (except Ginger and Douglas), William spoke up firmly from the foreground.

'GO AWAY, YOU YOUNG DEVILS!' HE SPLUTTERED. 'HOW DARE YOU COME KICKING UP THAT DIN.'

'Please, sir, we're c'lectin' books for our library. Please, sir, can you give us a book for our lib'ry?'

Mr Solomon gaped in open-mouthed amazement at this statement. He tried to utter some protest, but could only stutter.

MR SOLOMON'S VOICE IN THE REAR KEPT UP ITS SHRILL PLAINT. 'COME AWAY, BOYS! IT'S THE WRONG HOUSE!'

Uncle George, however, could do more than stutter. He answered the question in the negative with such strength, and at such length, that the waits' admiration of him became a sort of ecstasy. William answered the refusal by bursting with amazing promptitude and discord into 'Good King Wenceslas'.

The Outlaws followed his lead. The rest of the waits joined in, most of them showing their conservative spirits by clinging still to 'The First Noel.' Not that it mattered much. No listener could have told what any of them was singing. Words and tune were lost in a tornado of unmelodious sound. Each wait tasted the rapture of exerting the utmost force of his lungs, and trying to drown his neighbour's effort.

In front of them Uncle George hung out of his bedroom window gesticulating violently, his complexion changing from purple to black.

Behind them Mr Solomon clung to the gatepost of the Cedars moaning softly and mopping his brow.

A second time the waits stopped suddenly at a signal from William. The nightmare sound died away and there followed a silence broken only by the moans of Mr Solomon and sputtering from Uncle George, in which could be recognised the oft-returning words 'the police.'

But something of Uncle George's first fine careless frenzy was gone. There was something broken about him, as there would indeed have been something broken about anyone who had listened to the ghastly sound. Again William spoke up brightly.

'Please c'n you give us a book for our lib'ry? We're collectin' books for our lib'ry. We want a book for boys – 'bout history, please. If you've got one to give us. For our lib'ry please.'

In the background, Mr Solomon, still clinging to the gatepost, moaned. 'I assure you, sir – mistake – wrong house—'

With admirable promptness and a force that was amazing considering the energy that he must have already expended, William burst with sudden unexpected violence into 'Fight the Good Fight', which Mr Solomon had been teaching them the Sunday before. It was taken up by the others, each, as before, striking out an entirely independent line in his rendering of it. It was the last straw. Uncle George was beaten.

With an expression of agony he clapped his hands over his ears and staggered backwards. Then he reappeared, and *The Kings and Queens of England* hit William a smart blow on the side of his head, and fell on to the gravel at his feet. William picked it up and signalled that the hymn should cease. A moment later the waits had gone. There only remained Mr Solomon clinging to the gatepost, stupefied by the terrible events he had just lived through, and Uncle George sputtering at the open window.

Uncle George's sputtering suddenly ceased, and he hurled at Mr Solomon's figure, dimly perceived through the darkness, a flood of eloquence which was worthy of a more discerning and appreciative audience.

Mr Solomon looked around him wildly. He looked for his lantern. It was gone. He looked for his tin of sweets. It was gone. He looked for his waits. They were gone.

Pursued by Uncle George's lurid invective he fled into the road and looked up and down it. There was no sign of lantern or tin of sweets or waits. He tore along to the village street where he had told them to go next and where presumably their next warned host awaited them.

There was no sign of them.

Distracted he tore up and down the road.

Then at the end of the road there appeared the tall burly figure of – a policeman. Unstrung by his experience, the blameless Mr Solomon fled from the minion of the law like a criminal and ran as fast as his legs could carry him homewards.

Meanwhile the waits were joyfully approaching the house of Douglas's Aunt Jane on the hillside. William swaggered at the head of them, carrying the lantern in one hand and the tin of sweets in the other. Behind him followed the others, each sucking happily a mouthful of sweets.

Kings and Queens of England had been flung into the village stream on the way. None of them except the Outlaws knew what it was all about. All they knew was that what had promised to be a dull and lawful expedition, organised by the Sunday School authorities, was turning out to be a thrilling and lawless expedition organised by William.

They followed him gladly, thinking blissfully of that glorious medley of sounds at which they had assisted, looking forward to another, and enjoying the delightful experience of having their mouths filled to their utmost capacity with Mr Solomon's sweets.

William led them into the garden of Rose Cottage, where Douglas's Aunt Jane lived. There they massed themselves ready for the onslaught. Those who had not finished their sweets swallowed them whole, and all drew in their breath.

They looked at William. William gave the signal. The outburst came. The effect was more powerful even than before, because no two of them were singing the same tune.

William, tiring of carols, was singing 'Valencia' at the top of his voice.

Ginger, who had not moved with the times, was singing, 'Yes, We Have No Bananas.'

Douglas was still singing 'Good King Wenceslas'.

Of the others, one was singing 'D'ye Ken John Peel?' and others were singing 'Coal Black Mammy', 'Fight the Good Fight', 'The First Noel', 'Tea for Two', and 'Here We Are Again'. They all sang with gusto.

They had been singing for nearly ten minutes, when Douglas stopped them with an imperious gesture.

'I say,' he said to William, 'I forgot – she's deaf.'

The Outlaws were obviously nonplussed by this. They stared blankly, first at Douglas, then at his aunt's house. Suddenly Ginger said excitedly, 'Look! She's come downstairs.'

Certainly a lighted candle could be seen moving about in the downstairs room where before all had been darkness.

'Well,' said Douglas simply. 'I'm not goin' away without that tie now we've come this far for it.'

'I'll go,' volunteered William, 'an' see if I can get it off her. You'd better not, 'cause she knows you – Go on singin', the rest of you.'

With that William advanced boldly into the enemy's country. He had no clear idea of what he was going to do. He would simply await the inspiration of the moment which so seldom failed him.

He was afraid that the deaf old lady would not hear his knock, but she opened to him almost immediately and dragged him within with a suddenness that amazed and perturbed him. There was something witch-like about her as she stood, tall and gaunt, her grey hair over her shoulders, wrapped in a long grey dressing-gown. She held an ear-trumpet in one hand.

'Come in!' she said excitedly, 'come in! Come in! Saw you coming through the window – What is it?'

She held out her trumpet to him and he repeated into it nervously: 'What's what?'

'That sound,' she went on. 'It roused me from sleep; the roaring of wild animals or – is it an air raid? Has some enemy attacked us?'

'No,' William hastened to assure her through the trumpet, 'it's not that.'

'Animals, then,' she went on, still excited; 'it sounded to me like the baying of wolves. Did you see them?'

'Yes,' said William into the trumpet.

'And came here for protection? I thought so— They must have escaped from the circus at Moncton. I heard that there was a pack of live wolves there – most dangerous, I've always thought this exhibiting of wild animals — Are they round the house, boy? Listen!'

Outside arose the glorious medley of 'The First Noel', 'Good King Wenceslas', 'Fight the Good Fight',

'D'ye Ken John Peel?', 'Yes, We Have No Bananas', 'Tea for Two', 'Coal Black Mammy', and 'Here We Are Again'.

Aunt Jane shuddered.

'All round the house,' she said, 'even I can hear it, a most blood-curdling sound. I have often read of it, but never thought that it would fall to my lot to hear it. The first thing to do is to barricade the house.'

William, slightly bewildered by the turn events had taken, watched her move a table across the window and block up the door with a tall cupboard.

'There!' she said at last. 'That should keep them away. And I have provisions for several days.'

Aunt Jane seemed almost stimulated by the thought of the pack of wolves howling around her lonely hillside house.

'Listen,' she said again as the hideous uproar outside continued, 'listen and imagine the tawny brutes with ravening open fangs. Listen to that,' as Ginger's strong young voice proclaimed above the general uproar that he had no bananas. 'Did you hear? – that voice speaks of greed and cunning, of lust for blood and a passionate hatred of the human race.'

As she spoke she moved to and fro, moving pieces of furniture across doors and windows.

William was utterly at a loss. He didn't know what to do or say. He watched her in open-mouthed

'HAS SOME ENEMY ATTACKED US?' SHE ASKED. 'NO!'
WILLIAM ASSURED HER THROUGH THE TRUMPET.

bewilderment. Whenever he looked as if he were going to speak she placed the ear-trumpet in place for him so much that he gave a sickly smile and shook his head.

He watched her blocking up every available entrance to her cottage and wondered desperately how on earth he was going to get out of it. He wished to goodness that he'd never come in – that he'd let Douglas get his own silly tie. The waits outside were chanting as merrily and discordantly as ever.

Suddenly Aunt Jane left the room to reappear triumphantly a few minutes later carrying a large and old-fashioned gun.

'It's a long time since I used it,' she said, 'but I believe it might get one or two of them.'

William's annoyance turned to dismay.

'Oh, I wouldn't. I – er – wouldn't,' he protested.

She could not hear what he said, but seeing his lips move she presented him with the other end of her ear-trumpet.

'What do you say?'

He gave his sickly grin.

'Er – nothing,' he said.

'Then I wish you'd stop saying nothing,' she said tartly; 'if you've anything to say, *say* it, and if you haven't, *don't*, instead of mumbling away there and saying you're saying nothing.'

William gave her the sickly smile again and blinked.

She clambered on to the table before the window and opened the window very slightly. Through the small aperture thus made she projected the muzzle of her gun. William watched her, paralysed with horror. Outside the medley of song rose higher and higher.

William could dimly discern the forms of his companions through the darkness. Aunt Jane was as shortsighted as she was hard of hearing.

'I can see them,' she said eagerly, 'dim, lean, sinister shapes out there – now I *really* think I might get one or two. Anyway, the sound of the shot might drive them farther off.'

William felt as though in a nightmare, powerless to move or to speak as the old lady pointed the deadly weapon at his unsuspecting friends chanting their varied repertoire of songs so merrily in the darkness. Then, before the fatal shot rang out, William plucked her dressing-gown. She turned to him irritably and held the ear-trumpet to him again.

'Well,' she snapped, 'what's the matter now? Got anything to say yet?'

William suddenly found both his voice and an inspiration.

'Let's keep the gun for a – for a sort of last resource,' he yelled into the trumpet, 'case they sort of attack the house.'

She was obviously impressed by the idea. She took

'I CAN SEE THEM,' SHE SAID EAGERLY. 'DIM, LEAN,
SINISTER SHAPES OUT THERE.'

in the gun, closed the window and descended from the
table.

'Something in that,' she said.

The success of his inspiration restored William's
self-respect. Something of his dejection vanished and
something of his swagger returned. Suddenly his face

shone. An idea – an idea – an IDEA – had occurred to him.

'I say,' he gasped.

'Well?' she snapped.

'I've heard,' he yelled into the aperture, 'I've *heard* that wolves are frightened of green.'

'Of green?' she said irritably, 'of green what?'

'Jus' of green,' said William, 'of green colour.'

'What nonsense!' she snapped.

'Well, I've *heard* it,' persisted William. 'Heard of a man drivin' away a whole herd o' wolves by jus' goin' out and showin' 'em a green tablecloth.'

'Well, I've not got a green tablecloth, so that settles it.'

But William didn't think it did. 'Haven't you got *anythin*' green?' he persisted.

She considered.

'One or two small green things,' she said, 'but green varies so. What sort of green should it be?'

William considered this question in silence for a minute. Then, 'Can't quite describe it,' he yelled, 'but I'd know if I saw.'

That, he couldn't help thinking, was rather neat.

After a slight hesitation Aunt Jane went from the room and soon returned with an olive green scarf, a bottle green hat, and a new tie of a most virulent pea green.

William's eyes gleamed when they fell upon the tie.

'That's it!' he shouted, 'that's the green.'

Aunt Jane looked rather annoyed. 'I particularly wanted that for tomorrow,' she said peevishly, 'won't the scarf do? I've no further use for it.'

'No,' said William very decidedly, pointing to the tie, '*that's* the green.'

'All right,' she said, 'but it's too dark for them to see it.'

'I'll take a lantern. I've gotter lantern in the porch.'

'They'll attack you if you go out there.'

'Not if they see the green,' said William firmly.

'Very well,' said Aunt Jane, who was beginning to feel rather sleepy, 'take it if you like.'

William slipped out into the night with the green tie. Aunt Jane waited.

The noise outside died away, and all was silent.

Aunt Jane suspected that the boy had been devoured by the wolves, but the thought did not trouble her very much. She merely strengthened her fortifications and then went to bed. There was something rather inhuman about Aunt Jane. There must have been something rather inhuman about anyone who could choose a tie that colour.

The green tie had been torn into a thousand pieces, and trodden into the ditch. The toffee tin was almost empty. The waits were growing sleepy. Their songs, though no less discordant than before, were beginning to lack verve. Only Uncle Charles remained to be dealt with. Headed by William they marched upon Uncle Charles's house. Boldly they surged into Uncle Charles's garden. There they stood and upraised their strong young voices, and sang. Uncle Charles's window was flung up as quickly as Uncle George's had been.

'Go away, you young rascals,' he boomed.

The singing ceased.

'Please, sir—'

In the meek falsetto Uncle Charles did not recognise his nephew William's voice.

'Go away, I tell you. You won't get a halfpenny out of me.'

'Please sir, we're trying to go, but I've got all caught up in the clothes-line what was out in the grass.'

'Well, uncatch yourself.'

'I can't.'

'Cut it, then, you young fool.'

'Please, sir, I haven't got a penknife.'

Uncle Charles cursed softly, and after a short silence a penknife struck Ginger's head and fell on to the lawn. William seized it eagerly and examined it. It was the one! It was the penknife he couldn't do any harm with.

'Cut yourself loose with that, you young scoundrels, and get off with you, disturbing people's rest like this – if it wasn't Christmas Eve I'd have the whole lot in jail. I'd—'

But the waits had gone. Sucking the last of the sweets and still singing horribly, they were marching back through the village.

It was the day after Christmas Day. William and Ginger and Douglas foregathered in Ginger's back garden. It was the first time they had met since Christmas Eve. Christmas Day had perforce been spent in the bosoms of their families.

'Well?' said William eagerly to Ginger.

'He didn't say anything about the book,' said Ginger. 'He jus' gave me five shillin's.'

'An' neither did she about the tie,' said Douglas, 'she jus' gave me five shillin's.'

As a matter of fact Aunt Jane had gone to a neighbour the next morning to pour out the wolf story, but the neighbour (who was boiling with that indignation which only a disturbed night can produce) got in first with the wait story, and after hearing it Aunt Jane had become very thoughtful and had decided to say nothing about the wolf story.

'Uncle Charles,' grinned William, 'said that some fools of choir boys got tied up in the clothes-line 'n' he'd thrown 'em the penknife he'd got for me 'n' they'd pinched it 'n' he gave me five shillings.'

Each of the three produced two half-crowns upon a grimy palm.

William sighed happily.

'Fifteen shillin's,' he said. 'Jus' *think* of it! *Fifteen shillin's!* Come on. Let's go down to the village an' spend it.'

CHAPTER 10

WILLIAM TO THE RESCUE

O N the whole the Outlaws had had a very happy morning. They had been playing at 'Cannibals,' a new and absorbing game invented by William. The game originated with William's mother's cook, who had presented William with a tin of sardines. She was 'turning' out the store cupboard, and finding that she had many more sardine tins than she needed, and being in a good temper, she gave a tin to William, knowing by experience that there were few things for which William's ingenuity could not find a use.

William and his friends were greatly thrilled by this windfall. They bore it away to the woods and made a fire. Any excuse for making a fire was welcome to the Outlaws. The process involved much blackening of hands and faces, much puffing and blowing and crawling about on hands and knees, and the collecting of enough firewood for a Crystal Palace demonstration. They killed several fires by kindness before finally they got one going.

Thrown in with the tin was an opener, and first

of all the Outlaws wrestled with this in turn. William wrenched his finger, Ginger cut his thumb, and Henry dislocated his wrist before they got the tin sufficiently open to extract bits of sardine with the help of twigs. The next question was how to cook the sardines.

William was not a boy to do things in any ordinary way. William liked colour, romance, adventure. Sardines for breakfast or tea eaten with fish knives and forks and bread and butter and good manners were so dull as to be beneath contempt. Sardines cooked like this in the open over a glorious fire made a matter for the exercise of that imagination which was one of William's particular gifts.

The Outlaws could be pioneers, gold-diggers, robber chieftains, anything. Yet William, never satisfied till he had attained perfection, thought that there must be yet another and more exciting rôle to play. And suddenly it came to him.

'*Cannibals!*' he said.

The Outlaws thrilled to the idea.

In a few seconds the scene was laid. Ginger was the unsuspecting traveller making his way through the boundless forest, and Henry and Douglas were cannibals under William's leadership. They fell upon the unwary traveller and dragged him with savage whoops and cries to the fire. There they bound him to a tree and danced around him brandishing sticks. Then they cooked him.

The first sardine (selected at random from the heap turned out upon Douglas's handkerchief) now represented Ginger, and the sardine tin, insecurely fastened to a stick and held over the blaze, represented the cauldron, and Ginger himself, to increase the verisimilitude, hid behind a bush. Then they ate Ginger, chanting wild songs.

The sardine gone, Ginger emerged from the bush and joined them in the capacity of cannibal, and Henry in his turn was the unwary traveller proceeding through the boundless forest. He was captured, danced round, and eaten like Ginger. Douglas and William followed as unwary travellers in their turn, and the performance each time grew more realistic and bloodcurdling by the addition of such things as tomahawks and daggers and swords, and a horrible show of torturing and scalping the victims invented by William.

But when each one of the Outlaws had impersonated the unwary traveller (and William's dying groans had aroused real admiration and envy in the breasts of his companions), no one felt any desire to repeat the performance. For one thing the taste of burnt sardine is an acquired taste, and the Outlaws had not been wholly successful in acquiring it. Yet they were loth to relinquish their rôles, which were gaining in realism each minute. In fact, Douglas, dispensing altogether with the sardine substitute, was at that minute sitting on Henry and making a most effective pretence of gnawing off his ear, while Henry's screams of agony would have done credit to a hyena.

It was William who thought of varying the proceedings by introducing the fresh character of a rescue party. Ginger was to be a fair damsel captured by Henry and Douglas, the cannibals, and William, a passing traveller, was to hear her cries for help and come to her rescue.

Beyond Ginger's inability to resemble a fair damsel (except for a rather good falsetto 'Help! Help!') it was a great success, and the battle between William and Ginger (who proved quite a creditable Amazon) against Henry and Douglas was an enthralling one.

Henry had entered into the spirit of the thing so much that he retired behind a tree with a little clump of moss which he pretended to eat with much show of enjoyment, persisting (to William's indignation) that it was William's scalp. This new version of the game might have gone on indefinitely had not one of the keepers heard their voices, and, recognising his inveterate enemies, charged them on sight.

Cannibals, traveller, and distressed damsel fled to the road like four streaks of lightning, leaving only a smoking fire, a sardine tin, a few bits of dismembered sardine and a perspiring keeper to mark the scene.

On reaching the road the Outlaws discovered that it was lunch time, and wended their way back to the village, carrying on a cannibal v. traveller guerrilla warfare all the time, while Ginger (who fancied himself very much as the distressed damsel) practised his 'Help! Help!', making it higher and higher and shriller and shriller till it almost wandered off the scale altogether.

At the cross-roads they separated to go to their respective homes. Their rôles were by this time slightly mixed. Douglas was making a great play of eating a large stone, which he said was William's head, and William was licking his lips and evincing every sign of satisfaction over a stick which he said was Douglas's leg.

Ginger was still chirping his 'Help! Help!', trying to solve the difficult problem of reconciling highness in the scale (which he associated with the female voice) with that resonance and loudness that he felt to be an essential part of any cry for help. Henry was leaping and brandishing a stick and practising his war-whoop.

William threw away Douglas's leg in his garden and entered the house. The spell of his morning's game was still upon him. He had enjoyed being a cannibal, and he had enjoyed rescuing distressed damsels from cannibals. He entered the hall. He could hear his sister Ethel's voice from the morning-room.

'I don't love him at all. I'm being *forced* to marry him against my will. I have no one to turn to for help. My heart fails me. He presses his suit every day. He is coming this afternoon and my parents will *force* me to accede to his proposals. Alas, what shall I do?'

William, open-mouthed with amazement, eyes nearly starting out of his head, went upstairs to his room. *Poor* Ethel! What a rotten shame – his father and mother *forcing* poor Ethel to marry a man she didn't love. Of all the *cheek*. Why *should* poor Ethel marry a man she didn't love?

Between William and his sister there existed, as a rule, a state of armed warfare, but William's heart was now full of indignation and pity. He had spent the morning rescuing one distressed damsel in the shape of Ginger, and he was quite prepared to spend the afternoon rescuing another in the shape of Ethel.

'Gosh!' he muttered to his reflection as he brushed his hair savagely. 'Fancy them *forcin*' her to marry someone she doesn't love! *Rotten!*'

Downstairs in the morning-room Ethel closed the book and yawned. 'It *is* piffle, isn't it?' she said.

Mrs Brown looked up from her mending.

'Yes, dear, it is. I don't think we'll read any more.

But they hadn't any of my list in, and I just took it at random from the shelves. It's nearly lunch time, isn't it?'

Ethel rose, yawned again, and went out into the hall. She met William coming downstairs. He threw her a mysterious look of sympathy and indignation.

''S all right, Ethel,' he whispered huskily. 'Don' you worry. *I'll* see you through.'

She gaped at him, but he had disappeared into the dining-room.

'Now we mustn't forget,' said Mrs Brown at lunch, when she had made suitable comments on the state of William's hair and hands and face and nails, 'that Mr Polluck's coming today, and I told your father that one of us would meet him.'

Again Ethel met William's eye and again he threw her that mysterious glance.

Mrs Brown intercepted and misinterpreted it. 'Don't you feel well, dear?' she said solicitously.

'Yes thanks,' muttered William.

'I thought he was looking queer when I saw him in the hall,' admitted Ethel. 'I believe he's been eating green apples again. You know what happened last time.'

'Oh, no,' said William, nobly forgiving her for her unfeeling tone, and for her callous misunderstanding of his signals of sympathy, and added meaningly, 'It's

''S ALL RIGHT, ETHEL,' HE WHISPERED HUSKILY. 'DON'
YOU WORRY. I'LL SEE YOU THROUGH!'

not *that*. Oh, no, it's not *that* – it's somethin' very different to *green apples*.'

And again he gazed fixedly at Ethel, who returned his look blankly. The Brown family were quite accustomed to mysterious remarks and tones from William, and attached no meaning to them whatever.

After lunch he followed his mother into the drawing-room.

'What time is this Mr Polluck comin'?' he said to her coldly. He felt that he had declared war now on both his parents in defence of the deeply-wronged Ethel.

'His train gets in at four o'clock. Oh dear, that reminds me, somebody must meet him. Robert dear,' as her elder son entered, 'are you doing anything this afternoon?'

'Yes,' said Robert, very quickly, 'I'm going to tennis at the Maylands', and I've promised to be there by four.'

'Well, you could easily go round by the station and meet Mr Polluck and bring him here before you go, couldn't you, dear? It would be *so* kind of you.'

Then, lest Robert should discover some irrefutable reason why he could not possibly meet Mr Polluck's train, she went quickly upstairs for her afternoon's rest.

'Oh, yes,' said Robert bitterly, as the door closed behind her. 'Oh, yes, go and meet him and the train's

sure to be late, and get to the Maylands' when everybody's made up fours for tennis and me have to talk to
old Mrs Mayland. Oh, yes, very nice that, very nice
indeed.'

He was speaking to himself more than to William
but William (whose fertile brain had already formed
a plan), with his most innocent expression and in
his meekest voice said: 'What about me goin' for
you, Robert? I'd *like* to do jus' that little thing for you,
Robert. What about me meetin' him an' bringin' him
home? I could easy do that.'

Robert looked at him suspiciously. 'What do you
want?' he said brusquely, 'because you jolly well aren't
going to get a *penny* out of me.'

William looked shocked and hurt at this interpretation of his offer.

'I don't want anythin', Robert,' he said more
meekly than ever, ''cept jus' to *help* you. I'd jus' *like* to
do that little thing to *help* you.'

Robert looked at him more suspiciously than ever.
William's expression, almost imbecile in its meekness
and innocence, did not deceive him for a minute. He
knew the kid too well for that. The kid was after
something – a tip probably. He'd come cadging round
for a tip when he'd done it. Well, he jolly well wouldn't
get it, but – but there wouldn't be any harm in his
doing it.

Robert had a particular reason for wishing to be early at the Maylands'. He had met only yesterday the most beautiful girl he had ever seen in his life (Robert met the most beautiful girl he had ever seen in his life on an average once a week), and she was staying with the Maylands, and he'd determined to be a very early bird indeed at the Maylands' party. The rôle of the worm would be undertaken (he hoped) by the beautiful visitor. And now, if he had to 'muck about' (as he inelegantly put it to himself) meeting people at the station and carting them home she – She – SHE would be nabbed by someone else – probably someone quite unworthy of her – and he'd never get a look in at all. She was probably the most beautiful girl any of them had ever seen in their lives – but if he got there first he could hang on to her with both teeth (metaphorically speaking) and refuse to let go for anyone.

'Well,' he said, as if conceding a great favour, 'you won't be up to any of your tricks, will you? Because if you *are*—' he ended with an eloquent threatening silence.

Again William looked pained and shocked. 'Of course not, Robert. I only want to *help* you, Robert.'

'Well,' said Robert, after a moment's consideration, during which the claims of duty wrestled feebly and ineffectively with the claims of the most beautiful girl he had ever seen in his life, 'well, I suppose there's no harm in your just meeting him and bringing him home – only don't tell them you're going to.'

Robert was (and not without justice) afraid that William's reputation would prevent his being accepted as a substitute meeter of guests at stations and bringer of them home.

'No, Robert,' said William, 'I'll jus' go quietly an' meet him at the station – that's all. I – I'd *like* to do jus' a little thing like that for you, Robert.'

'All right,' said Robert, and added, warningly, 'but none of your tricks – and anyway, you won't get a *penny* out of me for it.'

'No, Robert,' agreed William unctuously, 'I don' *want* to be paid jus' for doin' a little thing like that for you. Yes, I'll cert'nly meet that train for you, Robert.'

He went away leaving Robert gazing after him. He wasn't *sure* about that kid. He never was sure about that kid. But – but he'd take any risk for the chance of hanging on to the most beautiful girl he'd ever seen for a whole afternoon.

So he forgot about William, and turned the whole force of his mind and soul and intellect upon the problem of his costume for the afternoon – which pullover, which blazer, which shoes, and which socks. Such little things settled one's fate; for instance, she might like white silk socks, or she might think them foppish. It was so difficult to tell, and so much depended on it.

Outside in the road William was meeting his Outlaws.

'What we goin' to do this afternoon?' said Ginger.

William wore his stern and frowning air of leadership.

'We've gotter *work* this afternoon,' he said, 'we've gotter make plans. Poor Ethel, she's being forced to marry a man she dun't love, an' he's comin' this afternoon an' she's bein' *forced* to recede to his proposals. He's pressin' his suit now so as to be smart for comin' over, but we've gotter *save* Ethel from bein' forced to marry someone she dun't love – poor Ethel with her heart failin' an' all that.'

'We can't fight him – not if he's grown up,' said Douglas gloomily. Douglas was always something of a pessimist.

'No,' said William, 'but – but we've gotter make *plans*.'

At four o'clock the visitor – a blameless man of middle age, the sole object of whose visit was a quiet business chat with William's father – stepped out of the train and looked around him.

The only person on the station was a small boy of not very prepossessing appearance who approached him with what was evidently meant to be a smile of welcome. It was Douglas.

'You Mr Polluck?' said the boy.

'Er – yes,' said Mr Polluck.

There was something strange about the boy's expression – something that he didn't quite like.

'I've come from the Browns' to meet you, an' take you there,' said the boy.

'Oh, thank you,' said Mr Polluck, 'thank you very much indeed.'

So he set off with the strange boy. He accompanied the strange boy, all unsuspecting, along the road that led in the opposite direction to the Browns' house. He talked of things which he thought should interest boyhood – of school life, of lessons, and of schoolmasters, and what an easy time boys had nowadays compared with the time when he was a boy.

He found the strange boy unresponsive. He began to find the walk a long one, too. It occurred to him that they might have sent some sort of conveyance to meet him. He'd no idea that Brown lived so far from the station as all this. He wasn't used to walking. Looking round, he saw that they had now left the village far, far behind them. Brown must live quite out in the wilds.

On and on, up and up – for the road led up the side of a hill. He certainly thought Brown might have warned him, or sent a conveyance or – or something. He stopped once or twice to recover his breath. Bitter feelings against Brown began to stir in his usually kind and placid heart. He took out his handkerchief and wiped his brow.

'Is it far now?' he panted.

The boy stopped and pointed upwards. 'You can't miss it now,' he said. 'House on top of hill – scuse me if I go now.'

And then he seemed to disappear as if the earth had opened to swallow him up.

Mr Polluck gazed about him despondently. The house seemed inaccessibly above him. On the other hand, the station seemed equally inaccessibly below him. After a brief rest to allow his breath to return and his perspiration to depart he decided that less effort would be involved in scaling the heights than in making his toilsome way down again to the station. Moreover, he didn't want to miss that little business chat with Brown.

So with that bull-dog determination that has made the British race what it is, and in the spirit of the youth who bore through snow and ice the banner with the strange device, he started again, puffing, gasping, panting, up the hill.

Douglas meanwhile rejoined the Outlaws, who were waiting for him near the station.

'Sent him up to the empty house on the hill,' he said laconically. 'I bet he'll jus' go straight home after that.'

But they were mistaken in their man. They remained at their post for about half-an-hour playing a desultory game of marbles and practising cart-wheels and at the end of the half-hour they were rewarded by the sight of Mr Polluck, footsore and breathless and weary, descending the hill and coming slowly along the road to the station.

Near the station, however, he stopped and looked about as though for someone of whom to make inquiries. Suddenly a boy stood in his way – a boy with fair bristly hair and a very round face. It was Ginger. In spite of his appearance he looked, thought Mr Polluck, a nice kind obliging sort of boy.

'Excuse me, my little man,' he said, 'can you tell me the way to Mr Brown's house. I have been misdirected and have been far out of my way.'

Ginger smiled brightly.

'Oh yes,' he said, 'I know it. I'll take you there, shall I? There's quite a nice short cut from here.'

Mr Polluck looked at him gratefully.

'I'd be so glad if you would, my little man,' he said.

Ginger set off briskly. Mr Polluck did not this time try to enliven the way by conversation. He walked rather slowly and in silence.

Down the hill this time into the valley. The 'short cut' seemed to involve innumerable ploughed fields, and innumerable stiles (Mr Polluck wasn't very good at stiles), and innumerable herds of cows (of which Mr Polluck was terrified).

'It's rather a long way, isn't it?' moaned Mr Polluck at last.

'Let's have a little rest, shall we?' said Ginger kindly.

They sat down on a heap of stones by the roadside, and Mr Polluck covered his face with his hands. When he uncovered it his companion had vanished. He gazed around him in the gathering dusk. He was alone – alone in a wild cow-infested countryside down in a deep, deep valley far from human habitation.

Meanwhile, Ginger was rejoining his friends near the station. 'I bet he'll be ready to go straight home *now*,' he said with satisfaction.

But again they reckoned without their man.

Footsore, weary, dusty, toil-worn, but with the pertinacity of Bruce's spider itself, Mr Polluck came clambering up the hillside from the valley, and looked around him as though again to ask the way.

And this time Henry stood before him wearing an engaging smile and the expression of one who is ready to direct anybody anywhere.

But Mr Polluck had had enough – and more than enough – of small boys. He ignored both Henry and the engaging smile and stopped a passing labourer who was wearing neither an engaging smile nor an expression of readiness to direct anyone anywhere. But the passing labourer did direct him, and quite correctly, to the Browns' house, and, ignoring Henry and his engaging smile, the way-worn but resolute wanderer set off to it.

There was consternation among the Outlaws. They held a hasty meeting.

'We've gotter stop him goin' there,' said William. 'We've simply *gotter*. If once he goes there, Ethel'll be *forced* to marry him same as what she said.'

'Well, 's no good *me* sayin' anythin' to him,' said Douglas, who had a fairly well-founded suspicion that if he should again present himself to the wanderer, the wanderer would slay him on sight.

'No, nor me neither,' said Ginger.

'And he wun't take any notice of me,' said Henry mournfully.

'Well, *I'll* have to do somethin', then,' said William, who had reserved himself for the *grand finale* if necessary.

Mr Polluck walked slowly and painfully, but with a lightened heart, through the dusk down the road at the end of which was Mr Brown's house. He was certainly on the right track at last. He'd asked twice since the passing labourer directed him, and he was certain that at last he had won through to his goal.

And suddenly a small boy seemed to spring up in his way. Mr Polluck, who at that moment hated all small boys with an almost Herodian hatred, made as if to pass by without looking at him, but William, raising his cap and saying, 'Scuse me,' stepped right into his path.

'Yes?' said Mr Polluck impatiently.

'Please, I'm William Brown,' said William politely.

Mr Polluck looked at him with a softened expression.

'Oh, Mr Brown's little boy?'

'Yes,' said William.

'He – he does live at the end of this road, doesn't he?' said Mr Polluck hopefully.

'Oh, yes,' said William, 'but – but you'd better not go there – not today.'

'Why not?' said the mystified stranger.

''Cause of Ethel—'

'Ethel?'

'Yes, Ethel – my sister. She's dead.'

'Good heavens!' gasped poor Mr Polluck.

'Yes, she's jus' died,' went on William fixing him with a stern and accusing eye. 'Died of a failin' heart. It happened 'cause of being *forced* to marry someone she didn't love.'

'G-good heavens!' gasped Mr Polluck again.

His consternation and amazement had to William all the appearance of remorse and guilt.

'Yes,' he muttered. 'I 'spect you're sorry now.'

At this moment Mr Brown suddenly loomed up through the dusk.

'Oh, *there* you are, old man,' he said to Mr Polluck. 'I came out to see if I could find you. Couldn't think what had happened to you. I suppose you missed your train.'

Mr Polluck grasped him by the hand.

'My dear fellow,' he said brokenly, 'you should have stopped me – I'm so distressed. I've just heard – your terrible loss.'

'My loss?' said Mr Brown.

'Yes,' said Mr Polluck, 'your – your daughter's death. I assure you I'd never have come if I'd known – I assure you – my deepest sympathy—'

'My d-daughter's d-death?' sputtered Mr Brown.

'Yes, your little son has just been telling me about it – I can't *tell* you – how deeply I sympathise—'

They both looked round for William, but William was not there.

William had hurried indoors to warn Ethel in secret of the advent of her wooer.

He found Ethel with her mother in the drawing-room.

'Well, he may have missed his train,' his mother

WILLIAM FIXED HIM WITH AN ACCUSING EYE. 'IT
HAPPENED 'CAUSE OF BEING FORCED TO MARRY
SOMEONE SHE DIDN'T LOVE,' HE SAID.

'GOOD HEAVENS!' GASPED MR POLLUCK AGAIN.

was saying, 'but I think he might have telephoned or something. It's most inconsiderate to be as late as this.'

William, who was standing by the table, happened to glance down at an open book. His eyes met the sentence, 'I don't love him at all. I'm being *forced* to marry him against my will. I have no one to turn to for help. My heart fails me. He presses his suit every day. He is coming this very afternoon and my parents will *force* me to accede to his proposals. Alas! what shall I do?'

He gasped.

'I say,' he said hoarsely, 'I – Ethel, I thought I heard you *sayin*' this this mornin'.'

'I expect you did,' said Ethel. 'I was reading it aloud to Mother. She'd lost her glasses.'

William blinked.

'Then – then what was this ole Mr Polluck comin' for?' he said.

'Just to have a talk about business with Father. Oh – here they are.'

There came the sound of the opening of the front door and of Mr Brown's and Mr Polluck's voices in the hall. Mr Polluck was speaking. He was saying: 'There were four boys altogether. The first took me right up the hill and the second right down into the valley, and this last – your little boy – said that your daughter was dead. He said, "Ethel's dead – she's just died," most distinctly.'

'Where are you going, William?' said Mrs Brown, who, being slightly deaf, had not caught the words.

But William was already far away.